Readers

MW01172187

"I started reading *Lucy's Voice* at 8 a.m. Pausing only to refresh my cup of coffee, I read on and on. Even knowing the Lucy Hale story, I kept going until I reached the final chapter. Robinson serves up an intriguing blend of fact & fiction sprinkled with local history and tightly wrapped in a tasteful, twisty mystery."
—*Thom Hindle, photographer, antiquarian, former Woodman Museum curator and trustee*

"*Lucy's Voice* is a delightful adventure, juxtaposing the joys and sorrows of modern fictional characters with voices from the past. Robinson's excellent research invites readers to join in and become history sleuths. New Hampshirites will see familiar places and figures in new ways. A wonderful read!"
—*Genevieve Aichele, NH State Artist Laureate, author of "Dreaming Again," "Neighborhoods" and "Ocean Secrets"*

"*Lucy's Voice* beats even *Point of Graves*. Robinson's second mystery weaves a tale that will appeal to anyone interested in American history. I particularly liked the witty repartee between the characters. An excellent piece of work. I thoroughly enjoyed it."
—*David Griffiths, traveler, writer, and former Canadian naval officer from Halifax, Nova Scotia*

"The author infuses *Lucy's Voice* with such rich detail, even with an intimate knowledge of area history, I found myself lost in that wonderful space between fact and fiction."
—*Jennifer Gray, historian from Kittery Point, ME*

"J. Dennis Robinson blends historical fact and fiction into a fantastic, fun, and engaging mystery set at one of my favorite museums in the country!"
—*Jonathan Nichols, Executive Director, Woodman Museum, Dover, NH*

"History-meets-fiction at its best. Lively, intriguing, poignant, and crafted by a master. Can't wait for history sleuths Levi Woodbury and Claire Caswell to stir the dust of time again."

 —*Patricia Q. Wall, author of "Lives of Consequence" and "Child Out of Place"*

"Levi, Claire, and Corey reunite in a remarkable new history mystery about New Hampshire socialite Lucy Hale and her fiancé, John Wilkes Booth, and a polar bear named Namuq. Another great Robinson read."

 —*Nancy R. Hammond, author of "The Life and Times of Jonathan Mitchel Sewall, 1748-1808, Poet-Lawyer-Patriot"*

"In a nation racked by the Civil War, Lucy Lambert Hale was desired and courted by the most eligible bachelors in the nation's capital. To her family's horror, the belle of Washington, DC became infatuated with the most dangerous man of all. In *Lucy's Voice*, the senator's daughter must protect her dangerous secret. Robinson's latest page-turner picks up speed throughout. A must-read."

 —*Scott R. Scribner, PhD, Social Science researcher from Los Angeles, CA.*

"Combining historic events and familiar contemporary settings, *Lucy's Voice* is an adventure. The likable yet flawed characters keep readers guessing and lead us to want to follow their adventures after this story ends."

 —*Terry Cowdrey, college enrollment management consultant and avid reader*

LUCY'S VOICE

*New England
History Mystery #2*

Harbortown Press
Portsmouth, New Hampshire
www.jdennisrobinson.com

Cover Art: Robert Squier
Production Design: Grace Peirce

This is a work of fiction. Unless otherwise indicated, all the names, characters, businesses, places, events and incidents in this work are either the product of the author's imagination or used in a fictitious manner. any resemblance to actual persons, living or dead, or actual events is purely coincidental.

Special thanks to all early reviewers and to a hardy band of proof-readers including Terry Cowdrey, Nancy Hammond, Wendy Pirsig, and John B. Robinson. I'm indebted to Thom Hindle for use of rare Hale family portraits in the appendix, and as always, to the saving grace of Grace Peirce.

For Ann & Caitlin

Selected Books by J. Dennis Robinson

POINT OF GRAVES
New England History Mystery #1

1623
*Pilgrims, Pipe Dreams, Politics
& the Founding of New Hampshire*

NEW CASTLE
New Hampshire's Smallest, Oldest, & Only Island Town

PORTSMOUTH TIME MACHINE
(With illustrator Robert Squier)

MUSIC HALL
How a City Built a Theater & a Theater Shaped a City

MYSTERY ON THE ISLES OF SHOALS
Case Closed on the 1873 Smuttynose Ax Murders

UNDER THE ISLES OF SHOALS
Archaeology & Discovery on Smuttynose Island

AMERICA'S PRIVATEER
Lynx and the War of 1812

STRAWBERY BANKE
A Seaport Museum 400 Years in the Making

WENTWORTH BY THE SEA
The Life & Times of a Grand Hotel

LUCY'S VOICE

New England
History Mystery #2

J. DENNIS ROBINSON

HARBORTOWN
PRESS

Portsmouth, New Hampshire
2024

Contents

Chapter 1

The heavy barn door was as reluctant to open as Lucy Chandler was willing to go inside. She glanced back once more, just to be certain none of the servants were watching. In defiance of her age, Lucy gave a mighty pull on the oversized metal latch. Sunlight cut the empty darkness in half and there it was. Immediately her tears began. Lucy dabbed her eyes with the sleeve of her white bistro blouse and stepped boldly ahead.

What had been her parents' worldly goods were now stacked in a corner of the barn next to an abandoned sleigh. The lesser items—bedding, crockery, curtains, and such—had been disbursed when her mother died back in 1902. Lucy's father, the distinguished Senator John Parker Hale, had gone to his grave long before, leaving his wife a widow for nearly three decades. Lucy's mother had carried on with dignity, living alone in the brick mansion on the main street in the city of Dover, surrounded by the objects that defined her.

How strange, Lucy thought, that she too had become the dutiful helpmate of a famous but controversial New Hampshire politician. Now in his 70s, her husband Willie, thankfully, was out of the limelight. For Senator William E. Chandler there would be no more battling railroad tycoons, exposing election fraud, or reinventing the U.S. Navy.

Of course, Willie's illustrious career could never outshine her father's reputation as a staunch abolitionist. Lucy flashed on the day, years ago, when the larger-than-life statue of John Parker Hale was unveiled in front of the New Hampshire state capitol building. A plaque at the base of the imposing bronze figure proclaimed Hale's legacy as the nation's "first anti-slavery U.S. Senator." No man could ever eclipse her papa's deeds, she knew. No other man had captured her heart . . . No! More tears. Lucy pushed the memory that had haunted her life back into its hiding place and recovered her composure with practiced care.

What remained of her parents' Dover home was mostly furniture—heavy, hulking and ornate wooden monsters dating from before the Civil War through to the Victorian Era. There was even a well-worn butter churn and a spinning wheel. They had belonged to Lucy's Gramma Abigail, born in 1779 amid the chaos of the American Revolution.

Lucy knew at a glance where each table, bureau, ottoman, and lamp had once lived inside the Hale House in Dover, now stripped bare and soon sold off to strangers. Stepping closer, she spotted a fabric-covered footstool, once tucked beneath her mother's favorite chair. There was a photograph in the family album showing JP's widow sitting in this very chair. In the picture, light poured in from a window that rose fully ten feet from the carpeted floor to the intricately detailed crown molding above. Lucy's mother, forever dressed in black, dozed in the sunlight. That room, she recalled, smelled of lavender, bergamot, and furniture polish.

She bent to brush a coating of sawdust and hay from the marble surface of a turtle-top parlor table, its curving dark legs now hopelessly out of fashion. The dust made her sneeze. She shrieked and jumped back when the figure of her elderly mother appeared. Only it wasn't her mother. The all-but-identical form, impeccably dressed but stooped and bone weary, was Lucy herself. She cocked her head, examining the 69-year-old woman reflected in a massive gold-framed mirror.

How was it possible, she asked herself, that this was the vibrant young daughter of Senator Hale? One newspaper had called her "the belle of DC." Another said she was "the toast of Washington society."

"What a foolish child you were," Mrs. William E. Chandler scolded herself aloud, her voice echoing in the cool, empty barn. Amid the carnage of war, as brave men in gray and blue lay dying on the battlefield, what had she been doing? Dancing, shopping, dining, and flirting—that's what!

A vision of the elegant National Hotel came to mind. She and her mother were sitting at a neatly appointed table topped with freshly cut spring flowers. Music from a small band mixed with the tinkle of silverware and chiming glasses. The murmur of conversation flowed like voices underwater. And there he was again. The handsome man with a thick mustache and wavy hair reached for her hand. Lucy's new silk dress swirled around her. They whispered secrets. Her face flushed and his dark eyes danced. Everyone was watching.

Lucy almost swooned. She pushed the memory back down, way down where it belonged. This barn was not a safe place, Lucy reasoned. Too many ghosts. Turning to leave, she steadied herself against a chest-high dresser. Its touch was instantly familiar.

"It's my . . ." she whispered. And it was.

The unique dresser, handmade of hardwoods, had been a gift from her father, a peace offering, really. Lucy, her parents, and an older sister Elizabeth, were then living in Madrid, terrible Madrid.

Their time in Spain quickly followed "the incident" of 1865, as her father called it. The assassination that galvanized the nation and Lucy's connection to it had become a taboo topic in the Hale house. For five years adrift in Europe and for ever after, no one spoke of that day.

Her father, meanwhile, hated his assignment as United States Ambassador to Spain. A sharp-tongued country lawyer from New England, JP Hale was not cut out to be a diplomat. No one in the Hale family had ever been out of the country. They didn't speak Spanish. And while Lucy enjoyed the lavish dinners and elegant balls, the Hales were fish out of water.

Her behavior, at first, only made the journey worse. She sulked, wept, and usually kept to the room she shared with sister Lizzie, often scribbling in her journal. Lucy was angry with her father, with the world, with fate and with God. The gorgeous dresser, a true work of art, had done its magic. She would come to love it like a friend. Her initials had been delicately carved into the bottom of each drawer.

"And just for you, my dear," her father had said, "a special place to hold your deepest feelings." He showed her where to place her hand against a secret latch in the bottom drawer. Pressed, it revealed a hidden space just large enough for her diary.

"If you are determined to record your feelings of these tragic days," her father said, "I cannot prevent it. But those words must never be seen by anyone but you. Do you understand?"

She did.

His kindness had touched her heart. In the coming years, as the senator's health and memory faded, Lucy would become his caregiver and constant companion. In time, purged of the trauma of 1865, she abandoned her private writing. Before spotting her old dresser in the barn that day, she had forgotten about the journal entirely. Now, she couldn't push it from her mind.

Bending to grasp the handles on the bottom dresser drawer, she was stunned by her wobbly knees and aching hips. So old. So sad. So lonely. The finely crafted drawer slid open easily. About to trip the hidden latch, she heard her name.

"Lucy? Lucy, are you in here?"

Chapter 2

"I don't believe it!" Claire Caswell said with undisguised relish. "You? Therapy?"

This was not the news Levi Woodbury wanted broadcast to the other lunch patrons as they hovered in line at the Bow Street Eatery, a popular spot for locals.

"Little help?" he asked Claire, pointing to the daily specials menu above a glass case heaped with cookies, pies, cakes, tarts, and loaves of fresh-baked bread.

She knew the drill. In contrast to the rugged features, Levi was, in his own words, "hard of seeing." Despite eyeglasses, the condition rendered him unable to read the text in a standard book, to drive a car, or to decipher the words on the menu just above his head. In his mid-forties, Levi was the reclusive live-in caretaker at the John Paul Jones House Museum, a few blocks away in the center of Portsmouth, New Hampshire.

A decade earlier, then the city's dominant newspaper reporter, Claire had fallen hard for the handsome, sometimes sullen handyman. Back then, Levi rarely ventured outside the mustard-yellow fence that surrounded the mustard-yellow gambrel-roofed mansion that had dominated the intersection of Pleasant and State streets since 1758.

Levi occupied a tiny apartment, constructed by his own hands, in what had been the hayloft of the mustard-yellow carriage house. Almost invisible from the street, the building sat at the back of the museum grounds, beyond the terraced green lawn and colorful garden. The dark-haired, hard-charging reporter with wild eyes had tried her best to draw Levi out of his hideaway.

That was, what, eight years ago now? The couple had tried their hearts out. But the loss that anchored Levi to the past could not be moved. It was up to Claire, who had built the bond, to break it, she knew. Within a year of their brief affair, she was married to Corey Caswell who, uncomfortably at first, was Levi Woodbury's closest friend. Amazingly, a partnership was forged. The Caswells' unflappable daughter Heather, aged four, had since become the light of Levi's life.

"We'll have the ham wrap with honey-garlic aioli, romaine, fresh red onion and cheddar," Claire told the young woman behind the counter at the Eatery. "Plus an order of white bean chicken chili with your amazing cornbread."

The detailed recitation was for Levi's ears. Long gone were the days when Claire would recite the entire menu, and then wait for Levi's response. They had been a couple less than a year but lunch-mates ever since. She knew what he liked to eat, so why bother asking? She knew what had broken his heart, and that she alone could never fix it.

Ten minutes later, they were tucked around their favorite tiny table in the Eatery back room. The intimate area, no bigger than an apartment bedroom, was hung with green plants on salmon walls and flooded with noonday sunlight. Claire set down her bag, shook back her hair, and shot her companion a look with dark, wild eyes.

"So, this therapist," she asked, chewing her honey-glazed sandwich. "You like her?"

"Him," Levi corrected.

"Name?" Claire urged.

"No way," Levi said. "You'll google him to death, expose his secrets in the newspaper, and I'll have to start all over with a therapist who isn't a serial killer."

"You know I'll just stalk you until I find out," she said casually. "I am an award-winning investigative reporter—and your best friend."

"Third best," he said, blowing gently on a steaming spoonful of chili. "It goes: Corey, Heather, then you."

Claire made her hurt-face. "So you'd tell my husband and my daughter before you'd tell me?"

"Yep," he teased. "But I'll give you a hint. He's not in Portsmouth."

Her hurt-face turned curious. "But you never leave town! You hardly leave the museum grounds. If you're not with Corey at the Athenaeum, or here, or at our house, or maybe three other places . . ."

For the record, Origen "Corey" Caswell was the "Keeper" of one of the nation's last surviving membership libraries. Founded in 1817, the Portsmouth Athenaeum still occupied a handsome brick building in Market Square.

"It's called a bus," Levi said, cutting Claire off. "They're like big cars, only you're not at the wheel. I'm learning to use them."

"But I like driving you around," Claire insisted, the hurt-face back. "Sometimes. When I can . . . which is . . . not very often," she admitted.

"You've been on my case to be more independent since we met," he said. "You got me that carpentry job with old Mr. Ladd. You talked me into buying that stupid bicycle, even though riding it makes me look like a middle-aged dork."

"No, Lee," she soothed. "It makes you look, um, environmental."

"Well, I feel like a ten-year-old. And it's not like I can bike to Dover in this weather."

"DOVER!" she shouted, almost knocking over their table. Seconds later, smartphone in hand, she was calling off the surnames of therapists based in the nearby seacoast town.

"Becksted?"

"No."

"Carter?"

"No."

"DeRochemont?"

"No."

"Will you tell me if I hit the right one?" she asked.

"No," he replied.

Chapter 3

The chicken chili was delicious, but Levi knew it wouldn't last. At some point, any moment now, Claire would slide the other half of her ham sandwich his way and swipe the warm, soothing bowl from his grasp. It was an opening, he knew, to shift the conversation from therapy to another topic. But timing was critical. So he waited and he watched.

The wobbly table separating them was barely two feet wide. And yet, Claire's face was already in the fuzzy-zone of his poor vision. The effect, like the portrait lens in an old-time movie, was to make her attractive features even more so. That was one advantage of being visually impaired. The mind filled in the gaps and softened the edges as, given time, it also did for memory. Levi scanned the room enjoying the impressionistic artwork hanging on the walls and the impressionistic customers dining beside them. His world was more like a painting than a photograph.

As if she had never done it before, Claire casually switched meals. He watched her savor the first spoonful, like a judge in a chili cook-off.

"Good, huh?" he queried.

"Ummm," she moaned.

"So, how's work?" he asked, picking up the abandoned half sandwich. She had also bitten the dill pickle precisely in half, he noticed, and consumed half the potato chips. He swallowed his pickle ration. Share and share alike.

"Sucks," she said. "Ever since that giant corporation bought up a couple hundred newspapers, including us, they've been dumping freelance reporters left and right. It was a massacre. We're down to a skeleton staff."

Levi set the sandwich down and grunted encouragingly.

"We've already lost the Saturday print paper," she continued. "They've sold off the printing press and sublet much of our building. Most of us work remotely, paying for our computers and supplies, our gas. In a year or two, according to rumor, we'll be entirely digital, except for maybe the Sunday edition thick with ads."

"I guess it's happening all across the country," he said with authentic concern. "Can't really take it personally, though."

"You bet it's personal," Claire snapped. "We used to be a team. Hell, one of my new assignment editors works from Chicago. I've never met the woman. The layout guy is in Texas. Texas! What does he know about New England news? He makes the photos on the front page so big there's no room for the words."

Claire paused for a bite.

"And what qualifies as news these days?" she asked rhetorically, making air quotes with her fingers. "I'm out covering restaurant openings and restaurant closings. It's all about cute animal stories, high school sports, and the latest multi-million-dollar real estate sale."

Levi made a mental note to never use the word

"personal" again. "And how's my girl Heather doing?" he asked, hoping to cool the tension.

"Exactly," Claire continued. "Did you know 19,000 journalists were laid off in America last year? What happens to Heather when her mom gets the boot? Corey's salary won't keep us afloat. My last editor is driving a UPS truck."

Her rant was interrupted by a buzzing phone. She extracted it from her coat pocket. She tapped in the security code, scanned the message, and made a squeaking sound like an animal trapped in a cage.

"Breaking news! Hold the presses!" she said. "My next assignment is in."

Claire stood abruptly, downing the last of their shared soda, and slid the chili bowl back in Levi's direction. She pulled on her parka and gloves in anticipation of the December weather outdoors.

"Well, my friend, I'm off to Dover. Someone just donated a priceless piece of furniture to a local museum," she said. "This might be worth a banner headline."

"To the Woodman Museum?" Levi perked up. It was a good guess, since it was the only history museum in Dover.

"I love that place," he said. "It's only a couple of blocks from my . . ." He stopped himself. But nothing got by Claire, who gave him a sly wink.

"Did you say furniture?" he asked, hoping for more. But she was on the move.

"I don't know, Lee," she said, hiking her laptop bag over one shoulder. "Something about an antique dresser made in Spain, the Civil War, Abraham Lincoln, blah-blah, and a woman named Lucy."

"Lucy Hale?" Levi jumped to his feet, eyes wide.

"Gotta run," she said. "You can read all about it in the morning paper."

"Hey," she said, turning back. "Maybe when I'm in Dover, I'll bump into your therapist. Maybe he can tell me why I'm reporting about furniture instead of making millions writing mystery novels."

With a swirl of her scarf, she was gone, leaving Levi with half a sandwich and a room full of people all wondering why this seemingly normal-looking guy needed a shrink.

Chapter 4

Despite its tenuous link to the Atlantic Ocean—barely 18 miles of beach, marsh, and rock—the New Hampshire seacoast is crammed with historic sites, characters, and stories. Along with Portsmouth, Exeter, and Hampton, the town of Dover was founded by English colonists in the early 1600s. It is among the oldest settlements in the state, if you don't count 12,000 years of Indigenous occupation.

Tucked a few miles up a tributary of the fast-flowing Piscataqua River, Dover is best known for its 19th-century textile mills. The sprawling brick factory buildings, now converted to office space, still define the city center. And while Portsmouth (population 21,000) sold its soul to tourism long ago, Dover (population 33,000) remains largely working-class and family-oriented.

Half an hour after abandoning Levi, Claire snagged a parking spot smack in front of the Woodman Museum. She knew the basics from a quick Google search.

Like so many New England schools, museums, hospitals, and libraries, this cultural treasure was the gift of a female benefactor. On January 7, 1915, according to the *Dover Democrat*, "an estimable lady of Dover passed to a higher life." Five days later, locals discovered that Mrs. Annie E.

Woodman had bequeathed $100,000 to three trustees. The funds, worth $3 million today, were earmarked to promote the education of science, art, and history for residents.

The unique museum campus, Claire read from her phone online, included three brick homes built in the early 1800s, plus a preserved wooden garrison dating to 1675. According to her editor's texted notes, Claire was headed to the Hale House, once owned by the nation's first abolitionist senator. Bill Wiggin, the museum curator, was standing at the back door of the house, waving her in his direction.

"You must be Claire," he said with evident excitement and held out a pink hand. "I'm Bill, or Billy. Either one works."

William Wadleigh Wiggin was tall, white-haired, of Puritan stock, probably in his sixties, but with a boyish face and no glasses. He wore classic L.L.Bean with hints of Eddie Bauer. His parents, in their effort to imbue their son with a distinctive name, could not foresee the trouble it would create at the dawn of the internet era. Billy's vanity license plate, MR-WWW, didn't help matters. So, to avoid lengthy introductions, he had come to join countless hundreds, maybe thousands, of Wiggin men and women called Billy.

Claire accepted the hand. Cold, she thought, because he had been outdoors awaiting her arrival. Firm and rugged, calloused, not clammy. His grip was confident, without being clingy. She trusted him immediately.

"Would you like the grand tour, or should we hop right to it?" he asked.

Good, Claire thought. The man respected her time, of which she had little to spare. She knew from the internet that the Woodman Museum featured a ten-foot-tall stuffed

Siberian polar bear, a 37-pound lobster, dead snakes floating in bottles, a giant clam, and a four-legged chicken. The little museum was known for its extensive collection of rocks and minerals, luminescent moths, vintage dolls, bird eggs of every size, pin-mounted insects, and lifelike stuffed birds, many now extinct. These treasures rested behind glass in wooden cases seemingly unchanged in the last hundred years. It was, as the brochure announced, "a museum within a museum."

All those items were in the Annie Woodman House next door, plus 800 colonial artifacts in the preserved garrison nearby. Impressive, Claire thought. She would have to bring Heather here soon, while her daughter was still in a state of constant curiosity.

A wave of emotion caught Claire off-guard as she pictured her daughter sitting at the breakfast table that morning. She had not expected to become the mother of the smartest, liveliest, and most beautiful child ever to walk the Earth.

"What is this cereal made out of?" Heather had asked, pushing the floating objects around in her bowl with one delicate index finger as Claire studied her laptop.

"Um, oats, I think, baby, or maybe made of wheat."

"OF FEET!" Heather screamed. "We eat feet?"

Claire closed her computer and looked directly into Heather's shining eyes.

"You said no screens at the table!" Heather demanded, punctuating each word.

"You're right," Claire agreed. "How about this? No screens for me, no screams from you. Deal?"

Heather pondered the agreement.

"Deal!" she said and, having achieved victory, Heather picked up her spoon and went to work.

That, Claire thought, was the world she was missing in order to spend her afternoon writing about some dead old lady's dresser.

Chapter 5

"**I**'m afraid we're on a tight deadline, Mr. Wiggin," Claire said while extracting an old-school pocket tape recorder. She pressed a button and eyed the player to make sure the tape was spinning. "Do you mind?"

"Go right ahead," he said, opening the heavy Hale House back door. "And it's Billy. The kids think I'm Mr. Woodman, but I'm not that old. This house was built in 1813, by the way. Senator Hale bought it from John Williams in 1840. Williams was the founder of the Cocheco Mills, the first cotton factory here in town. Watch your step."

From a hallway, they descended a few stairs into a massive room filled to capacity with a dozen glass-topped display cases. Every square foot of wall space was hung with portraits, old signs, framed photographs and documents, textiles, ship models, toys, and artifacts.

"Wow," Claire whispered, mostly to herself. "There's a lot of stuff in here." And this was only the museum annex, her guide told her. He continued his narrative as they navigated to the far side of the room.

"When he wasn't in Washington, DC, JP Hale lived here with his two daughters, Lucy and Lizzie, and his wife, also named Lucy. This was the downstairs ballroom, dining area, and kitchen."

"The family lived on the second floor," he continued, "with servants' quarters above them. The senator died here in 1873, four years after the Hales returned from Europe. His widow lived in the house for another three decades. The house was largely abandoned until the museum trustees bought it in 1915."

The dresser was lovely, as advertised, with intricate patterns made of beech, ash, and walnut, all hand-inlaid by Spanish craftworkers. It stood in an alcove next to a full-length gold-framed mirror, a floral sculpted gas lamp, the ambassador's desk, and two finely detailed wooden chairs. A life-sized portrait of John Parker Hale, painted in his slimmer years, held sentry over the family heirlooms.

"Most visitors never get this far into our collection," Claire's guide explained. "The display here represents the four and a half years the family spent in Europe while JP was our emissary to Spain. It has never received the attention it deserves."

"Can't compete with a four-legged chicken or a polar bear?" Claire joked.

"Precisely," Billy said. The curator seemed to give off a shiver of emotion, Claire thought. Then he carried on.

"Spanish artisans were considered the best of the best. All of these items were commissioned by Ambassador Hale and later imported to New Hampshire at considerable cost. In fact, they incited quite a firestorm when Hale's political enemies accused him of enriching himself at public expense."

Against her initial annoyance at this assignment, Claire found herself drawn into the story.

"The Hales returned to this house from Spain in 1869,"

Bill continued. "JP was pretty sick by then. Lucy stuck by him. I mean, she didn't have much choice. By this time her sister Elizabeth . . ."

"That's Lizzie?" Claire held up her hand like a traffic cop and pointed to her tape recorder.

"Right, right," Billy confirmed. "Lizzie had married while the family was in Europe to a lawyer named Edward."

"Edward who?" Claire gestured again for clarification.

"You don't want to know," Billy winced. "His full name was Edward von Schoonover Kinsey."

"No way," the reporter groaned, her interest now waning.

"You can look it up," the curator nodded. "But the point is, with Lizzie wedded to Edward, Lucy was kind of trapped here in the house until her father passed on. I mean, a decade earlier, when JP was a senator, she had been one of the most desirable young ladies in Washington, DC society. By the time her dad died in 1873, she was an old maid, if you'll pardon the sexist expression. The senator's funeral, by the way, was a huge event in Dover. This city loved him."

Claire pointed to the historic dresser and shrugged.

"I'm almost there, I swear," Billy Wiggin said. "So, a couple of years after dad died, Lucy Hale married William E. Chandler—right here in this room! Chandler had been one of Lucy's suitors back in the day."

"In fact," he whispered, one hand to his lips as if breaking a solemn vow, "when Mr. Chandler was a student at Harvard, he began sending love poems to Lucy. She was barely 12-years-old."

"That cad!" Claire hissed.

"Nothing came of it, of course, not for years anyway."

Billy was back to his tour guide voice. "Chandler became a lawyer and a journalist. He married another woman, but she died of cancer, leaving him a widower with three boys. So fate brought them back together a generation later."

Claire glanced at her watch and the narrator picked up the pace.

"Fast forward 30 years. The Chandlers kept houses in Concord and Warner, New Hampshire. Lucy's mother finally died and the house we're in went on the market. What was left of the Hale family possessions, including Lucy's old forgotten dresser, were shipped to the Chandlers in Warner and stored in a barn."

Billy Wiggin paused to catch his breath. "And?" Claire prodded.

"Lucy died in 1915, around the same time Annie Woodman bequeathed a bunch of money to start this museum. The Woodman trustees bought the Hale House. By then, it was completely empty. All the stuff you see here was donated during the last century. We knew from inventories and shipping bills that there was a missing dresser, but we could never find it—until now."

The curator paused again. Claire's fading interest was palpable.

"And my 40,000 distracted newspaper readers care about this because . . . ?"

"That," William Wadleigh Wiggin said, clasping his hands as if in prayer, "brings us to the man who pledged to marry Lucy, but murdered President Lincoln instead."

Chapter 6

"It's not just a legend?" Levi Woodbury asked his best and smartest friend. "John Wilkes Booth was actually engaged to a woman from Dover, New Hampshire?"

"Shhhh," Corey Caswell held a finger to his lips. "You'll wake the Kraken."

"She's here?" Levi whispered. They were seated at a long table in the research room of the Portsmouth Athenaeum surrounded by books on all sides. Some of the leather-bound volumes had rested on shelves untouched for centuries. Through the opposite door was a small exhibition gallery, and beyond that was Corey's office where Heather lay curled out of sight in an ancient leather loveseat, her tiny nostrils flaring with each breath.

"Claire was supposed to take her this afternoon so I could get some work done," Corey said, "but she got that Dover thing."

"Something about Lucy Hale's bureau or dresser?" Levi asked.

"Billy Wiggin, he's the curator over there, has been searching for this object for ages. And yes, all signs point to the fact that Lucy Hale was engaged, or thought she was engaged, to Booth. A witness spotted them dining together at the National Hotel in Washington a few hours before Booth shot President Lincoln at Ford's Theatre, although that eyewitness report is in dispute."

"And when Booth was captured and killed days later," Levi said, "he had a picture of Lucy in his pocket, right?"

"Lucy and four other women," Corey corrected. "They had apparently exchanged rings. But most historians think Booth was probably playing Lucy for access, since Lincoln was friendly with her dad, Senator Hale. You know Booth's original plan was to kidnap Lincoln and trade him for Confederate prisoners of war."

"I read about that," Levi confirmed.

They were interrupted by a gray-haired woman seeking Corey's help in tracing her family tree.

"God, I'm starving," Corey said, returning to the table minutes later. "I'd love to chat, but . . ."

Before he could finish, Levi pulled half a ham wrap from his canvas messenger bag.

"Your wife ate the other half," he said. "And I only took a bite."

"Bless you, my son," Corey said, seizing the sandwich. "For this offering, you may continue to bask in my wisdom."

Levi let the man eat for a full minute. It was not a pretty sight. Corey had an interesting look not unlike a John Wilkes Booth impersonator, but with the prominent forehead of an Edgar Allan Poe. He ate, to put it politely, with gusto.

"So what's with the dang dresser?" Levi said at last.

"Okay," Corey said, wiping his mouth with the sleeve of his flannel shirt. "But you didn't hear this from me."

"We never had this meeting," Levi nodded. "But why the secrecy?"

"There is the possibility," said Corey, "that I may have been the guy who suggested that Bill Wiggin call Claire's boss at the *Portsmouth Journal*."

"You're a dead man if your wife finds out!" Levi said.

"I know." Corey contemplated the last of a truly excellent sandwich. "I should have told her directly, but I wanted to make sure she got the story—and had to do it. Bill's been good to me over the years and I wanted to return the favor."

"I will raise Heather as if she were my own," Levi deadpanned.

"Thank you," his friend replied before swallowing the final bite. "No pickle?"

"Claire ate it. So spill!" Levi commanded.

Corey stood, turned, bent low, and opened a small wooden door at the bottom of a line of bookshelves. He withdrew a thick, expandable manila folder and slid the contents onto the table in front of his friend. Corey fanned out the paper and, as if playing a card trick, extracted a cluster of pages housed in a plastic sheet. Although Levi couldn't read the text, he could tell these were pages copied from books and early newspapers.

"Lucy's father was a leader in the anti-slavery movement," Corey began, ticking off the facts. "JP Hale was a close ally of Abraham Lincoln. Lincoln emancipated Union slaves in 1863. Hale had been stumping to abolish slavery since the 1840s, making him an unpopular figure in Washington."

Levi twirled his index finger to speed up the narrative. Corey continued.

"John Wilkes Booth was a pro-slavery racist, but he was also a handsome, seductive, and popular actor. He was angry when Lincoln was re-elected and enraged when the

Civil War ended on April 9, 1865. When his little gang of conspirators failed to kidnap the president, Booth elected to kill Lincoln, thinking he would be embraced as a hero in the South."

"This is old news," Levi said. "I remember reading that Senator Hale did his best to cover up his daughter Lucy's engagement to Booth after the assassination. Then he rushed her off to Spain. Tell me something I don't know."

Corey picked up one of the Xerox copies from the table.

"This contemporary account," he held the page in the air, "says Lucy Hale continued to profess her love for Booth, even after he became the most hated man in America."

"But is it reliable?" Levi asked.

"You'd make a good historian," Corey said. "Much of our work is trying to sort fact from fantasy. Without a word on the topic from Lucy herself, it's easy to put too much weight on hearsay or untrustworthy reports. When it comes to Lucy and Booth, we have a ton of pundits and almost no data. In my opinion . . ."

Corey stopped in mid-sentence. Levi followed his gaze to see a sleepy figure standing in the doorway clutching a battered cloth bunny.

"Uncle Leeeee!" Heather shouted and hopped into his lap.

Chapter 7

"Let me get this straight," Claire said to Billy Wiggin. "You think this piece of furniture was a gift to Lucy from her father?"

"I don't think, I know." The curator extracted a pair of white cotton gloves from his pocket and pulled them on.

He slid aside the plexiglass wall in front of the dresser and gently placed one hand on each brass handle of the top drawer. He drew the drawer open with a slow even motion and beckoned Claire in for a closer look. The initials "LH" were expertly carved within a circle at the bottom of the empty drawer.

"Oh, my!" Claire gasped. "That's pretty convincing."

"And that's not the half of it," Billy said. He closed the top drawer and, as if handling a newborn, opened the second, third, and fourth to show identically carved initials. Each drawer, Claire noticed, was slightly deeper than the one above it.

"Like many girls and young women of her era, Lucy kept a diary," the curator said. "We have a few of them, spanning from age ten up to age 22."

"Have them here?" Claire asked.

"Lord, no," he laughed. "Way too fragile. They're

archived in a special vault at the state historical society collection in Concord. But we have a reproduction."

Billy reached into the display and extracted a small leather-bound volume from beside an early photograph of Lucy Hale. He handed the book to Claire. The letters "LH" were precisely embossed on the cover. She traced the initials with her thumb before spreading the pages open and skimming the handwritten text.

"A local bookbinder made this reproduction for us," Billy said. "Isn't it exquisite?"

"Are all of Lucy's diaries this fancy?" Claire asked.

Billy nodded.

"She got a new one from her father every year on her birthday from age ten. She was born on New Year's Day, so it was the perfect gift."

"But this is huge!" Claire said. "I mean, the private diary of an assassin's fiancée!"

Billy Wiggin half-shrugged, half-winced. "Well . . ." he spoke cautiously, eyeing Claire's tape recorder.

"Lucy wasn't exactly Jane Austen or Virginia Woolf. Her observations, when she got around to writing, were, to be honest, pretty mundane. A ride in a carriage on a sunny day, what she fed her pony, the purchase of a new dress, a letter from an admirer—that kind of thing."

Claire frowned as the curator continued.

"I mean, it's a gold mine for a thesis on women's studies. And there are occasional historical references to her father's job in the Senate. But Lucy lived a life of privilege and was quite sheltered, even from most of the horrors of the Civil War. She was more interested in, you know, in parties and young men. And they were interested in her."

Claire opened the facsimile journal to a random page and began reading aloud: "Some rain showers. Papa says Lizzie can ride out with Mr. Jonas, and that I must not protest so much. Mama says my time will come and that I will be a great beauty soon."

Claire hummed and handed the journal back.

"She was only 15 then," Billy said. "Eventually she would attract a host of suitors, including Oliver Wendell Holmes Jr., a future Supreme Court justice. Holmes, according to his letters, was quite love-struck. So too, legend says, was Robert Todd Lincoln, the president's son, though Lincoln later denied he even knew her. There are coded references in Lucy's diaries—but this is no kiss-and-tell."

"Remember," he continued, "this was a time when women wore layers on top of layers. Lucy got up each morning and put on a chemise, under-drawers, and a corset. Then she slipped on a hoop skirt and petticoats before picking out a dress that was as big as a pup tent. Her writing is also buried in layers of meaning we may never unravel."

"So no revelations about a hot and heavy affair with John Wilkes Booth?" Claire said, her disappointment showing.

"It's important to remember Booth was an actor. Theater people were generally considered well below the social status of a senator's daughter. Despite the fame the Booth family enjoyed, Lucy's parents would certainly have disapproved, if they knew what was up."

"She never recorded her feelings about the man she was secretly engaged to?" Claire was perplexed.

"Never say never," Billy beamed. "I want to show you something that only a few museum trustees have seen. And then, I'm going to put my reputation on the line."

The curator squatted to the level of the bottom dresser drawer. "Notice anything strange?" he challenged.

"I really don't," Claire admitted, dropping down so they were eye-to-eye. She stared into the empty drawer.

"Good," Billy said. "Neither did I, at first. We're not supposed to."

He moved one gloved hand inside the empty drawer. He extended an index finger and pressed firmly on Lucy's initials. Claire could feel her jaw fall as the panel slid aside to reveal a hidden space.

Chapter 8

PORTSMOUTH JOURNAL
DECEMBER 3
MUSEUM GIFT SPARKS LINCOLN MURDER MYSTERY
BY CLAIRE CASWELL

PORTSMOUTH—A secret drawer and a missing journal may offer clues to one of the biggest crimes in American history. The arrival this week of a long-lost artifact has rekindled a debate at the Woodman Museum in Dover, New Hampshire. Hand-crafted in Spain around 1865, the dresser is the gift of an anonymous donor. Deftly constructed of walnut, cherry, ash, and teak, the decorative dresser once belonged to Lucy Hale Chandler (1841-1915), daughter of John Parker Hale, the nation's first abolitionist senator.

"We've been looking for this item since the Woodman opened in 1916," says curator William "Billy" Wiggin. "It literally turned up on our doorstep the other day in perfect condition."

According to legend, Wiggin says, Lucy Hale of Dover was secretly engaged to actor John Wilkes Booth, who fatally shot President Abraham Lincoln at Ford's Theatre in Washington, DC. The couple were reportedly seen together at the National Hotel on April 14, 1865, the day of the assassination. Booth was fatally shot in Virginia after a 12-day manhunt.

Lucy and her family spent the next four years in Europe, where JP Hale served as the U.S. Ambassador to Spain.

Lucy's influential father largely managed to keep the scandalous engagement story out of the media, Wiggin explains. But Lucy was devastated by the death of her fiancé, according to a contemporary report.

"I believe this beautiful dresser was a gift from Ambassador Hale to his grief-stricken daughter, and that's where the mystery starts," Wiggin claims.

He believes a secret compartment in the dresser, now empty, once held Lucy Hale's lost 1865 diary. The contents of the diary could reveal whether Miss Hale knew of Booth's assassination plan or, perhaps, offer details of the couple's alleged plans to elope. It might also expose Lucy Hale's reaction to Lincoln's murder and to the 12-day manhunt and killing of Booth that followed.

"We have recovered some of Lucy's diaries," Wiggin says. "And now we have her dresser from that very year with a hidden compartment. I'd call that super suspicious, wouldn't you?"

Wiggin has been curator of the Woodman Museum for almost four decades. He notes that Lucy Hale's initials, "LH," were professionally carved into the bottom of each drawer in the newly acquired dresser. Her initials were also embossed on the journals she kept from 1852, when she was ten years old, until 1864.

"We don't know if Lucy recorded the events of 1865," Wiggin says. "But if she did, that volume might have been secreted in what is now an empty drawer."

Best known for his outspoken stand against American slavery, Senator Hale died at his Dover home in 1873, following his term as ambassador to Spain. A life-sized bronze statue of Senator Hale can be seen in front of the State Capitol building in Concord, NH.

In 1874, one year after her father's death, Lucy Hale married William E. Chandler, a lawyer, journalist, state senator, and Secretary of the Navy.

The dresser was known to have resided at the Chandler home in Warner, NH, but it disappeared after the couple's deaths early in the 20th century. Its whereabouts were unknown until it reappeared at the Woodman Museum last week. The donor of the item remains unknown. Lucy (Hale) Chandler and her parents are buried in Pine Hill Cemetery just up the street from the museum.

"Lucy never spoke publicly about her scandalous connection to John Wilkes Booth," Wiggin says. "In the dark days that followed Lincoln's assassination, hundreds of people were arrested, Booth was killed, and four alleged conspirators were hanged. Lucy Hale, however, was never even questioned by the authorities."

Trustees of the museum were unavailable for comment during the preparation of this article.

Lucy's dresser is currently on display in the Hale House gallery along with hundreds of historic artifacts and natural history wonders. The Woodman Museum is open daily from 10:00 a.m. to 5:00 p.m. except on holidays. Call or visit the website for details on tickets and tours.

Chapter 9

Getting on the bus in Portsmouth was the easy part, Levi discovered. You stand at the right spot at the right time and, when the door opens, you step inside. Knowing when and where to get off the bus in Dover, however, was nerve-racking.

"And how did that make you feel?" the therapist asked in a practiced, soothing tone.

"Like a little kid. Like an idiot," Levi responded. "I feel vulnerable on a bus, panicky, dependent."

"And why do you think that is?" the therapist oozed.

"Are you kidding me?" Levi almost shouted. He was irritated despite the extremely comfortable couch. The therapy walls were a soft relaxing color, somewhere between white eggs and brown eggs. There were healthy green plants while, just outside the door, a white-noise machine whooshed.

"Have you ever been on a bus around here?" Levi asked.

"Not since high school," the therapist smiled. He was a nice guy, Levi thought. He had dark skin, a salt-and-pepper beard, and an almost eerily peaceful aura. They were probably about the same age, but there was no question which of them would play the father on TV.

"Well, you should try it sometime as an adult," Levi said.

"You pull a wire to let the driver know you're getting off at the next stop. The bus barrels along and, if you have crappy eyesight, it's really hard to know what's going on outside. Pull the thing too early or too late and you have to hoof-it to your therapy appointment. Oh, and the local bus line only runs once per hour. So even if I get off at the right stop, it's half a mile to your office."

"Have you considered other methods of transportation to reduce the stress?" the therapist asked.

"Let's tick down the options," Levi said. "It's a 20-minute ride from my place in Portsmouth to here. A taxi costs about $80 each way. I could rent a car for that—if I could drive a friggin' car! Uber is about $50 or $60 round trip, versus three bucks for the bus."

"You sound angry," the calm man said.

"I guess I am, a little," Levi admitted. "You don't make much money as a museum caretaker, but I love my job. And I'm good at it."

"Maybe we should focus on that," the therapist said. "On what you're good at."

Levi shook his head. "No, I'm here to fix what I suck at."

"Like your eyesight? That sucks, right?"

Levi laughed. "Good one," he said. "But according to a shitload of doctors, my poor vision has something to do with the optic nerve, not the eyeball itself. It falls, experts agree, into the unfixable category."

"Like Julianne," the therapist added. "You can't fix that situation either."

The reference to Levi's dead former girlfriend made him sit up straight.

"Okay," he said, almost choking. "I did say I wanted to play hardball in here."

"What you said exactly," the therapist glanced at his notes from the previous session, was that you 'don't want any of that namby-pamby, Rogerian, bullcrap talk therapy'."

"Point taken," Levi nodded. "I can't fix my eyesight and I can't stop my old girlfriend from being dead."

The therapist said nothing.

"And this is where you remind me that my low-vision impairment kicked in 20 years ago right after Julianne died. One doctor suggested it might have been the stress. But it was probably something called Leber Hereditary Optic Neuropathy. It's a DNA thing, so I should blame my mother—who is also deceased, by the way."

Dr. Gerome Goldman, PhD (he preferred being called "Gerry") jotted down the medical term but said nothing.

"I guess what I suck at," Levi said, "is dealing with unfixable things."

"And yet, you've managed to make a career for yourself at the museum fixing things. Am I right?" Gerry struck a pose, one elbow on the arm of his chair, his head on his hand.

"I guess. If you call pruning bushes and repairing shutters a career," Levi hedged.

"I do indeed, and an honorable one," Gerry said. "But let's move on. At our first session, you said you recently managed to build up the courage to visit Julianne's grave."

"Finally," Levi agreed. "But it took me 20 years."

"And you got on that scary bus to come see me," Gerry said.

"Okay, I see where you're going with this," Levi said. "You're trying to twist things around to make me feel good about myself."

"Is it working?" Gerry asked.

"A little," Levi sniffled. He bent towards the box of tissues on the table between them. "Maybe I could learn to give myself a break now and then. Is that what you're saying?"

"Visiting a cemetery, taking a bus, talking to a therapist—sounds like somebody is playing a little hardball already," Gerry said.

Chapter 10

After 45 minutes (one therapy hour), Levi found himself back on the sidewalk in Dover. The season's first half-hearted snowfall was already melting and the temperature at 11:00 a.m. was a balmy 45 degrees. Having missed the return bus to Portsmouth by two minutes, Levi had nearly an hour to kill.

"Why not?" he asked himself and headed toward the center of town on foot. The Woodman Museum was a few blocks away and it was apparent, even with his faded vision, that Claire's newspaper article had done its work. Standing in front of the metal fence surrounding the museum campus, Levi could see a line of people waiting to enter the Hale House to view the now famous dresser.

He had fallen in love with this museum during a grammar school visit decades ago. It was, as Mrs. Woodman had intended, a curiosity shop for kids. Despite the crowd, after buying his ticket, Levi found the main museum building almost vacant and everything still in the places he remembered.

With the excitement of a ten-year-old, he revisited the man-eating clam shell, the last mountain lion shot in New Hampshire, the giant Siberian polar bear. Pressing his face to a glass case, he examined the same arrowheads and Indian artifacts he had seen as a boy. The thrill he felt was unchanged. It was as if someone had shrunk the Smithsonian Institution into a single museum exclusively for him.

He was studying the rocks and gems, one of the largest collections in New England, when a tsunami of uniformed children swept in. A blonde woman in a maroon blazer positioned herself near Levi and quieted the troop. She smiled in his direction as if to say, "This is your chance to run for the hills."

But he smiled back and stood his ground. Her practiced lecture drew him back until he, too, was hearing about the Earth's fiery formation for the first time. She was a good speaker. Levi found himself wondering what his mother had packed in his lunch box and hoping there would be a cupcake instead of an apple.

"Do you come here often?" the teacher said when her lesson was done and a couple of parents began urging the children into the next room. "That came out like a pickup line," she said, but without a drop of embarrassment. Levi blushed.

"I come here every decade or so," he managed. "And you?"

"First week of December, every year like clockwork," she said. "It's a godsend having this museum so close by. It's a great change of pace for the kids, I mean, with their noses stuck in front of a screen all the time—cell phone, TV, computer. Everything here is so . . ."

"Three-dimensional?" he offered. "Analog?"

"Exactly!" she said, presenting her right hand. "I'm Emily. Saint Seton's Elementary. And no, I'm not a nun."

"Neither am I," Levi said, accepting her hand.

There might have been a spark. He wasn't sure. More likely, he was lightheaded from the faint scent of ancient things infused with the woman's shampoo. It could be the lingering therapy high, or the rush of getting out of town on his own for a change. More likely, he reasoned, he was woozy from missing lunch. Levi didn't wear a watch. He didn't carry a phone. So he said the dumbest thing possible.

"Do you have the time?" Levi asked Emily, pointing at his naked wrist.

"Time for what?" She paused for two beats, then laughed. "Sorry. I can't resist a straight line. I do a little stand-up comedy when I'm not cloistered with the kids. Just local stuff. Open mic, that kind of thing. Are you ever in Portsmouth?"

"I live there," Levi said.

"Cool. Um, well . . . Maybe you can catch my set sometime."

"EMILY?" a chaperoning parent shouted from the next room. "WE'RE READY!"

"Duty calls," she shrugged and reached to shake his hand a second time. "To recap, me Emily, you . . . ?"

"Levi," he stammered. "Woodbury."

"Delighted to meet you, Mr. Woodbury. I'm Emily Smyth—Smyth with no I, don't ask me Y." Her face reddened. "Sorry, again. That's what I say to the kids. It works better on Comedy Night at the Bistro."

"The one on State Street?" Levi brightened.

"Ever been?" Emily, too, thought she felt a spark.

"Not yet," Levi said. "But I'm trying to reinvent myself."

"Yoo-hoo, MIZZ SMYTH!" the voice from the next room rang out.

Chapter 11

THE WHITE HOUSE
WASHINGTON, DC
APRIL 14, 1865

It was a great day to be alive. Spring had sprung and the dogwood trees were in bloom. Five days earlier, General Robert E. Lee had surrendered his Confederate forces to General Ulysses S. Grant at Appomattox Courthouse in Virginia. After four years, one month, and two weeks, the war that had taken at least 620,000 American lives was over.

By 10 a.m. President Abraham Lincoln had already gotten in a little office time and breakfasted with his wife, Mary Todd, and his sons Robert (Todd) and little Tad. He had read the morning paper and met with Speaker of the House Schuyler Colfax. General Grant was in town and promised to attend a meeting of Lincoln's Cabinet in an hour. The President was determined that the reconciliation between North and South would be firm, but forgiving. "Enough lives have been sacrificed," he had said. But first, there were the morning meetings.

Seated at a mahogany desk in his second-floor office, Lincoln pulled a bell cord and instructed a secretary to usher in the next visitor. The president greeted John P. Hale warmly. Hale had been battling the evil institution of slavery back when Lincoln was still an Illinois lawyer. The two had sometimes sparred. The New Hampshire politician had run for president twice, for the Liberty Party in 1848 and as the Free Soil candidate in 1852. Once known as a dogged warrior against government corruption, having earned too many enemies along the way, Hale was now being put out to pasture by his fellow Republicans. His dark mass of hair was now thin and gray while his keen roguish eyes were sunken and faded.

"Please sit, old friend," the president said, gesturing to a chair. "Is your family excited about departing for Spain?"

"Yes, Mr. President," Hale said. "All but my Lucy, I'm afraid." Lincoln knew of Lucy, both from her doting father and from the president's son, Robert Todd.

"Too fond of social life in Capital City?" Lincoln grinned.

"And too fond of a handsome young actor." Hale shook his head. "And a Booth, no less."

"Not Edwin?" Lincoln asked in surprise. "But he is a fine Unionist. I have conversed with Edwin Booth at length in this very room. Some say he is our finest man on the stage."

"Sadly, no," Senator Hale confessed. "She is besotted with Wilkes, the brother."

"I have seen him too," Lincoln said, searching his mind for details. "It was perhaps two years ago . . . Dammit! The name of the play escapes me. It was right before I spoke at Gettysburg," the president said, still lost in thought. "What was that play?"

Senator Hale shifted uncomfortably. Rather than reviewing United States foreign policy, the newly re-elected president seemed more interested in . . .

"I have it!" Lincoln shouted with obvious delight. "The

play was called *The Marble Heart*. Young Wilkes was an athletic fellow, if I recall, but nowhere close to his brother's skill in language or form."

"My wife and I will be happy to see the back of him soon," the former senator added. Booth's Southern sympathies were well known, rendering the possible romance untenable.

From the corner of his eye, JP Hale saw a White House secretary discreetly trying to signal his boss.

"Mother and I are considering a carriage ride this afternoon after the Cabinet meets," Lincoln said absently. "She has tickets to Grover's Theatre, but has a mind to see the performance of *Our American Cousin* at Mr. Ford's instead."

"Well, sir . . ." Hale said, rising from his seat. The president seemed not to notice.

"Mother has invited the Grants to accompany us to the stage this evening, but he is fresh from the battlefield and I'm dubious he will accept."

Seeing his guest standing, the president turned and again the two men shook hands.

"I don't suppose," he said tentatively, "that you and Mrs. Hale might consider accompanying . . . No, no, of course not. Forgive me. You are trying to escape the seductive allure of Dionysus."

"That we are," Hale said.

"I envy you," Abraham Lincoln said. "Off you go to the court of Queen Isabella. A reward you richly deserve."

"Thank you, Mr. President," Hale said, bowing deeply. "It has been an honor serving in your administration. You have preserved our Union."

"We have done that together, my friend," Lincoln said,

returning to his desk. He signaled his secretary to send in the next visitor. "Bon voyage, sir!" he said to the new ambassador.

"Enjoy your evening," the ex-senator replied.

"I could use a good comedy," the president agreed.

Chapter 12

"Crap!" Levi muttered to himself. According to the wall clock at the Woodman, he had missed his bus connection again. Such are the wages of curiosity, he mused, and of not wearing a watch. Oh well, he'd catch the next hourly trip back to Portsmouth. And to be honest, this was starting to feel like an adventure.

Emily Smyth and her rambunctious students had moved on to the old Damm Garrison next door. It was a favorite among kids, and not just because saying the names John and William Damm felt like swearing. The 17th-century building was packed with strange and wonderful objects from the past, including touchable exhibitions for students to explore.

"Nice to meet you, Mr. Woodbury," Emily had said on her way out. "Maybe we'll bump into each other in Portsmouth soon."

The words "bump" and "soon" held promise, Levi thought. Now he was wandering alone in the Civil War room on the third floor of the museum while replaying the Emily encounter in his mind. He might, he half admitted, have a crush on the teacher. No lunch, therapy high, whatever it was, he felt uncomfortably good.

There was something disrespectful about being happy amid all the trappings of a terrible war. The tattered flags, the rusty guns, the faded military badges and medals, the maps and the Matthew Brady photos—all somber reminders of a dark period in American history. And yes, these same objects had thrilled him as a boy standing in this very room. It was combat, after all, that had sparked his interest in history. Men with guns, knights in armor, dueling pirates, plus a dash of dinosaurs, mummies, and superheroes made his days back then.

As he had done on earlier visits, Levi made his way to the sacred Lincoln saddle. According to legend, the president had rested his private parts upon this very saddle on March 26, 1865. Lincoln was then reviewing the troops in Virginia during the final days of the Civil War. It was his last formal military action. Twenty days later, Lincoln was murdered by Lucy Hale's boyfriend.

Daniel Hall, a veteran of battles at Gettysburg and Antietam, had saved the saddle. It was Hall, a Dover lawyer, who later helped Annie Woodman craft her will, who founded the Woodman Museum, and who preserved the Hale House and the ancient William Damm Garrison.

Levi stretched his hand toward the saddle, once ornate, now sad and faded. At the sound of a voice, his arm retracted.

"Our desire to touch the past is powerful, isn't it?" the speaker said.

Levi spun around to see the kindly face of William Wiggin.

"Go ahead," the curator said. "I won't tell anyone."

Levi did as he was told. His index finger connected to the dry leather. For a split-second, he was jolted by the thunder of war mixed with the acrid smell of gunpowder and blood.

"You know," the curator continued, "Lincoln visited our little town in 1860 while running for president. At first, the locals thought he was homely and uncouth. He seemed too honest, too simple to be a politician, but the longer he spoke, the more they were enraptured. Abe didn't have his signature beard back then. He wore a long black coat. Lincoln spoke for two hours, and then wandered around town, chatting with people in the streets until after midnight."

"You know how I knew that story, Mr. Wiggin?" Levi asked when the tutorial was over.

The curator was surprised to hear his name.

"I was here when you told my fourth-grade class," Levi continued.

"Oh, so you're a teacher?" The curator brightened.

"No," Levi laughed. "I was in the class. I was ten when you gave us the tour."

"My God! That must've been 20, 30 years ago?"

"Thirty-five," Levi corrected. "But who's counting?"

"Certainly not me," the curator chuckled. "And what brings you back to our little campus today, Mr . . . ?"

"Woodbury, Levi. I'm a friend of the Caswells, Claire and Corey."

"Of course, of course," the curator said, shaking Levi's hand with obvious affection. "Lovely people. And as you can see by the attendance today, true friends of the museum. Have you had a chance to view our new acquisition in the Hale House?"

"Not yet," Levi admitted. "Too busy visiting old familiar artifacts." He gestured toward the Lincoln saddle. "This was one of my boyhood favorites."

"Mine, too," the curator agreed. Then, noting Levi's expression, he added, "Hey, that saddle has been here since 1920. I'm not that old!"

A visitor in a colorful winter sweater stuck his head into the Civil War exhibit room.

"Hi," he said awkwardly. "Either of you guys know where they keep that desk that belonged to that lady who helped shoot Lincoln?"

Bill Wiggin groaned, but his response was kindly and respectful. After giving the stranger directions to the Hale House, he turned back to Levi.

"I hope I haven't opened Pandora's box," he said.

"I don't remember hearing much about Lucy Hale during our fourth-grade tour," Levi said.

"Our emphasis has always been on Senator Hale as an abolitionist, but lately . . ."

"If it bleeds, it leads, as Claire always reminds me," Levi filled in the silence.

"An impressive woman and a fine reporter," Billy said, changing the subject. "I've known and respected her husband for years."

"Wasn't Lincoln in New Hampshire," Levi asked, changing the subject back, "because he was visiting his son?"

"Exactly," the curator said. "Robert Todd Lincoln was then at Phillips Exeter Academy in nearby Exeter. Poor Robert had applied to Harvard the year before, but he flunked 15 out of 16 topics on his entrance exam. His dad sent him to New Hampshire to study up. Robert passed his test and got into college the following year."

Levi paused to calculate. "So Robert was at Harvard

while his dad was president during the war?"

"Mostly," Bill Wiggin agreed. "He later enlisted, much to his mother's dismay, and saw a bit of action. In fact, Robert was at Appomattox Courthouse when General Lee surrendered in '65."

A museum volunteer dressed in Civil War garb appeared at the door. At first, neither man noticed.

"So didn't Lincoln's son also have a crush on Lucy Hale around this period?" Levi asked. The curator shook his head.

"You're opening a can of worms, my friend. The short answer is . . ."

"Billy!" The costumed woman was waving nervously with both hands. Her hoop skirt brushed both sides of the door frame as she entered the room.

"Marybeth!' the curator responded, then turned to Levi. "Meet Mrs. John Parker Hale."

"How do you do, sir? "Marybeth said, half in character. She then focused her nervous energy on Billy.

"We need you at the house! The visitors are piling up at the Hale exhibit to see the dresser. A bus group just appeared without reservations. And there's a reporter with a TV camera. I don't have a script for this!"

"It's okay, Marybeth. I'm with you. Just breathe. Everything's going to be fine. Duty calls," Billy Wiggin said over his shoulder to Levi as the couple hurried from the room.

Chapter 13

L evi never did get to see Lucy's dresser that day. It was dark by the time he found his way from the Portsmouth bus stop in Market Square down Congress Street to the John Paul Jones House Museum. He deftly unlatched the wooden gate with one hand, a warm boxed meat-lovers pizza in the other. With his path lit only by a distant streetlamp, Levi walked a few yards along a slate walkway, past a dogwood tree and an ancient white birch. There he turned left and stepped beneath an arched trellis leading to the carriage house.

A square pink envelope was pinned to the building's only door. The word "LEE" in large, unmistakably childish block letters filled the page. Balancing the pizza on bended knee, he unpinned the letter, replaced the thumbtack, and opened the unlocked door. The bottom floor was his workshop. Up a short steep stairway was Levi's miniature world. It consisted of two small rooms and a bath. The kitchenette at the back of the main room would seem modest even in a camper van. The back window looked out onto an alley, while two front windows, in season, offered a gorgeous view of the flower garden Levi had nurtured for the last two decades.

Tossing off his boots and jacket, the caretaker withdrew a soft drink from a tiny fridge. He carried the pizza to a couch that doubled as a fold-out bed. Minutes later, with only a single pizza bone left, he set the flat cardboard box aside and reached for the pink envelope. He knew what it was, of course. Heather was turning five.

Levi unfolded the computer-generated message. Clearly Claire's work, it was printed in bold letters so large that he could read them unassisted:

Please join us to celebrate the fifth anniversary of the arrival on this planet of Ms. Heather Caswell. Smiles required. Gifts optional. No sugar, dolls, screens, or batteries. She loves books. Saturday 2:00 p.m. at Casa Caswell.

Despite dark skies, it was not much beyond 5 p.m. and still time to get a little work done. This being New England, the weather had morphed into a winter storm. What would have been snow, thanks to global warming, was instead a pelting rain delivered in ferocious gusts of wind. Levi made a cup of Earl Grey tea and headed downstairs.

There were no windows in the workshop. Built around 1830, the ground floor of the carriage house was constructed of brick. A former colonial stable was gone. Naval hero John Paul Jones was long dead before the carriage house appeared, but the legend that he had boarded at the main house during the American Revolution lived on. In fact, the story had saved the 1758 gambrel-roof mansion from being razed by bulldozers in the early 20th century.

No one had lived in the "Jones House" since 1917, when the local historical society adapted it into a museum. Like the Woodman in Dover, the Jones House was packed with remnants of the old city—from furniture and dishware to portraits, ship models, walking sticks, and wedding gowns. And for six months each year, beginning in November when the docents went home until they returned in the spring, Levi Woodbury was the only living creature to wander the premises. He kept the house temperature cool, but not freezing. He patched the leaks, plunged the pipes, replaced the rotted bits, and patrolled the rooms like a night watchman.

. Late this rainy, chilly day, he was reproducing one of the large egg-shaped wooden finials that adorned the waist-high, cedar fence surrounding the property. Even through the brick wall, he could hear the howling wind. It rattled the door that suddenly flew open. A dark, hooded figure was framed in the entranceway. Levi, who had been hovering over his work, stood stiffly, a chisel clutched in one hand, a hammer in the other.

"My wife hates me," the hooded man said.

"What did you do this time?" Levi responded, recognizing the voice. He relaxed his grip on the tools.

"She found out that I leaked the Lucy Hale story to her boss at the newspaper," Corey Caswell moaned. Water dripped from his dark slicker.

"Wasn't me," Levi protested.

"No, it was the rugrat again," Corey said, slipping off his hood. "I think she heard me on the phone in the office, and ratted me out to her mother."

"Clever girl," Levi said. He knew he wouldn't get any more work done this evening.

"It's like living with a miniature CIA agent. Now I'm in the doghouse for doing a good deed." Corey had his coat off and shook it like a wet dog. He hung it on a hook by the door.

"What's her beef? You tipped off her boss and Claire got a good story. I was there today. Mr. Wiggin was drowning in visitors."

"The story was too good," Corey fumed. "Assassin's girlfriend, secret drawer, lost diary, dead president. Claire's article blew up the internet."

"And that's a bad thing?" Levi stretched out his question.

"You know Claire," her husband said. And, for a moment, this naked fact hung uncomfortably in the air.

"I mean," Corey began again, "you know she's pissed off at work with all the corporate takeover crap. She's the best reporter they have. Hell, she's the only real reporter left. Still, she gets all these dip-weed assignments designed to attract digital readers. There's no possibility of climbing the ladder or getting a raise anymore. The handwriting is on the wall. Reporters across the country are getting dumped by the thousands."

Levi nodded along. He knew the story well from Claire's own lips.

"Then along comes a story with sex, politics, murder, mystery. And what happens? It gets stolen right from under her nose. Two days! Two freaking days after her article appears, some 20-year-old social media influencer has half a million hits on his Lucy Hale podcast. Claire didn't even get a credit line!"

"And she blames you because?" Levi trailed off.

"Because I'm there when she comes home?" Corey wondered aloud. "She claims I should have given her fair warning to do some advanced digging, to get her arms around the story before she went to Dover to interview Billy Wiggin. I dunno. I thought I was doing us a favor."

Corey slumped against the wall. "I'm an idiot," he sighed. "I didn't even think she'd be interested if the story came from me. I don't have a great track record for earth-shattering ideas."

"Really, man," Corey said at last. "What do you think I should do?"

"What we always do," Levi said, taking his friend by the arm and pushing him towards the carriage house stairs. "Drink beer."

Chapter 14

"**I** tell you, man, I think I'm losing her," Corey said as he flopped down on Levi's worn couch/bed. "It's that seven-year itch thing."

"No, no," Levi said, popping a can of beer and handing it over. "You guys have been married eight years. It was a squeaker, but technically, you're in the clear."

A decade earlier, in the same room, their roles had been reversed. Back then, it was Levi, still obsessed over the loss of Julianne, who had come to his closest friend for support.

"Can I give you the same advice you gave me years ago?" Levi asked.

"I guess," Corey grumbled.

"You told me to trust Claire. That she was smarter than both of us put together, and she would do the right thing."

"BUT SHE DUMPED YOU!" Corey shouted.

"EXACTLY!" Levi yelled back. "Dumped me for YOU, you idiot! She made the right choice. She wanted a house and a family, not some messed up guy living in an apartment the size of a hamster cage."

Levi's words seemed to hit their mark.

"This place is pretty dinky," Corey said, glancing around.

"Microscopic," Levi agreed.

"And you were pretty screwy back then," Corey added.

"No question," his friend nodded.

"Still are," Corey deadpanned.

"Don't push it," Levi laughed. He summarized his visit to Dover, meeting Emily and chatting with Corey's mentor, Bill Wiggin. Claire's article, he confirmed, had worked like a charm, drawing in visitors and beefing up ticket sales.

"Therefore, you did a good thing," he concluded. "Claire will forget about it by tomorrow. Now take me to school about Miss Lucy Hale."

And for the next hour, they did what they loved most— talk history. From boyhood, they had shared a family curse. Corey, short for Origen Caswell, had inherited his strange name from a teetotaling, abolitionist fisherman who ran a 19th-century rooming house on the Isles of Shoals, a few miles off the New Hampshire coast. Levi Woodbury's namesake had been a prominent lawyer, politician, and justice of the New Hampshire Supreme Court. Neither man, they liked to say, had lived up to his ancestor's potential, but both shared a passion for the past.

Corey, in his role as "Keeper" of the Portsmouth Athenaeum, was a walking Wikipedia of regional history. Lucy Hale, he explained, was an enigmatic character. By some accounts, she was a raving beauty who drove young men wild. Early photographs, however, did not do her legend justice.

"Lucy was 12 when she began receiving love letters from suitors," Corey said. "Oh, I almost forgot."

He rummaged in his pocket for a few sheets of folded paper. "Listen to this!"

"Dear Miss Hale, After leaving you at Dover, I am sorry to say, for the next three days I was so cross that no one could come within a mile of me. What a disappointment it was to hear that you were not coming to Boston."

"That's from?" Levi asked.

"Sent in 1858 from future Supreme Court Justice Oliver Wendell Holmes, Jr. when Lucy was 16 years old. Holmes was at Harvard and super jealous of her other male friends," Corey said.

"Impressive."

"Holmes mentions their dalliance inside a private railroad car in Maine. Lucy replied in a letter scented with a perfume called *Kiss Me Quick*," Corey added and read another passage from the letter by Holmes. "How many young gentlemen do you keep going at once on an average?"

"Whew," Levi breathed. He pretended to mop his brow as if overheated by the steamy language.

"It was four years later, in 1862, when Lucy got a weird anonymous Valentine's Day letter from John Wilkes Booth. She was 21 by this time, and living at the National Hotel with her parents in Washington."

Corey unfolded another sheet of paper and was about to read it when Levi's phone rang.

"Yes, he's here," Levi told the caller. "Uh-huh. I know. Yes, I'll deliver your message. Yes, word-for-word. OK, see you at the party. Ba-bye."

"Are we getting divorced?" Corey winced as if the words might sting. "Give it to me straight."

Levi cleared his throat and spoke as if addressing the House of Lords. "I'm sorry I was so mean to you. There are two pieces of pizza left. Please pick up a half gallon of two-percent milk on your way home."

Corey sighed with relief. Rising from the couch and donning his jacket, he came perilously close to thanking his best friend for the intervention.

"Well, gotta run," he said. "It's not safe for us married men to hang out with you screwed-up bachelor types."

"See you at the birthday party, Big Daddy," Levi replied.

"Please read this with your magnifier," Corey said, handing over a Xerox of Booth's Valentine's letter to Lucy. "The guy creeps me out."

At the top of the carriage house stairs, Corey turned. He gave his friend two thumbs up, descended the carpeted steps, retrieved his raincoat, and disappeared into the howling wind and rain.

Chapter 15

NATIONAL HOTEL
WASHINGTON, DC
VALENTINE'S DAY, 1862

My Dear Miss Hale,

Were it not for the license which a time-honored obser-
vance of this day allows, I had not written you this poor
note. . . .

You resemble in a most remarkable degree a lady, very
dear to me, now dead and your close resemblance to her
surprised me the first time I saw you.

This must be my apology for any apparent rudeness
noticeable.—To see you has indeed afforded me a melancholy pleasure, if you can conceive of such, and should we
never meet nor I see you again—believe me, I shall always
associate you in my memory, with her, who was very beautiful, and whose face, like your own I trust, was a faithful
index of gentleness and amiability.

With a thousand kind wishes for your future happiness
I am, to you—

A Stranger

Chapter 16

Six smiling faces greeted curator Bill Wiggin as he stepped into the conference room at the Dover Public Library, just a hop and a skip away from his museum. Hanging his coat on a wooden peg, he settled at the large oak table and raised both hands.

"What's up, gang?" he said.

Bethany Waldron-James spoke first. A dark-haired former city councilor, her family had been pulling strings in town for centuries. Her red blazer sported a lapel pin of a snowman holding an American flag.

"I'm sure you know everyone," Bethany said but proceeded to introduce members of the Dover Pioneers all the same. Among them was Jenna Labreche, the bookbinder who had created the reproduction of a Lucy Hale diary. Jenna winked knowingly at Bill.

The mission of the Dover Pioneers was to promote the city's past in the most positive light. They might as well be wearing cheerleader outfits and waving pom poms, Bill thought. He stifled a laugh at the image playing in his head.

"We were wondering . . ." Rusty North said and paused for effect. The owner of North Motors was movie-star handsome and among the wealthiest men in town. The fact that pretty much everyone referred to his dealership as "Rusty Motors" did nothing to diminish his success.

"As to your wonderful discovery, if I may get right to the point, we were wondering if it might be possible to ease off a little on the negative angle when speaking with the media," Rusty said.

Thanks to Jenna's intel, the curator knew this was coming.

"To be clear, you'd like me to tap the brakes on the John Wilkes Booth narrative?" Bill said calmly.

"Exactly," Rusty said. "I'm no historian like yourself, but I've done a little reading. And it appears that Mr. Booth was in the habit of proposing marriage to quite a number of vulnerable young women."

"At least three others, besides Lucy, I'm aware of," Bill replied.

"And when he was killed, weren't there pictures of four other women in Booth's pocket besides Lucy Hale?"

"Rusty, you have been doing your homework," Bill said.

"So you would agree that Booth was both a villain and a Lothario," the auto dealer pressed.

"No doubt," the curator replied. This quick admission brought Mrs. Waldron-James back to life.

"Can we not then dispense with any speculation that Miss Hale had any knowledge of Mr. Booth's evil plans?" she said. "Or that there is some secret diary floating around out there."

Bill Wiggin pondered the questions.

"I'm not sure it's a good idea for historians to ever stop asking questions," he said. "What do you think, Jenna? You know Lucy's journals better than anyone."

Although soft-spoken and outwardly shy, Jenna sported a single braid of bright green among her otherwise auburn hair. And hidden from view was a tattoo that would have made Bethany blush.

"Lucy was a flirty one," Jenna replied. "A bit of an airhead as a girl, in my opinion. My guess is that she was very much in love with Booth, whether he reciprocated or not. As to the missing journal, it's anyone's guess. But a conspirator to Lincoln's murder? I think not."

This was apparently not the full-throated denial that Wagner Hilton was looking for. The CEO of Founder's Point Estates, a sprawling new retirement center for seniors, rose ominously from his chair.

"This has to stop!" he demanded, and banged the table for emphasis.

"Sorry?" Bill Wiggin said.

"You know," Wagner insisted. "All this negativity about our ancestors has to stop. It hurts our reputation. It hurts our kids. It hurts our economy. People don't want to take a vacation or retire in a community full of negativity."

"I'm not following the logic here," Bill said, but he was. He had tangled with the outspoken Mr. Hilton before. "We're only following up on the latest . . ."

"No!" Wagner interrupted, his face shifting from pink to crimson. "The past is the past."

"Here we go, again," the curator mumbled.

"I heard that, Billy!" Wagner shouted. "You've been telling people for years that my ancestors didn't land at Hilton's Point in 1623."

"Probably because they didn't," Billy said. "Do we really want to go there again?"

"Then why is the date on the town seal?" the businessman demanded.

"Because politicians don't know anything about history?" Bill countered.

"Gentleman, gentleman," Rusty North raised his hands in a calming motion. "I think we were making progress."

But the dam had broken. Bethany cracked next.

"I've seen the way your revisionist tour guides talk about the 1689 massacre in which Major Richard Waldron was tortured and killed by the Indians."

"You do know," Bill said as politely as he could manage, "that Major Waldron cheated the Pennacooks in business, broke signed treaties, and eventually sold 300 Indigenous men, women, and children into slavery."

"So you say," Bethany pouted.

"I don't say it," the curator protested. "In his own handwriting, Waldron proudly recorded how he tricked the Indians—whom he called 'Savages'—and captured them. They killed and mutilated him in revenge. A bit over-the-top, perhaps, but they made their feelings known."

"He's right on that," Jenna said meekly. "I helped restore those Waldron documents for the university."

Silent until now, a woman in a plaid coat made an effort to turn down the temperature.

"Mr. Wiggin," she said politely, "I certainly hope the story of the brave girls who protested against the textile mill owners is true. I've heard the girls were forced to work six days a week for up to 12 hours a day on deafening and dangerous machines under horrific conditions."

"Definitely true, Mrs. Dawes," Bill said.

"And they walked out in defiance, girls as young as eleven?"

"Right again," the curator said. "That was in 1828. The girls were making less than $15 a week in modern money."

"Well, that's a heart-warming Dover story from the past, isn't it?" Mrs. Dawes, a real estate agent, seemed to be addressing her ruffled colleagues.

"Except," Bill couldn't help himself. "The strike failed," he said. "The mill girls were forced back to work at a reduced pay rate. And, of course, our whole textile industry wouldn't have existed had it not been for enslaved Africans picking cotton in the South."

Mr. Hilton was back on his feet. "You want me to believe that our textile economy was tied to slavery?"

"Well, of course," Bill said. "Everyone knows that."

"Next thing you'll be telling me is that people in Dover kept slaves," the CEO sputtered.

"Only if they were rich enough," Bill replied, scanning the table for millionaires.

"Well, I've had enough of this enlightening and educational discussion for one day," Mr. Hilton said, donning his coat and making a beeline for the door.

"Good talk!" Bill shouted after him. The curator turned to see Jenna gritting her teeth and shaking her head.

"Nice job applying the brakes," she whispered.

Chapter 17

Controlled chaos reigned at the Caswell house. For the first hour, before the birthday party was in full swing, Claire and a couple of newspaper colleagues held court in the modest kitchen/dining room of her equally modest home.

The neighborhood, known as Atlantic Heights, had a history of its own. Built in a rush during World War I, it was the nation's first low-income housing project. Over 200 units, mostly of brick, were created to house shipbuilding families. But the war ended and the contracts dried up, leaving a cul-de-sac full of unemployed workers. A century later, the quaint little neighborhood, looking much like an English village, was among the last of the affordable housing in the gentrified city of Portsmouth. But what had been affordable two decades ago when an unmarried Corey Caswell signed the lease, had quadrupled in value. Property taxes, keeping pace, now required both Claire and Corey's modest incomes to stay afloat.

"I'm sure we could sell this place in a minute," Claire was saying to a woman clutching a Bloody Mary. "But where would we go? Corey is an expert in local history. I've been covering local news for two decades. Heather has friends in daycare, when we can afford to send her."

"Tell me about it," the journalist said, swirling the celery stick in her drink. "I used to edit the Arts and Culture section full time."

"Arts and what?" a young writer with a designer beer laughed. "I heard the publisher sold off Culture and outsourced Arts to India."

"It's true," the Bloody Mary guest said. "I was paid actual money to review books, movies, theater, and restaurants. Can you imagine? Now I'm lucky to get 20 hours a week turning crummy press releases into mediocre articles."

There was a sharp squeal from the living room, but the journalists didn't flinch. Another mother was monitoring Heather and her friends. Zeke, a year younger, had an obsession with vacuum cleaners. Minda was all about superheroes while Rosa was still in her dinosaur phase. Heather was teaching them all to do the butt-butt dance, one of her signature moves.

Upstairs in what doubled as an office and family room, Corey and Levi were in full swing.

"So you actually believe there is a lost Lucy Hale journal?" Levi said.

"I do," Corey confirmed.

"That was once hidden in a ˌsecret drawer in Lucy's dresser?"

"Correct."

"And it will tie Lucy to Booth's assassination plot?"

"No, no, no!" Corey protested. The buzz from his second beer was beginning to hit. "Lucy was just a pawn in Booth's game. But her insights might be revealing."

"That reminds me," Corey said, rising from an heirloom Caswell chair. He took two steps to a filing cabinet and began wrestling with the metal drawer.

"I wrote a whole research paper on this topic in college. That's how I met Billy Wiggin."

"You interviewed him like 20 years ago?" Levi asked.

"It was more than that," Corey said, cursing at the stuck drawer. "I remember because it was before Julianne . . ." He stopped mid-sentence. "I'm sorry."

"It's all right," Levi said. He settled his second empty bottle back into the cardboard six-pack sleeve and retrieved a fresh one. "Julianne died. Someone killed her. The murderer was never caught. I'm alive. It wasn't my fault. See, my therapy is finally working."

"Wow. It is, buddy. I'm proud of you," Corey said, truly moved.

An awkward silence followed.

"My wife ever come up in your shrink sessions?" Corey teased.

"You bet," Levi replied. "She did kind of save my life, you know, when I was still . . ."

"A basket case?" Corey offered.

"Pretty much," Levi agreed. "I mean, you were there from the start, but she kind of . . ."

The silence was back. Corey opened his mouth, but thought better of it.

"Enough bonding!" Levi commanded. "Back to Lucy."

Corey gave a mighty yank and the file drawer opened at last. He fingered his way down a row of manila files.

"Eureka," he said. He extracted a file and placed it in Levi's free hand. "Take this home and read it with your magnifier."

The "magnifier" he referenced was a bulky monitor

attached to a moving platform. A closed-circuit camera allowed the user to blow up the size of a book or document placed on the platform. Corey had three of them at the Athenaeum, and since they were rarely used, he had donated the oldest model to Levi for use at the carriage house.

"Give me the CliffsNotes version," his friend said.

"It's about Lincoln's second inauguration on the front steps of the Capitol building on March 4th, 1865," Corey explained. "Hundreds of people attended."

"I've seen the photograph. It's incredible," Levi said.

Corey wheeled around to grab an oversized book off a shelf. He flipped it open to the center spread, showing a beehive of black and white bodies swarming the steps of the Capitol. He flipped the page and Levi saw a full-sized blow-up detail of Lincoln. Although fuzzy, the hatless figure with a beard was recognizable. Lincoln was holding his inaugural speech. Corey struck a pose, ramrod straight, a hand to his heart, and began to recite from memory.

"With malice toward none, with charity for all, with firmness in the right as God gives us to see the right—let us strive on to finish the work we are in—to bind up the nation's wounds . . ."

"Okay, Abe," Levi said, applauding. "We get the picture. Now, what's the point?"

Corey leaned down and flipped the page to show another fuzzy, but recognizable image. John Wilkes Booth was standing among the crowd in the balcony above the president as he was speaking. Booth wore a silk stovepipe hat. Corey tapped the photo with his finger.

"Crap," Levi said. "Are we certain that's Booth?"

"Pretty much," his friend replied. "In 1956, some

researcher spotted a bunch of famous people in the photo of the crowd. Booth once told a friend he had attended the inauguration and was within striking distance of the president."

Levi rubbed his eyes and looked again. "It must have rankled Booth no end to hear the re-elected president talking about binding up old wounds."

"No doubt," Corey said. "Two weeks later Booth and his henchmen tried to kidnap the president and ransom him for Confederate prisoners. But the plan fell apart when Lincoln changed his itinerary at the last minute."

"Close call," Levi said.

"But here's the kicker," Corey said. "Guess who got Booth a ticket to attend the inauguration?"

"Not?" Levi said.

"Yup," Corey replied. "None other than Senator Hale's daughter Lucy."

"Friends in high places," Levi whistled.

"That's my theory," he said, bowing slightly as if to a room filled with applause. "Booth was using Lucy and her father to get access to Lincoln."

Having made his point, Corey turned to shove the filing cabinet drawer shut. As he did, there was an odd tearing sound as a thick, tightly wrapped packet fell to the floor. Bands of gray duct tape sprouted from all corners of the packet. Corey picked it up and saw a message inked in large, bold letters on the outside. He read it aloud:

PRIVATE! DO NOT OPEN!
YOU LOOK, YOU DIE!

"Open it. Open it." Levi chanted.

"Not me, man. That is Claire's angry handwriting," he

said. "She'll burn down the house with us in it if she catches me with whatever this is."

Corey was struggling to reattach the duct tape to the bottom of the file drawer when he heard a small whimpering. Heather stood in the doorway, her little lip quivering.

"Why is Mommy going to burn us up in the house?"

Chapter 18

Levi saved the day. Heather had trusted him since birth. He could calm her restless spirit with an ease that almost made her parents jealous. Heather, in return, seemed to sweep away all the grief and guilt Levi had been carrying since the night Julianne left the world.

"How's she doing?" Corey asked, now secure that Claire's mystery file was back in its hiding place.

"Are we good?" Levi asked Heather, who was hanging around his neck like a 35-pound scarf.

"YOU'RE good!" She giggled.

"Ready to turn five?" he said, struggling to extricate himself.

"No, YOU'RE five!" she said.

"More like a hundred-and-five," he managed, breaking free and settling her dinosaur-slippered feet gently on a braided rug. She was also wearing a frilly tutu, a Hulk t-shirt, and a purple hand-knit hat with mouse ears.

"You're OLD," Heather quipped, now clinging to his leg.

"CAKE!" Claire shouted from the bottom of the stairs.

No one solved the journalism crisis in America that day or the mystery of Lucy Hale's diary, but everyone agreed, despite the sugar-free cake, that Heather's birthday party was a blast. She didn't get the hamster she wanted, but she did get the unbearably cute replica her Uncle Levi had carved from a block of lime wood. It would live in her backpack for years to come.

During the educational portion of the afternoon, Zeke demonstrated how the Caswells' vacuum cleaner worked. Minda explained Wonder Woman's invisible lasso, and Rosa threw up.

"Mom?" Heather whispered during a cuddling session. "If I don't like being five, can I be four again?"

But it was the dance party that sealed the deal. Claire wasn't certain she had ever seen Levi dance, and yet, there he was with Ms. Bloody Mary cutting a pretty impressive figure. She was even a little . . . no, she was definitely not jealous. Heather was, of course, and continued to butt-butt her way between the two dancers. Amid the mayhem, Levi signaled Corey, who was acting as designated DJ. The music abruptly halted.

"Ladies and gentlemen!" Levi announced. "We have a special request. The birthday girl wishes to join her mother for a special song."

With a nod from the DJ, the room began to vibrate with the pulsing rhythm of the Talking Heads playing "Burning Down the House." With a martini in one hand and no clue what was going on, Claire Caswell joined her daughter on the living room dance floor.

"Do you think she bought it?" Levi shouted into the DJ's ear.

"Heather? Sure looks that way," Corey shouted back. "But Claire is going to grill me later."

"Not if you make her another drink," Levi shouted, only

half kidding. He was wondering about the hidden file. Best to let sleeping dogs lie.

And everything would have been perfect had Claire's cell phone not begun vibrating in her back pocket. She made a motion for her husband to tone down the music. Claire held her phone to one ear and covered the other ear with her hand.

"Okay, okay," she said. "I understand. Okay. No problem. Got it."

"That was your buddy, Billy Wiggin," she said, sidling up to her husband. "Something big is going on and he wants to meet with you first thing tomorrow."

There was no recrimination in Claire's voice, or in her smile, or in the way she put her arm around her husband and gave his waist a little squeeze. But her eyes told a different story. Corey smiled back with the most innocent expression he could muster, kissed his wife, and tugged her closer. They watched, both lost in thought, as their dancing daughter, surrounded by her friends, continued to burn down the house.

Chapter 19

"Is this secure enough?" Corey Caswell asked Bill Wiggin as they settled into metal folding chairs and faced each other across a small work table.

"Quite satisfactory," Bill said. They were, after all, locked in the anteroom of the giant vault on the third floor of the Athenaeum. Only one other staff member had a key, and she was out sick. Rows of gray archival boxes stood like little tombstones on shelves ten-feet high. The temperature and humidity were carefully regulated to preserve the ancient documents.

Dispensing with his usual history chit-chat, the Woodman Museum curator hoisted his vintage leather briefcase onto the table and snapped it open.

"What I'm going to show you, Corey, could be a forgery," he said. "If it is, it's a helluva good one."

Bill brought out a large standard-sized envelope. He made a motion to open it, then paused.

"You need to know," he said wearily, "that there's trouble afoot in the Garrison City. A few Dover muckety-mucks are up-in-arms over Claire's story—and by that I mean, my comments in her excellent article."

There was no need to prod, Corey knew. The details

were forthcoming. He nodded attentively.

"Well, you know how the museum business is these days. Preservation is super expensive. Restoring one old portrait can cost thousands of dollars. Archival materials are costly and storage is at a premium. We've got 40,000 artifacts and four buildings to care for. Museum attendance is down nationally, and so is volunteerism. Young people don't value their parents' old stuff anymore, so family heirlooms are winding up on eBay."

Corey nodded along like a bobblehead doll until Bill paused. The curator seemed to consider the enormity of what he had just said. Then he continued.

"When the Lucy dresser came in, well, it seemed like a gift from heaven. I thought we might get a little media attention for a change. A little intrigue. A little fundraiser. Maybe we could hook a big new Connecticut or New York donor from one of those multi-million-dollar seacoast McMansions. A guy can dream, can't he?"

Bill Wiggin slid three 8x10-inch glossy photographs from the envelope and pushed one slowly toward Corey. It showed the cover of a battered leather book. The initials "LH" were clearly embossed on the cover. The curator removed an identical-looking journal, encased in a plastic pouch from his briefcase and placed it next to the photo.

Corey made an admiring little grunt. "I remember that Lucy diary from my research all those years ago," he said.

"That was a great research paper," Bill said. "It should have been published."

"I was never the professor-type," Corey admitted. "I've always been a hands-on kind of guy."

"Me, too," Bill agreed. "No tenured college track for us."

"This Lucy volume is from 1862 when she was about 21. I was able to borrow it back from the historical society in Concord for comparison," Bill said. "As I'm sure you know, we have only five extant volumes of her diaries, but I've always believed she kept writing one every year, including 1865."

"I've never doubted your theory," Corey said. "Or your belief that Booth was just using her to get to Lincoln through Senator Hale."

"Which is what makes what I'm about to show you, all the more disturbing," Bill said. "He carefully removed Lucy's diary from its plastic pouch and lovingly opened it to a page marked by a slip of paper.

"You're okay without the white cotton gloves these days?" the curator confirmed. The long-held belief that documents had to be protected from the oils carried by human hands was in decline.

"Washed and dried," Corey said, displaying his fingers.

"Remember this one?" Bill asked, pointing to a passage.

Corey shivered as he touched the page where a 21-year-old Lucy Hale had recorded the day she saw John Wilkes Booth onstage. His photographic memory kicked in.

"That's the day Lucy attended a performance called *The Robbers* by the German playwright Friedrich Schiller. It's about two warring brothers, not unlike John Wilkes and his more famous brother Edwin. Anyone can read the whole play on the internet these days."

"I forgot what an egghead you are," Bill Wiggin laughed. "You could always turn a footnote into a short story. But the point remains . . ."

"The point remains," Corey picked up the thread, "that Lucy Hale was the worst journalist ever."

"She was no Boswell, that's for sure. Heck, there are 20,000 books about Lincoln, and not one scholar—present company excepted—has paid any attention to her diaries."

"Because they are so dull and reveal next to nothing," Corey said. "She found Booth's performance fascinating that night, but recorded nothing else. She sent flowers to his dressing room, a bold move. But we only learned that from other sources. Her diary didn't mention it."

"Perhaps because she didn't want her father to know," Bill offered.

He slid two more photographs across the table. Each was a photo of a handwritten page. Portions of each page had been redacted with a thick black line, apparently edited in a program like Photoshop, leaving only a few sentences visible.

The first excerpt, dated March 8, 1865, read: "W has been inconsolable since Richmond fell. He speaks openly of revenge."

"What the hell?" Corey's voice echoed inside the vault. "Where did you get this?"

"I know, I know," Bill soothed, his hands raised and open. "It has to be some sort of prank. But Lucy did call him 'Wilkes.' The date is six days after Richmond fell to Union forces and two days before General Lee surrendered at Appomattox. And the handwriting is spot on."

"Anybody could look that stuff up on Wikipedia," Corey countered.

"It gets worse." Bill swapped the sheet for one nearly identical. The date in early May was impossible to make out. The only unblocked text read: "My beloved W is alive! He was not the man killed in the Virginia barn and I told them so. My heart is beating again."

"Okay, that's just nuts!" Corey said, shaking his head wildly. "Lucy never wrote that."

The implication, both men knew, was based on an unreliable report. It was rumored that Lucy Hale was among a small group called to identify the body of John Wilkes Booth following the 12-day manhunt. The rumor sparked a theory that Booth had escaped being killed and lived incognito for decades following the assassination.

"These three photos," Bill said, "arrived in the museum post office box. They were addressed to me with no return details. The envelope was postmarked in Dover. There was no note."

"This has to be some conspiracy theory nut!" Corey was still vibrating with emotion.

"Agreed. But the nut has done his homework. Even a few reputable scholars have suggested Lucy might have been the mysterious woman seen at Booth's autopsy aboard the ship *Montauk*. Some still believe Booth was not shot in Richard Garrett's barn."

"That's right," Corey snorted. "I forgot. Wasn't he picked up by a flying saucer along with Elvis and Amelia Earhart?"

"Crazy as it all seems, as a historian and museum curator, I have to keep an open mind." Billy stood and began repacking his briefcase.

"But if this gets out before I can track down the source, the Dover Pioneers will roast me in the town square."

Corey saw the next line coming like a freight train.

"Oh, no!" he said. "You want me NOT to tell Claire that Lucy was in on the conspiracy and John Wilkes Booth lived to a ripe old age?"

"Please! Just until I prove where these forgeries came from and nip this in the bud," Bill begged.

"I've got a better solution," Corey said. "Let me flip that little switch on the wall. It will suck all the oxygen out of this vault. We'll die a horrible death gasping for air, which is easier than keeping a secret from my wife."

Chapter 20

MADE ABOARD THE IRONCLAD USS *MONTAUK*
WASHINGTON, DC NAVY YARD

To Secretary of War Edwin Stanton
Sir,

I have the honor to report that in compliance with your orders, assisted by Dr. Woodward, USA, I made at 2 PM this day, a postmortem examination of the body of J. Wilkes Booth, lying on board the Monitor *Montauk* off the Navy Yard.

The left leg and foot were encased in an appliance of splints and bandages, upon the removal of which, a fracture of the fibula (small bone of the leg) 3 inches above the ankle joint, accompanied by considerable ecchymosis, was discovered.

The cause of death was a gun shot wound in the neck—the ball entering just behind the sterno-cleido muscle—2½ inches above the clavicle—passing through the bony bridge of fourth and fifth cervical vertebrae—severing the spinal cord and passing out through the body of the sterno-cleido of right side, 3 inches above the clavicle. Paralysis of the entire body was immediate, and all the horrors of consciousness of suffering and death must have been present to the assassin during the two hours he lingered.

Signed: Surgeon General Joseph K. Barnes

Chapter 21

"In other words," Levi was straightening up his messy apartment as Corey finished reading the autopsy report aloud, "Booth was dead."

"Definitely," Corey confirmed. "He shot Lincoln at the theater and broke his leg leaping from the opera box to the stage. Twelve days later, he was shot inside a burning barn in Virginia. Soldiers sewed his body up in a horsehair blanket. It was transferred from a wagon to a steamer to a tugboat and into the ship USS *Montauk*. They laid his corpse out on a carpenter's bench for examination. His leg was broken. There was a scar on his neck from a recent operation. The initials JWB were tattooed on his hand. A dozen people identified him."

"So what's the big fuss?" Levi said. "You wanted tea, not a beer?"

"Tea, please. Gotta keep my mind sharp. Claire knows I met with Bill. She's gonna want answers and I'm a terrible liar." Corey accepted the steaming mug.

"I offer this advice as your best friend." Levi popped the tab on a can of beer. "Stab your old history friend Billy in the back and tell your wife the truth. Claire will track down the forgers, win a Pulitzer, and you don't end up covered in honey and stuffed down an anthill. Can we go get lunch?"

Corey was pacing. The floor space in Levi's living room was not much bigger than that in the Athenaeum vault. He found himself sipping and staring out the window. Nature's next attempt at winter had also failed, leaving only a white frosting on the lawn of the old Georgian mansion next door.

"But what if it's real?" he said at last. "I mean, the dresser was real. The secret drawer was real."

"You're starting to freak me out," Levi warned.

"There's a legend that Lucy was among the witnesses taken aboard the USS *Montauk* to identify Booth's body. I always figured it was crap, but . . ."

"Maybe Lucy did see the body. She was probably traumatized. Booth was so beaten up from his two-week manhunt and having his corpse dragged around in a blanket that she didn't recognize him. Or she was in denial. C'mon! How dark would it be in the hold of a warship in 1865?"

Corey moved from the window to the couch. "Pretty good deducting, Mr. Watson," he said.

"Thanks a pant-load, Sherlock." Levi was already putting on his winter coat and retrieving his boots. "Good enough for soup?"

The Bow Street Eatery was packed as usual. But their plan to bag lunch back to the Athenaeum shifted when Corey spotted a young couple wrapping their leftovers and swooped in. He settled his bowl of tomato florentine and a slice of zucchini, red pepper, and cheddar quiche on their table. Levi followed suit with a plate of Jamaican chicken over black beans and rice. Three minutes into the feeding frenzy, Levi spoke up.

"Feeling better?"

"A little," his friend admitted, although he kept glancing nervously at the doorway.

"Relax, Sherlock. Your wife is out of town on an interview, remember? At the birthday party, she kept saying— Just what we need, an article about another spa opening!"

Corey searched his memory.

"And you're picking up the rugrat from daycare at 3 p.m."

"Right, right, I knew that," Corey said.

But his mind was churning with the legend of the assassin's escape. It began, as Corey told Levi, when a dying man named John St. Helen confessed to a Texas lawyer. St. Helen confessed he was John Wilkes Booth. St. Helen claimed he had escaped from Garrett's burning barn and, with the help of President Andrew Johnson, hid his identity for decades. St. Helen miraculously recovered. The Texas lawyer, a guy named Finis L. Bates, would never see him alive again.

"Pull the other one," Levi said, blowing on a forkful of hot chicken as Corey resumed his summary.

John St. Helen, a drunk by reputation, changed his name again—to David Elihu George. While living in Oklahoma, Mr. George ingested strychnine and died in 1903 at age 64. On his deathbed, once again, he claimed to be the man who assassinated Lincoln. The town undertaker embalmed him, but no one claimed the body. The mortician then dressed Mr. George-St. Helen-Booth in a suit of clothes and placed the body in a chair in front of the funeral home.

"A promotional embalmed cadaver," Levi said. "Truth in advertising."

"Exactly," Corey agreed and resumed his tale.

Years later, while passing through Oklahoma, Finis

Bates recognized the body on display as John St. Helen. Bates began exhibiting the mummified corpse as John Wilkes Booth, renting it to sideshows. The body was stolen, ransomed, battered in a train wreck, chipped by souvenir collectors, sold and resold. In 1907 Bates documented his version of the story in a popular book called *The Escape and Suicide of John Wilkes Booth*. The mummy was on display right up to World War II and is rumored to be in a private collection today.

"That, my friend," Levi said, having polished off a piece of cranberry pie, "is the dumbest, most implausible, load of horse manure I've ever heard."

"You'd think," Corey said. "But check the reviews online. People are still downloading digital copies of the book and giving it five stars. Apparently, if you believe the government is lying about everything from the moon landing to Area 51, this stuff has the ring of truth."

"And you're afraid, if the Lucy journal gets out, it will bolster the crazy conspiracy theory?" Levi was beginning to see his friend's dilemma.

"Have you read the news lately?" Corey said, growing sullen. "We're in a war for the truth in America. And I'm not sure we're winning."

Chapter 22

LATE SPRING, 1910
WARNER, NEW HAMPSHIRE

"Lucy?"

Lucy froze at the familiar voice.

"You out here?"

"Over this way, Willy," she said as cheerfully as she could manage.

Lucy Hale Chandler slid the bottom drawer of her dresser closed and stepped out from behind the gilded full-length mirror. Though graying and slightly stooped, William E. Chandler was still tall and handsome. Not leading-man handsome, but politician handsome, statesmanlike, academic. There was something dignified in his bearing. He was a man who carried his importance from room to room.

And important he had been—from Secretary of the Navy to a Senator from New Hampshire, to a lawyer and owner of the *Concord Monitor* newspaper. He had been, she sometimes thought, more than she deserved. William had, after all, rescued her from scandal and spinsterhood. He had given her a child, a home, a new name, and even a touch of social status, although tongues still wagged. It was a lot, considering the alternative. And if the arrangement didn't include love, well, love was a dangerous thing.

Hadn't her love for Booth, or infatuation, nearly destroyed her family and wrecked her father's career? She had been seduced by what the newspapers called "the most handsome man in America." She had treasured his words, worn his ring, and believed his plans for their future together. She had written about those events on paper. And now, decades later, those words could still destroy her family.

"What are you doing alone in the barn?" her husband asked, exposing only the edge of his annoyance. "The Quimbys will be here within the hour." He was immaculately dressed, as usual.

"I was just remembering," she said, stepping out of the shadows. "The old Dover furniture. It arrived. I was thinking of the house. Of Father, of Mother, of Spain. And . . ."

Lucy struggled for words. She moved closer until their shoes were almost toe to toe. She ached for the embrace she knew was not coming. Lucy reached up to brush a piece of lint from his suit.

"Remember how you fancied me back in the olden days?" she said, tugging the two sides of his suit coat together. He had put on weight. Not as much as she, but enough to create a roundness.

How different things might have been, she thought, had she accepted his attentions as a girl. But he was so serious back then, so stiff and awkward, so needy, while her head was full of dreams and promise. So he went off to marry another. William and his first wife, Ann, the daughter of a New Hampshire governor, had three boys. Lucy followed her family to Washington, DC, where she found parties and theaters and lines of young men ready to take her hand and dance.

It was Death, she knew, not Cupid, that finally brought them together. The passing of her father, the cancer of his wife. William had insisted on a strictly private wedding. The ceremony at the Dover house during the last week of 1874 was attended by a handful of discreet guests. It rated barely two sentences in most newspapers. Their marriage was less a bond than a contract of convenience. William needed a wife. Lucy needed a reputation. And it had been a successful bargain. She disappeared into the role of Mrs. William Chandler, her husband's "loyal helpmate," as once reported. And now they were old, their mission almost completed, their legacy intact. Neither would see the next decade, she predicted.

Lucy had no regrets, as she straightened her husband's tie. No regrets, save one. She wanted only to speak of the event that had changed her life, and the life of the nation. But William had said "No." Not a word of her dalliance with that cursed actor must leave her lips. Not once, not ever. And so it had been for almost four decades. And so it would always be.

"You run along, dear," she said like a mother sending her child off to play. "I'll be there in a minute."

She stood on her toes and tilted her head for a peck on the cheek. The ritual completed, he turned without another word and exited the barn.

Heart racing, Lucy Chandler hurried back to the beautiful dresser of Spanish wood. If it had come to set her world on fire, it would not succeed. She would destroy the evidence before it destroyed her. But first, just once, she would read what a very foolish young woman had written long ago.

Readjusting her skirts, bending on painful knees, she

pulled on the brass handles of the bottom drawer. Holding her breath and extending a trembling hand, she touched the initials "LH." She heard a familiar clunk as a panel opened to reveal the secret sacred space. It was empty.

Chapter 23

Corey Caswell came bearing gifts. The peace offering, he hoped, might soften the upcoming interrogation.

"Chunky Monkey AND peanut butter cups!" Claire exclaimed, emptying the bag.

"Shhh," Corey gestured, finger to lips, but it was too late. The little thing with elephant ears rushed into the kitchen. It was share and share alike.

"You first," Corey said, finally closing the door to Heather's bedroom hours later.

"I'll make you a deal," she said, pulling her legs under herself on the couch and grabbing a vintage afghan. "I won't ask you what Bill Wiggin said if you don't ask about the hidden file."

He made an effort to appear confused.

"I know you know," Claire said. "The thing taped under the filing cabinet. You look, you die."

Corey tried to look innocent.

"You did a great job putting it back," Claire said, patting the cushion beside her. "And I appreciate that you respect my privacy. But there are no secrets in the House of Heather."

"Sees all, hears all," Corey agreed.

Claire spat in her palm and thrust her hand out to

shake. When he took it, she pulled him toward her.

An hour later, nested in their metal-framed bed on the second floor, Corey broke the cozy silence.

"Oh hell," he said. "Levi was right. I'm going to tell you what Billy told me, and you're going to do whatever you do with the information."

Buried in blankets, he explained about the three photographs, the two conspiracy theories, and the possibility that Lucy knew Booth was planning something nefarious.

"But you believe it's all fake?" she said, vibrating with enthusiasm.

"I don't believe a word of it. And I'm not your source on this," he warned.

"Of course, of course! My lips are sealed. We never met." Grabbing her phone off the night table, she began tapping a few notes.

"You say the ship was spelled M-o-n-t-a-u-k?"

"Yes. It was a Civil War ironclad battleship, or what they called a 'monitor.' In pictures, it looks like an early submarine."

"And the dead mummy guy who claimed to be Booth was named John St. Helen?"

"Yes," Corey groaned. "I have a book about him in the family room. I'll get it for you in the morning."

Claire tried to sleep for five full minutes before leaping out of bed and pulling on her warmest night clothes. She grabbed her laptop and crept out of the bedroom. Five minutes later she was back, kneeling by the bedside, her face pressed to his.

"Thank you," she whispered directly into his ear.

"You're welcome," he muttered.

"But we had a deal," she said. "Now I have to trust you with my secret file."

Corey raised himself on one elbow and shivered as the chill hit his skin.

"Look, babe," he said. They were eye-to-eye in the room, lit only by a distant outdoor street light. "I know you were alive before you met me. So you had some nudie pictures taken, you robbed a bank and stole a horse—these things happen. You don't owe me an explanation."

She said nothing for half a minute and Corey almost dozed. When she sniffled, he opened one eye to see a glistening tear. That was the night, Claire decided, it was time to tell her husband the whole story. And that night, only Heather slept.

"You know you can never ever tell Levi what's in that file of yours," Corey said, his voice just above a whisper. They were at the breakfast table now, two totally exhausted humans drinking coffee.

"Never ever," she repeated.

And yet, as a historian, Corey couldn't condone destroying the documents. Claire, as a journalist, had reached the same conclusion. Truth be told, it had not started as a secret file. She wasn't hiding anything from Levi or Corey back in those days because she had never met them.

The Julianne Frost file had been one among hundreds from Claire's early articles in the *Portsmouth Journal*. Being first to arrive at a murder scene had, in fact, been a thrill for the reporter fresh out of college. And despite the horror of a woman her own age senselessly murdered on a beautiful spring day, Claire had learned a critical lesson. The news, she discovered, never stops. She was amazed how quickly an unsolved crime disappears from the front page, and eventually, from the public forum.

No one was ever charged in the Julianne Frost homicide. For years, Claire continued her investigation privately. The Frost file grew fatter as the case grew cold. It was ten years and two dates with Levi Woodbury before she made the connection. By then it was too late to identify herself to the attractive moody museum caretaker. To be honest, she had been hooked from the start. He was the nicest guy in town, she thought, broken, perhaps, but repairable. If she couldn't solve the murder, she could at least try to fix . . .

"You know this puts a whole new spin on everything," Corey interrupted her thoughts, "psychologically, I mean." He was cradling an aching head in his hands, elbows on the table.

"Can we not go there?" she said. "I didn't know you guys. I didn't know the victim. And back then, I thought I might have the makings of a true crime bestseller. It sounds cold now, but I was ambitious. Maybe I could parlay the book into a job at *The Boston Globe*, work my way up to *The Times*." She snorted a little laugh at the memory.

"The irony is," Corey gave her a wounded half-smile, "I was so busy protecting Levi from the newspapers back then. I never saw your byline. I never made the connection."

"And I was too scared to bring it up," she admitted. "I'm sorry. I didn't want to wreck what we were building together."

A thump from the small upstairs bedroom signaled the end of their heart-to-heart. A toilet flushed. Tiny footsteps descended the stairs. A sleepy Heather climbed into her mother's lap and placed a carved wooden hamster on the kitchen table.

"Hammy's hungry," Heather said, yawning.

Corey rose on command and gestured toward the cupboard door. "And what, pray tell, would Hammy like for breakfast this fine morning?"

"He only eats hamster food!" Heather said, striking an indignant pose.

"Of course. How forgetful of me," her father said, opening the cupboard door. "And hamster food is made out of what?"

"Cheerios!" mother and daughter cried in unison.

Chapter 24

Claire found Billy Wiggin upstairs in the museum struggling to dress a female mannequin in a World War II uniform.

"Need a little help?" she offered from the door.

Spotting Claire, the curator's face reflected a pallid blend of surprise, embarrassment, and fear.

"Corey told you," Bill said flatly.

"We're married," she replied. "It comes with the turf. But I'm not here for some cheap headline. There's a bigger story going on. I can smell it."

"Something stinks all right," he said, sinking into a folding chair. "Or maybe I'm just getting too old for this job. People don't seem to care about history anymore, real history, that is."

"Corey says the same thing sometimes when he's had a bad day," she soothed. "He says all people care about now are ghosts, pirates, scandals, and conspiracy theories."

"And good luck telling a fourth-grade class about John Parker Hale," Billy sighed. "Talk about America's first openly anti-slavery congressman, a member of five political parties, a guy who ran for president, who lived right here in town—and I get a room full of blank faces. All they see is the portrait of a chubby, uncomfortable-looking old man in a funny suit."

The curator looked like he might come undone, but carried on. "Do you know how many books there are about Abraham Lincoln?"

Claire shook her head.

"Zillions and counting," Bill said. "Not to mention an endless stream of books, movies, and research papers on the assassination. The two most photographed men of the era were Booth and Lincoln."

"And how many books about Senator Hale, do you think?" He quickly answered himself. "Two! That's how many. Both obscure, both out of print. I may be the only person alive who read them cover to cover."

Claire raised her hand as if in school. "Did you say Hale was in five political parties?"

"Democratic, Liberty Party, Free-Soil Party, Opposition Party, and Republican," Bill rattled off the list.

"Look, Mr. Wiggin . . ."

"Billy," he corrected.

"Look, Billy, I'm here to get the facts. So far, from what Corey told me, you only have a couple of redacted photographs of what may or may not be from a missing diary by Lucy Hale. Correct?"

"Correct," he said.

"And these copies mysteriously arrived following the reappearance of Lucy Hale's lost dresser. I'd call that a whale of a coincidence," she said. "The dresser was an anonymous gift, right?"

A drop of sweat, a squint, and a hard swallow were all the clues Claire needed. "C'mon, Billy. Out with it," she said.

"Can I show you something?" he asked, heading for the door, not waiting for a reply.

Claire followed down a well-used circular staircase, past the looming polar bear, out the exit, across the lawn, and into the Keefe House next door. In the upstairs research room, the curator withdrew a faux leather-bound book from a metal shelf. The name JOHN P. HALE was embossed in thick gold letters on the cover.

"This is one of those two books about Hale I mentioned," Bill said, laying it open on a modern desk. The first two pages were blank, followed by an illustration of the senator. Hale was younger, thinner, and more handsome than in his full-length portrait, despite a three-way combover at the sides and top of his noble dome. A slice of tissue paper protected the illustration from the title page dated 1892. The book, nearly 250 pages, Bill explained, was a transcript of the speeches. They were delivered at the dedication of the larger-than-life-sized statue of Hale still standing by the front steps of the New Hampshire State House.

"Notice who paid for this costly bronze monument," Bill said, pointing to a line on the title page.

Claire read the name aloud: "William E. Chandler. That's Lucy's husband, right?"

Bill nodded. He licked his thumb and turned the page. A faded grayish photograph showed the heroic figure of JP Hale in bronze, one arm thrust out, fingers spread in an expressive gesture. His other metal hand, hanging towards the hem of his frock coat, appeared to grip a rolled document.

"The bronze figure is eight feet, four inches tall. It was cast in Germany," he explained with pride. "Senator Hale stands on a granite pedestal, making the monument 18-feet high. It's darned impressive standing next to the statues of Daniel Webster, the famous orator, and John Stark, our hero of the Revolution."

"I've seen it tons of times in Concord," Claire admitted, "but never bothered to read the plaque."

"You're in good company," Bill said. "I wonder how many of our 400 representatives and 24 state senators could identify the guy on the pedestal who they pass by on the way to govern New Hampshire."

"And like a good politician, you have cleverly evaded my question." Claire smiled. Billy, perking up, smiled back.

"Or have I?" he said.

"The Chandlers gave you Lucy's dresser?" she whispered, although no one else was in the room.

"Off the record?" Bill asked.

"Totally," she confirmed.

"There is a family connection, but the contract is specific. Lucy's dresser is on loan. That loan can be revoked at any time if the name of the donor is exposed."

"Whew," Claire breathed. "I see why you were freaking out."

"And why I need to trust you implicitly," he said.

"Where do you think I should start solving this mystery?"

Bill gestured back to the photo in the open book. For the first time, she noticed there was a boy at the foot of the monument. He wore knee-high boots, a wide-brimmed hat, a starched wide collar, a floppy oversized bowtie, and what appeared to be a girl's dress.

"He looks like the kid with the dog in the old shoe advertisements," Claire said.

"Buster Brown," Bill confirmed, enjoying the reveal. "He had a comic strip, too. But the little urchin in the photo is John Parker Hale Chandler."

"Lucy had a kid?" Claire hadn't seen it coming.

"You're looking at him," Bill said. "And you didn't hear it from me."

Chapter 25

It is a high pleasure to me to give the statue to my native state and city as an evidence of the strong affection which I bear to my home. As a work of art, it cannot, I think, be justly criticized; and, as a likeness in face and form, it must be received as being as good as could be expected in a design made from photographs never fully satisfactory to the family or friends.

Statues of the illustrious dead and memorial arches and monuments are principally valuable for the lessons which they teach to new generations. No inculcation has sprung from any life more noble than the one inspired by Mr. Hale's career: That there can be no higher aim in life than to espouse a humane and holy cause in the hour of its gloom and despondency, and to devote one's self constantly and fearlessly to its service.

Gifted with pleasing form, feature, and voice, receiving an excellent collegiate and professional education, and achieving success as a lawyer, at an early age John Parker Hale became the favorite orator of his political party, an associate and friend of Franklin Pierce, its greatest leader in the state, and was elected a representative in congress. But when he was called upon to support the forcible annexation of Texas and an unjust war with Mexico, in order to extend the domain of human chattel slavery, and to bring more slave states into the Union, he rebelled, for which he was expelled from his party and debarred from congress; and his now historic proclamation of resistance was the beginning of the political antislavery movement in New Hampshire.

The conflict upon which he then entered aroused the best elements of his noble nature, and enlisted every energy of his soul from 1845, when the struggle began, down to 1865, when every slave was free and liberty was universal in America.

Once engaged in Freedom's battle, Mr. Hale's hostility to every form of human debasement became intense, and his reverence for humanity, his respect for man made in the image of his Creator, became the absorbing and controlling principle of his existence.

It was alike abhorrent to him that black men, women, and children should be sold as chattels upon the auction-block, under national laws, and that the sailors of the republic should be flogged with brutal whips. To contend against the enslavement or degradation of either the bodies or the souls of human beings of any race, color, or condition, was the deliberate mission of his life.

No more inspiriting example can be studied by the ingenuous youth of New Hampshire than the life of him whose statue rises before us. His character and life should be imitated by the present and every future generation in the state he loved and served.

Chapter 26

"Great sleuthing, babe," Corey said, leafing through the John P. Hale dedication book. "You cracked our friend Mr. Wiggin like a walnut. And he just gave you this 1892 copy of it?"

"Turns out the museum has a boxful," Claire said. "People have donated them over the years. Nobody reads it, but I'm betting it's rich with clues. Both Lucy and her young son were in the audience at the dedication of her father's statue. That's little JPH Chandler in the Buster Brown costume."

Corey examined the image with a professional eye. "And you're going to plow your way through this dense mass of Victorian speechwriting?"

"No, you are!" she cooed. "Because you love me until death do us part. And because you're the history guy. And, I have to cover the annual Top Ten Seacoast Basketball Players front-page feature for the newspaper."

She groaned.

"I'm sorry about the death of journalism," he cooed back, as they snuggled on the couch. The couple had managed a rare lunch together at home while Heather was in daycare.

"It's either that article or Top Ten Depressed Reporters

Who Jumped Off the I-95 Bridge. Did I mention we lost Adam?"

"He jumped?" Corey mocked shock.

"He took the corporate buyout from the paper. Six months' severance. That's what we have come to. Do you think that's enough time to write and publish a bestseller?"

"You're not thinking of . . ." he let the sentence die.

"Don't worry," she said. "I'm aware that one percent of novelists earn 98 percent of the publishing royalties."

"What's Adam gonna do?"

"He's joining his brother's HVAC business. Beth, who got riffed, is driving a truck for Amazon. Rachel is doing PR for a pharmaceutical firm. I'm thinking more about becoming a stripper down at the Silver Pole on Route 1."

"I'll be in the front row every night with a fistful of dollars," Corey promised.

"And the rugrat?"

"Oh, she'll be back home with my second wife, who I don't love half as much as you."

Claire glanced at her phone. "Shoot! Ten minutes to lift-off," she sighed and set a reminder alarm.

"I've got to get back, too," he said. Her husband made an effort to stand, but she held him down.

"Ten minutes!" she repeated. "Cherish it!"

They shared a minute of silence that slowly filled with sounds. Even through the storm windows, they could hear a couple of dog walkers chatting outside. A hammer beat out a rhythm in the distance. Cars whooshed on the high-rise bridge and, further down the Piscataqua River, a tugboat tooted. Corey spoke first.

"It must have been weird."

"What?" Claire asked sleepily.

"For Lucy," he said. "Sitting there, probably on a wooden folding chair, in the crowd on a warm day at the dedication, looking up at a giant bronze statue of her father. By the size of this book, the speeches took hours. And she had to sit there, listening to people describing her dad as if he had been a god. Meanwhile, everyone was looking at her, judging her."

"Nobody wants to see their father on a pedestal," she said. "But Hale kind of earned it, don't you think?"

Corey had to agree. Fighting slavery, opposing the Mexican War and the Fugitive Slave Act, ending the flogging of sailors in the U.S. Navy—JP Hale was looking pretty heroic. But his battles had certainly earned him many enemies.

"Statues are all about legacy," Corey mused. "William Chandler was pushing really hard to preserve the memory of Lucy's dad."

Claire instinctively checked the time and groaned again.

"Billy Wiggin all but admitted Lucy's dresser came from the Chandler family," Claire pondered. "But why? He said they never spoke about Lucy's connection to Booth. It was a very public secret."

"They probably didn't know about the hidden drawer or the missing diary," Corey countered.

"If there is a missing diary," Claire corrected.

"Right," Corey agreed. "To the Chandler family, the old dresser was probably little more than a relic and a tax deduction."

"There's a dramatic story here," he continued. "William

Chandler was paying big bucks to build a monument to keep Lucy's dad in the history books. At the same time, he was trying to bury the scandal of his wife's past."

"BURIED ALIVE! The Lucy Hale Story, now in Technicolor at a theater near you!" Claire spoke in her best movie trailer voice.

"Imagine," Corey wondered aloud, "the impact those two warring forces might have had on their only child. He was half-Hale, half-Chandler. Poor kid."

"A BOY TRAPPED BETWEEN FAME AND SHAME!" Claire was on a roll.

"Okay. Got it, babe," Corey said as Claire's alarm sounded.

"You're on kid duty," she said, suddenly all business. "Don't forget she's at daycare." Claire pulled on her parka and grabbed her bag in a single swift motion.

Chapter 27

Linda, a long-haired research intern on loan from the local university, dropped a folder into Corey's inbox. Over two centuries old, the Athenaeum began as a shared resource for a cluster of ministers, merchants, and sea captains. Today 400 "proprietors" keep the nonprofit archive alive and located in a Federal-style building in the heart of Market Square.

"Here's that genealogy report Mrs. Pridham wrote about Puddle Dock, Mr. Caswell," she said.

"Thanks, Linda," the Keeper pulled his nose from an old book and smiled. "Hey, have you ever heard of Lucy Hale?"

"The singer from that American Idol spinoff?" she asked.

"Not that one. How about John Parker Hale?"

The intern shook her head.

"William Chandler?"

"The mystery writer? No, that was Raymond Chandler," she said.

"How about John Wilkes Booth?"

"C'mon, Mr. C. Everybody knows the actor who shot Lincoln. He's like super famous," Linda said.

"Fame trumps legacy," Corey muttered.

"What say, Mr. C?"

"Oh, nothing. Thanks, Linda."

An hour of googling later, Corey had gathered a basic biography of the boy in the Buster Brown outfit. John Parker Hale Chandler was born in 1885 when his mother, Lucy, was 44. He was seven years old when he pulled the cord to unveil the statue of his namesake in 1892, revealing the grandfather he had never met. The crowd cheered. The band played, and four hours of speechmaking began. By 1915, JPH Chandler was living in Portsmouth. He showed up in Tucson, Arizona, and was dead in California by 1940.

"I'll keep digging," he told Claire during an afternoon phone call. "But it's a fair guess he inherited his mother's dresser at some point. Although he had three brothers-in-law. Maybe we can track down a will."

"Thanks, dear!" Claire said. She was shouting into her phone from a noisy high school sports event.

"I can barely hear you," Corey shouted back.

"I just got a voicemail," the line crackled, "from a guy in California! He said he's doing a docu-(crackle) about Lucy Hale's journal for PBS or the History (crackle) or somebody. He read my story online. Wants to interview (crackle) on camera. This is not good."

"Stall him. We'll talk about it when you get home, probably late?"

Levi Woodbury stuck his head in the door.

"Yes. I pick her up in an hour. I know. Okay. Look, gotta run, Lee's here. Love ya, too." He hung up.

"Still hates her job?" Levi asked, already lounging in the overstuffed visitor's chair.

"Worse than ever," Corey nodded. "Another round

of corporate cuts and there'll be nothing left but an editor working out of his bedroom in his pajamas. If she takes their golden parachute offer—and it's more like a golden handkerchief—we can't live off my salary."

"She needs a hot investigative story to lift her spirits," Levi said. "Speaking of spirits, any news about Mr. Booth's mummy?"

"We've got pieces to the puzzle, but they don't add up," Corey stated. "It looks like Lucy's dresser was donated by a descendant of the Chandler family. That's not to be repeated. She had a son who lived right here in Portsmouth, not far from you down Middle Street."

"No way!" Levi said.

"John Parker Hale Chandler. Poor kid. His father was a pretty controversial guy, too. I was reading how William Chandler helped Teddy Roosevelt create the Great White Fleet of ships, turning the U.S. Navy from wood to steel."

"Oh, here's a flash," Corey added. "Frederick Douglass attended the dedication of a statue to Lucy's father, the one in Concord."

"THE Frederick Douglass?" Levi was impressed.

"The very one," Corey confirmed. "Former slave turned black abolitionist, friend of Lincoln. He even spoke passionately about JP Hale. Said when the senator fought against racism, it was like a HALE STORM. Get it?"

Corey held up the 1892 dedication book. "It's all in here. The more I learn about JP Hale, the more worthy he seems of his statue."

"There's a letter in here from John Greenleaf Whittier, the Quaker poet and abolitionist."

"Love that guy," Levi said. "He was a bachelor like me and wrote some pretty creepy poems."

"Whittier wrote Chandler to say how much he admired Lucy's dad. Whittier regretted he was too sick to attend the dedication of the statue in 1892. A few weeks later he croaked."

"Sounds like you're getting pretty caught up in the weeds of this Lucy thing," Levi said.

"Totally," his friend replied. "Claire too. Can I read you a little of what Douglass said?"

Levi propped his feet up on Corey's desk as Linda, the intern, poked her head around the office door.

"There's a Mr. William Wiggin on the phone from Dover," she said.

"I'm not here," Corey said, waving his arms in protest. He couldn't bear to face his old friend after breaking his oath.

"He sounds pretty stressed," the intern warned.

"Say, I'll call him back in 15. Thanks, Linda."

Levi grinned. "I can't believe you took my advice and ratted him out to your wife." Corey ignored the jab. He thumbed to a bent page in the Hale book.

"Listen to this," he said. "Imagine it's Frederick Douglass speaking."

Chapter 28

DEDICATION OF THE JOHN P. HALE STATUE
SPEECH BY FREDERICK DOUGLASS
AUGUST 3, 1892
CONCORD, NH

I have made no preparation to address this audience, and had hoped that the managers of this occasion would allow me to sit here and only give color to the occasion. (Laughter.) I hardly ought to be here today on account of my health. I am very feeble, and am suffering from an attack which would excuse me almost for my absence from this place; but I desired to be here, and I may say that I never in all my life desired more fervently to make a speech than on this occasion, and never felt myself less able to do so than now.

I want, however, to say that, in 1845, it was my pleasure and my privilege to look upon the manly form of John P. Hale, and thereafter to meet him often, and to hear his melodious voice and listen to the thrilling sentiments he was accustomed to utter in connection with the great cause of liberty.

I traveled with him some and one thing that struck me in regard to John P. Hale. It was this: Wherever he stopped, and there were any little children around, little girls and

boys, somehow or other they were irresistibly attracted to
John P. Hale. (Applause.) They would lean on his knees,
play about him; and I thought that was a good sign, a very
striking evidence of the greatness of the man. And if you
ever see a man in your travels anywhere in this world from
whom children shrink, there is something wrong about that
man. (Laughter.)

I remember the time that I came here, fifty years ago.
I was a slave, even here in New Hampshire. Indeed, in all
parts of the country I was a slave. The country was a slave
hunting-ground. Not only the South, but the North, was in
a state to make it dangerous for any man to take the side of
the slave. There was no valley so deep, no mountain so high,
no glen so secluded, no spot so sacred to liberty, in any part
of this broad land, whereon I could place my foot and say,
with safety, I am now secure from the slave hunters.

The thing that pleases me today is the vast and
wonderful change that has taken place. Yes, this audience is
full compensation for the slender audience that met me in
the old town hall, with its side benches. I can see it now, but
it is gone. This was not such a city then as it is now.

I wanted to be here because I am one of the vast multi-
tude of emancipated ones whom John P. Hale devoted his
heart and his transcendent abilities to liberate. I wanted to
be here to represent those millions; to show you that one,
at least, of those millions appreciates the greatness, the
grandeur, and the devotion and the courage of John P. Hale.
(Applause.)

I have often said that the want of congress now, or
want of the senate, is another John P. Hale. (Applause.) We
have a representative who has inherited his principles, and

has the nerve to stand up on the floor of the senate and that is your senator, Hon. William E. Chandler. (Applause.) He is no coward. But, great as he is, he will admit that John P. Hale was a little taller man. (Laughter)

We, in this day, can hardly understand the measure of the greatness of that man's courage, the greatness of the sacrifice he made, the greatness of his faith in the ultimate triumph of great principles. My friends, I have spoken longer than I intended. I did not expect to speak at all.

Chapter 29

Levi whistled. "Powerful stuff," he said as Corey concluded his reading from the Frederick Douglass speech and set his book down.

"It's got me thinking," the Keeper said. "I mean, who else comes to mind when you think of American abolitionists?"

Levi mused. "I'd say William Lloyd Garrison, Harriet Beecher Stowe, Lincoln, of course, and Sojourner Truth?"

"Same here. Plus Harriet Tubman. And maybe John Brown, if you include the radical fringe. But here we have Frederick Douglass, the greatest of them all, showing up in New Hampshire, despite being sick and frail, to shower praise on John Parker Hale."

"We may have underestimated Hale. And Douglass also mentioned William Chandler by name. That was impressive," Levi added.

"And yet," Corey opened both arms, palms up like a preacher, "nobody mentioned the elephant in the audience— the woman who almost married the guy who murdered The Great Emancipator himself."

"Call for you," Linda said, leaning into Corey's office.

"Shoot!" he almost swore. "I forgot about Billy."

"No, this one is from California," the intern said. "It's a

guy named Travis. Something about a history documentary."

"There's a form for that on our website," Corey said. "It's under Rights, Copyrights, and Usage Fees."

"Eww, Mr. Hollywood," Levi taunted as the intern hurried off.

"We get these requests all the time," the Keeper said. "Mostly for shows about haunted mansions and ancient aliens. The directors like shooting interviews with our old books and busts in the background. Gives them a false sense of legitimacy. Usually, they disappear after getting a look at our room rental rates."

"Back to our topic?" Levi asked.

"Hit me," Corey said.

"Isn't it possible that by 1892, the world had forgotten about Lucy's connection to Booth? She was 50 years old by then."

"If only," Corey said. "As you saw in my thesis, Senator Hale tried to hush up the engagement rumors after the assassination, and with considerable success. In the crazy days during the manhunt for Booth, anyone who knew him was arrested and grilled, including his brother Junius Booth Jr. and the actors at Ford's Theatre. It was Junius Jr.—he was performing in Cincinnati at the time—who told the newspapers the assassination must have been 'a sudden impulse'. Why else would JW throw his life away when he was planning to marry a senator's daughter?"

"Sounds like grounds for an insanity plea," Levi said.

"And not unfounded, as you probably know," Corey confirmed. "JW's father, Junius Brutus Booth, was considered the greatest Shakespearean actor of his day. But he was also a severe alcoholic. He suffered from emotional explosions, often violent, and sometimes in the middle of a performance. Junius abandoned his first wife in England and never married JW's mother. He sired 12 kids but was mostly away from home and on tour. Once, returning to find one of his daughters had died, Junius dug up her decomposing corpse and carried it back into the house."

"Jesus," Levi said. "Quite the father figure."

"It gets worse. Junius died while on tour," Corey said, his tone hushed. "His body was embalmed in New Orleans and shipped back to the Booth farm in Maryland. Apparently, the mortician did such a good job that JW's mother thought her husband was in a coma. She left the body lying in the parlor for days, hoping he would recover. Young John Wilkes was only 14 at the time."

From there, the conversation bounced from topic to topic, like the ball in an arcade game, eventually landing back on Lucy.

"For what it's worth," Levi was saying, "it's clear Booth and Lucy both had powerful, if not domineering, fathers. You could say the same for Robert Todd Lincoln."

"That's true," Corey agreed, bringing the discussion full circle. "While Booth's conspirators were hanged, his fiancée was never even interviewed. And while Lincoln's funeral train was winding through almost 200 cities, reporters danced around the topic without mentioning Lucy Hale by name. Two days before Lincoln was buried in Illinois, one writer argued that reckless women who hung out with men like Booth deserved to be exposed to the public."

"Things calmed down while the Hales were in Spain," he continued, "but there was another feeding frenzy after Daddy Hale died in '73. That's when Lucy was officially outed in the media as one of the five women whose photos were found in Booth's pocket."

Levi nodded enthusiastically. "It's like her father could no longer protect her reputation and she was fair game."

Corey nodded back. "Exactly. While it was improper to attack a high society senator's daughter, by 1873, Lucy was on her way to becoming a vulnerable spinster. Meanwhile, the penny daily newspapers were cropping up like weeds and ready to print anything, no matter how hurtful or opinionated."

Levi was on his feet now. He grabbed an umbrella leaning against the wall in the Keeper's office and brandished it like a sword.

"In swoops our hero, William Chandler," he announced, posing like Douglas Fairbanks. "I'll save you, Lucy! Down with those dastardly wordsmiths!"

Corey grabbed a reproduction walking cane and a brief battle ensued. It ended suddenly when Linda, stifling a laugh, announced her departure for the day.

"You gotta wonder," Corey said, dropping back into his office chair, "whether Mr. Chandler was rescuing Lucy's reputation or the reputation of Senator Hale. He was a staunch abolitionist too and, although it would take a decade to work his way up the political ladder, Chandler had his eye on Hale's seat in the U.S. Senate. He comes off in the history books as a highly educated Dudley Do-Right, well-intentioned and honest, but with none of JP Hale's charisma or charm."

"Let's face it, Mr. and Mrs. William Chandler were probably not a fun couple," Levi agreed.

"One of her stepsons later called Lucy, and I quote,

'a thoroughly unpleasant woman'."

Levi shook his head. "It's tragic," he said, "the way she went from being the toast of Washington, DC society to a media punching bag."

Corey shuffled the papers on his desk. "There was another big newspaper scandal a few years after Lucy married Chandler. I wanted to read it to you, but I may have brought my copy home."

The Keeper suddenly sat upright, eyes wide, mouth open, like a man in shock. Levi followed his eyeline to the vintage clock on the wall.

"Heather!" they cried in unison.

Chapter 30

Excerpt from an 1865 letter from JW Booth's mother,
Mary Ann Holmes (never married to Booth's father)

The secret you have told me is not exactly a secret, as Edwin was told by someone that you were paying great attention to a fine young lady in Washington. Now, my dear boy, I cannot advise you how to act. You have so often been dead in love and this may prove like the others, not of any lasting impression.

* * *

April 22, 1865
New York Tribune

The unhappy lady—the daughter of a New England Senator—for whom Booth was allianced, is plunged in profoundest grief, but with womanly fidelity, is slow to believe this appalling crime, and asks with touching pathos, for evidence of his innocence.

* * *

April 29, 1865
Bucyrus Ohio Journal

A correspondence of the *Boston Advertiser* writes: "I'm given a dispatch from Cincinnati stating that J. Wilkes Booth was to have been married soon to a daughter of Senator Hale. There is no truth in the statement, nor the slightest foundation for it: and I would request, that in justice to Senator Hale and his family, you will give this the same publicity you have the statement.

* * *

May 2, 1865
Springfield Times

BOOTH AND HIS INTIMACY WITH LADIES.

The story that has gained such wide circulation that Booth was engaged to be married to Senator Hale's daughter is formally denied here. I hear there is positive evidence, however, of its truth; but this evidence is in private letters which cannot be used. But it cannot be then denied that Booth was very intimate with the wives and daughters of prominent Republican Senators and Representatives, at the National Hotel last winter. They must have known that he was not only a secessionist but a gamester. Such was his general reputation, yet because he was handsome, and could spout Shakespeare by the hour, these ladies permitted intimacies that have carried them, with the infamous assassin, into the newspapers. All I can say is—served them right—good enough for them. When our women, married and unmarried, are so coarse, so reckless, so wicked that they like to dally with temptation, that they rather enjoy intimacies with scoundrels, let them take the consequences. They are none the worse for being found out.

* * *

May 22, 1865
Philadelphia
Excerpt from a letter by Asia Booth Clarke (John's sister) to her friend Jean Anderson in England.

My Dear Jean:

I have received both of your letters, and although feeling the kindness of your sympathy, could not compose my thoughts to write—I can give you no idea of the desolation which has fallen upon us. The sorrow of his [John Wilkes] death is very bitter, but the disgrace is far heavier.

I told you I believe that Wilkes was engaged to Miss Hale. They were most devoted lovers and she has written heartbroken letters to Edwin about it—Their marriage was to have been in a year, when she promised to return from Spain for him, either with her father or without him, that was the decision only a few days before the fearful calamity.—Some terrible oath hurried him to this wretched end. God help him. Remember me to all and write often.

Yours every time, Asia

Chapter 31

The figure in the pink knit hat and matching mittens was not to be trifled with. Arms crossed, jaw set, she glared at the two grown men.

"You're the wingman," Corey whispered to Levi. "Do your magic."

"I don't know," Levi whispered back. "She looks pretty pissed off."

"You're LATE!" Heather bellowed.

Levi inched forward carrying a familiar smile. "Wow! That's a pretty big voice for a pretty little girl," he said. "You must be at least five years old."

"You forgot me," she countered, but couldn't suppress a grin.

"Double wow," Corey said, scooping her up. "A person who's five probably wants something special for dinner."

Heather's grin broadened. She knew what she wanted all right.

An hour later, all three were seated at The Bistro in downtown Portsmouth. Unwilling to be bought off with ice cream or pizza, Heather had made her wishes known. She wanted dinner at a grown-up place. She also wanted a lobster, but Corey was able to compromise her selection down to a hot dog and fries.

The venue was classic New England, with a lot of brick walls and wooden tables. So many downtown restaurants had come and gone in recent years, Corey had to check the title on the menu to remember where they were. Heather insisted her two chaperones "get some beers," while she sipped ginger ale from an identical mug.

It was, according to the sign on the wall, Open Mic & Oyster Shuck-a-Buck Night. The performances were still an hour away, but a few potential acts were tuning guitars and tanking up at nearby tables. The trio was halfway through their hot dog specials when a young woman in skinny jeans put her hands on Levi's shoulders. He turned, and at close range, recognized her immediately.

"Emily," he said. "What a surprise."

"May I?" she said. Emily grabbed a chair from a neighboring table and settled provocatively close to Levi. Heather's gaze locked on.

"We met in Dover," Levi told Corey, anticipating his question. "Emily is a comedian, and a nun."

She punched his arm playfully. "I teach at a Catholic elementary school," she told Corey. "I have a stand-up spot coming later. Can you stay?" She addressed the question to Levi, who smiled in agreement.

"And who is this delightful young lady?"

"I'm five," Heather announced, pleased to finally be included in the conversation.

"Well, I'm pleased to make your acquaintance, Ms. Five!" Emily said, shaking the girl's ketchupy hand. "I'm 35, so we must be cousins."

"What's a nun?" Heather asked.

"Now that's an excellent question. A nun is . . ."

"Can you take me to the girl bathroom?" Heather interrupted.

"Of course," Emily said after searching the two men's faces for permission. And off they went.

"I'm pretty sure they don't hire serial killer teachers at Saint Seton's Academy," Levi told Corey with a shrug. "When I met Emily, she was herding a bunch of kids through the Woodman Museum."

The return from the bathroom trip turned into a social affair as Emily introduced Heather to the Open Mic regulars. She got to meet a juggler, strum a medieval lute, bang on bongos, and talk to a puppet. Meanwhile, at the adult table, the conversation returned to Lucy.

"Back in the office," Levi reminded Corey, "you said something about a scandalous newspaper account."

With one eye on his daughter, Corey outlined a lengthy story that appeared in a Chicago newspaper and instantly mushroomed across the country in the summer of 1878. According to a reliable "investigative reporter," JW Booth had murdered the president in a jealous rage upon learning Robert Todd Lincoln was also in love with Lucy Hale.

The account reportedly drew on interviews with a mysterious Mrs. Temple who, like the Hale family and Booth, lived at the National Hotel in Washington, DC. The article, Robert Todd protested angrily, was a libelous lie. But no matter, the story was in print and would enter the canon of assassination lore.

"Lincoln was murdered because of Lucy? It's insane." Levi signaled the waitress for another round, but Corey countermanded the order by gesturing for his check.

"It's bollocks," Corey agreed. "But like all false logic, it has a certain symmetry. It takes a footnote to history and twists it just enough to create a plausible new reality."

"Plausible?" Levi echoed.

"Maybe not to us," Corey explained. But to Victorians, the Hales and the Lincolns lived in a bubble. They were high class. Booth and his actor buddies were one social step above hookers and pimps. Second, it's possible that Robert Todd was attracted to Lucy. They ran in the same circles. One scholar pointed out that Robert Todd was college room-mates with John Hay, later Abraham Lincoln's private secre-tary. Hay definitely had a crush on Lucy."

"Hi, Dad! Hi, Uncle Lee!" Heather shouted from across the room. The two men waved back.

"Third, the Mrs. Temple character was living at the National Hotel where Booth and Lucy were staying. She had ample opportunity to observe what was going on in April 1865."

"Except you said there was no Mrs. Temple," Levi pointed out.

"And how perfect is that?" Corey said. "Once the reporter admitted Mrs. Temple was a fictitious name, there was no way to debunk her story when it came out 13 years later."

"It must have been awful for the recently married Mr. and Mrs. Chandler to pick up the newspaper and see that crap." Levi accepted his second mug of beer from the wait-ress and Corey placed a credit card on the table.

"Excruciating for Lucy and William," Corey said, "not to mention for Robert Todd and his wife. Both men were lawyers, but daily newspapers were filled with pseudo-reporting garbage back then."

"Not like today," Levi joked. "So the real damage came, not from the silly theory, but from the intimate details about Lucy embedded in a provocative widely read article?"

"Exactly," Corey said as he signed off on his bill and stood up from his chair. "As soon as I get home, I'm going to dig out the Mrs. Temple article and give it a fresh read."

Seeing Corey rise, Emily quickly ushered a smiling and sleepy Heather across the room.

"Had a good time, button?" Corey asked, employing the past tense. Heather instinctively understood and didn't resist. Her night out with the grown-ups, she knew, was the payoff for not revealing her father's late arrival at daycare. She would honor the unspoken bond, hoping it might lead to future rewards. Heather hugged Emily and dutifully took her father's hand.

"Your bedtime too?" Emily asked Levi.

"I think I can stay up a little longer," he said, directing his smile at the girl in the pink outfit.

"No fair!" Heather's weak protest ended in a deep yawn as Corey hoisted her into his arms.

Chapter 32

Levi hadn't seen a Caswell in the flesh for days, but he knew from his phone answering machine that chaos reigned. A documentary filmmaker from California, according to a message from Corey, had spotted Claire's article about Lucy's missing diary on the internet. Bill Wiggin's efforts to discourage the filmmaker only made the story more intriguing. The director and his two-person crew planned to arrive in chilly Dover, New Hampshire within days. Claire was annoyed, Woodman trustees were intrigued, and the Dover curator was apoplectic.

Levi, however, was busy. An ice dam on the third floor of the John Paul Jones House required his immediate attention. He was a man unafraid of ladders, and having patched what he could on the outside, the caretaker found himself checking for leaks inside the third floor of the old Georgian mansion. It was his favorite place. He climbed a narrow wooden stairway where a span of thick rope still functioned as a handrail. Unseen by the public, the top floor of the museum, with its low ceiling and slanted roof, had become a storage attic for unused mannequins, spinning wheels, furniture, and other treasures.

The space had long been sectioned off into small rooms

of unknown use. There was no record that Sarah Purcell, the 18th-century widow of an Irish sea captain, had kept enslaved workers here. More likely, the space had been occupied by Purcell and her eight children who, left in debt by her husband's sudden death, were forced to rent the best rooms below. Captain Paul Jones, legend claimed, was among the tenants. But try as he might, Levi couldn't get his mind off Lucy.

His work done for the day, Levi examined an old poster from the city's tricentennial in 1923. A battered wooden ship model, a child's pedal car, and a large sign for Frank Jones Ale stood nearby. After 20 years, the caretaker still cherished the opportunity to wander unchaperoned through the museum as it went dormant each year from November to May. He had examined every item in every room countless times, imagining their use and the people who used them in days gone by. But today, he had another long-dead person on his mind.

The phone machine in his apartment, the kind that still used a cassette tape, was only one symptom of Levi's addiction to the past. He had never owned a cell phone or a computer. It wasn't that he feared or despised technology. The modern items were simply of no use in his small sheltered world. But now and then, under Corey's tutelage, he had fiddled with the Keeper's desktop computer at the Athenaeum. And on rare occasions, like today, he did a little online research of his own in the museum office.

A basement furnace kept the old building pipes from freezing, but the winter temperature was never set above fifty degrees. The artifacts didn't seem to mind the cold, nor did the unused desktop computer, nor Levi. He fired up the system and settled into an old office chair, steam rising from his breath. The monitor flickered to life. The hard drive whirred. Magnifying the screen images, as Corey had taught him, Levi soon found himself inside the alternate internet universe of John Wilkes Booth.

"I don't believe this," he muttered to himself while reading a story from an early newspaper. The truth behind Lincoln's death, the author revealed, began with Lucy Hale. According to this account, the famous actor was so taken by the lovely Miss Hale, that he vowed to mend his ways. To win Lucy's love, Booth gave up his profligate lifestyle and abandoned his Southern pro-slavery sympathies. Senator Hale was so impressed with Booth's conversion that the two became fast friends. The senator even gave Booth permission to marry his daughter.

"Pull the other one," Levi groaned to himself. Face pressed close to the glowing screen, he read on. A friend of Mr. Booth, the story continued, a Confederate agent named John Beal, was condemned to be hanged. Booth and Senator Hale went to the White House. Together, they asked President Lincoln to grant executive clemency for John Beal. The actor, Levi read online, "knelt at the feet of Lincoln, clasped his knees with his hands, and begged him to spare the life of one man." The President, tears streaming from his eyes, promised Booth he would pardon Mr. Beal. But William H. Seward, Lincoln's Secretary of State, used every tactic from logic to threats to force the president not to release the southern traitor from the gallows. Beal was hanged. To avenge his friend's life, the article concluded, John Wilkes Booth shot Lincoln.

Levi sat back in amazement. He briefly closed his

tired eyes, then pressed on. This crazy account reportedly appeared in 1868 while the Hales were living in Spain. It was "rediscovered" and circulated in 1902. There really was a John Beal, Levi's study soon confirmed, who was hanged as a Confederate spy in 1865. Booth may even have known him. But the thought of Booth joining forces with Senator Hale to visit Lincoln—it was too much.

For the next hour, Levi wandered the murky world of Lincoln conspiracy theorists. There was, as Corey had mentioned, a 1907 book about John St. Helen, the man who claimed he was Booth. St. Helen had died from drinking poison and his mummified body was displayed at carnivals for decades. A photo of St. Helen's swollen corpse was widely distributed across the Web.

"That could be anybody," Levi said to himself, examining the photo.

He moved on to a 1937 book in what was called "the Booth Survived genre." *This One Mad Act* was written by Izola Forrester, a pioneer female journalist and silent film scriptwriter. Forrester, too, touted the theory that Lincoln's assassin escaped being shot. She claimed to be the granddaughter of Booth and his common-law wife. She argued that Booth was merely part of a plot by a radical group of Freemasons known as The Knights of the Golden Circle. The members helped Booth escape capture and live in exile until he died in 1879. Forrester admitted her story was filled with historic gaps and that "nearly all written evidence has been deliberately destroyed." But her book is still quoted today.

Shaking his head in disbelief, Levi moved on to a book titled *Why Was Lincoln Murdered?* According to Wikipedia, this bestseller created "a national furor" when it, too, appeared in 1937. The author, Otto Eisenschiml was an Austrian-born chemist who, like so many, was obsessed by the assassination. He proposed that Edward Stanton, Lincoln's Secretary of War, orchestrated Lincoln's murder and Booth's escape. Otto saw Booth as Stanton's tool, not the mastermind of a carefully planned plot. It was Stanton, he posited, who arranged to leave the president unguarded at Ford's Theatre. Stanton then arranged Booth's escape out of the city. Others have since suggested that Stanton also faked Booth's death and spirited him out of the country.

Last, but far from least, Levi discovered the nearly 600-page "Roscoe Theory." In 1957, Theodore Roscoe turned from writing pulp magazine fiction to release *Web of Conspiracy*. The Catholic Digest Book Club called it a "terrible drama . . . culled from two decades of research." According to Roscoe, Stanton was again the evil puppet master who plotted the assassination. The Secretary of War, the author argued, made certain that JW Booth "got away with murder" by employing a substitute corpse at Garrett's barn and spiriting the actor out of the country.

Levi powered down the computer in the museum office and rubbed his eyes. It must be exhausting, he thought, to believe in conspiracies—weaving elaborate webs, trusting no one, while clinging to a flat and cheerless world. He felt a headache coming on.

Chapter 33

Levi screamed.

"It's about time," Claire said weakly, lifting her head for a moment from the carriage house couch, then dropping back onto a cushion. She was lit only by the streetlamp in the alley through the back window.

"Jesus!" Levi said, one hand to his heart. "How about a little warning?"

"You don't text, don't email, don't carry a phone like a normal person. What should I do, send up a flare?"

He flicked on a small lamp, still breathing hard.

"If you don't want visitors, try locking your door. By the way, I ate the leftover pad thai in the fridge. It was pad thai, wasn't it?"

It was only 7 p.m., but the December sun had set hours ago. Levi stepped to the couch and, in one smooth motion, grabbed Claire's legs, swung her feet onto the floor, and plonked down beside her.

"Hey!" she protested. "I'm relaxing!"

"No, you're hiding," he said. "I'll bet Corey thinks you've been at work."

"I am at work," Claire grumbled. "I'm here to get your advice."

"You want my advice?" Levi said.

"Hey!" she feigned offense. "Just because we weren't the best at being a couple doesn't mean we're not the greatest crime-solving partners."

"What crime are we fighting?"

"The president has been shot, Mr. Woodbury, and I'm on the case."

"You're a couple of centuries late, Sherlock," he said. "And I think we know who did it."

"Ahhh, Mr. Watson, but do we know EVERYONE who did it?"

"I thought I was Mr. Woodbury," Levi said, wafting his hand in front of his nose. "How many drinks did you have?"

"Oh, right," she confessed. "You're out of beer. And chips."

"You drank both of my extra-large imported German lagers? I was saving those!"

Claire turned to face him, pulling her knees onto the couch and leaning in close.

"But you were gone a long-long-long time, Lee. I got lonely," she said in what came out as a sort of sexy whimper.

"I was right next door," he protested and drew back slightly. "I was using the computer in the Jones house."

"Are you sure you weren't out with your new girlfriend?"

Levi's expression showed his confusion.

"Emily, the cute little nun? You know what I mean."

"Oh," Levi exhaled.

"Heather says you two are in looovvve." Claire stretched out the last word. "What happened to that archaeologist you were dating?"

"Wanda?" Levi blushed. "She got a job on a dig in

Ireland. Won't be back for months."

"So, while the cat's away, eh?"

"I just met Emily," Levi stammered.

"Cradle robber," Claire taunted.

"She's 35. And you're drunk. And I do believe you're a wee bit jealous."

"Jealous!" Claire made a buzzing sound with her lips. "You wish."

Levi shifted from annoyed to amused. He hadn't seen Claire this playful in ages. It reminded him of their brief time together, sitting, sometimes lying on the same pull-out couch years ago.

Their relationship had begun joyfully. There were hours, even days, when he was able to stop thinking about Julianne. But every time he tried to commit to something new, like a hand from a grave, Julianne drew him back.

That wasn't Julianne's fault, he knew. She was dust. What remained, besides a few photographs and memories, was the paralyzing fear that it could happen again. It was simple math. If one lover could disappear so suddenly and so permanently and so horribly, why wouldn't the next, and the next?

The closer he came to giving life another shot, the more he pulled away until, after copious bouts of denial, Claire saw it too. And only she had the courage to react.

"I'm going to make you some coffee," he said, holding her at arm's length by the shoulders.

"Don't want no coffee." She shook her head.

"And then maybe we can talk about Lucy Hale."

Claire buzzed her lips. "She sure can pick 'em."

"Pick what?" Levi said.

"Men, Mr. Watson. Men!"

"I'm going to get you that coffee anyway," he said. But when he tried to rise, she wouldn't let go.

"You know what I really want?" she said, and her dark eyes widened.

"Another beer?" he guessed.

"Ya," she agreed.

"And a better job with more pay and greater respect?" he suggested.

"Sounds good," she nodded.

"And a million billion bucks tax-free delivered by hot men in skimpy bathing suits?"

Claire thought about that one for a moment. "But more than all those things," she said, and she was holding him now, hugging him. "What I want is a kiss."

"What I want," she continued, "is for you to kiss me one time every year."

She pulled out of the embrace to look directly at him. For untold seconds she stared, observed, read, and processed what she saw on his face.

"Ah, I can probably do that," he said, slowly rolling out each syllable.

"Here's the deal," she pronounced with only a slight slur. "We're talking about one honest, passionate, friendly kiss per annum. That's on the lips, no cheeks, no pecks, no hesitation, no guilt, no welching."

"But what if I . . . ?"

"And no discussion or analysis. One and done. Can you handle it?"

Mesmerized, he leaned toward her, only to be shoved back.

"Do we have a deal?" Claire insisted.

"Yes," he said. "On my honor as a nearsighted bachelor."

"Good, man," Claire said with an explosive smile. "I'll take that coffee now."

It was instant coffee and not the expensive kind, but by the time Levi stepped from his kitchenette to the couch, Claire was snoring like a lumberjack.

She probably won't remember a thing, Levi thought as he tapped the Caswell home number on his vintage telephone.

"Yep," he said a moment later. "Out like a light. I was working late next door and found her like Goldilocks . . . Yup, all three. One ale, two lagers . . . Okay, man, whenever you can get here."

Chapter 34

"Do you mind if we take a moment to summarize?" Dr. Gerome Goldman, PhD, asked his client.

"Go for it," Levi said. He stretched his long blue-jeaned legs and Timberland boots forward while extending both arms across the back of the therapist's comfortable sofa.

"Okay. You recently met a woman you quite like. You find her outgoing, intelligent, funny, and attractive. But you are hesitant because she is younger than you."

"Roughly half a generation," Levi acknowledged.

"Meanwhile," the therapist continued, "your best friend's wife has expressed lingering feelings based on your former relationship."

"While drunk," Levi said. "But yes, we have kind of a mutual, leftover, sort of unresolved, affection type thing. But it's in the bottle. Not a problem."

"I see," Gerry said, as if he didn't see at all.

"In fact," the client leaned forward for emphasis. "Her new one-kiss-per-year idea is brilliant. I mean, it acknowledges the chemistry, but keeps it in the bottle."

The therapist looked like a man about to fill his pipe and blow a smoke ring. "Except once per year?"

"Right."

"At Claire's discretion?"

"I guess. It was her idea."

The therapist puffed his invisible pipe and glanced, ever so discreetly, at the clock on the wall behind the couch.

"If I may borrow your metaphor, once every year, at a time known only to her, she gets to rub the lamp and let the genie out of the bottle."

Levi sniggered. "I guess. But it's just a teeny-weeny genie."

"You hope," Gerry probed.

"Hey, you can't tell me with everybody married and divorced and hooking-up and estranged from everybody these days, there must be a ton of bottled-up emotions, not to mention all the kids caught in the middle."

"But you and Claire are not married or divorced or estranged or hooking up. There are no children caught in the middle. I'm just making an observation."

"It sounds like you're observing the possibility that the genie might have a mind of its own," Levi said. He liked this guy and his imaginary pipe, despite the bi-weekly bus ride to Dover and the crazy hourly fee.

"I'm not trying to predict the future," the therapist said. "You two are definitely working on your relationship— acknowledging boundaries, avoiding triggers."

"Jargon alert," Levi grunted.

"Sorry," the therapist said. "Force of habit. I'm just reminded that your friend Claire is struggling with her career and your friend Corey is worried about their marriage."

"That's true," Levi said thoughtfully. "You do take good notes."

"And isn't there some sort of secret dossier taped inside a filing cabinet?"

"Oh, that," Levi said. "Shouldn't be a problem. You see, Claire was a reporter when my girlfriend Julianne was killed. Claire covered the story for the newspaper. When we started dating, years later, we never made the connection, or at least, I didn't."

The therapist did his best to disguise his fascination and scribbled a few notes as the client continued.

"Claire never told me about her professional connection to Julianne's murder. She still hasn't. But I figured it out. I couldn't say I knew she knew. But when that file popped up recently when I was talking to Corey, I was pretty certain what was in it. And when I could see Corey trying not to tell me, well, you get the picture."

"It's quite a picture," the therapist said. "And you appear to be handling it extremely well."

"Thanks," Levi said. "It's one of those things you try not to think about, like the Pope on the toilet or your parents making love. As much as she wants to fix me, Claire likes to protect me too. Sometimes, I just let her."

Feeling a surge of emotion rise, he reached for a tissue from a box on a small table.

"You're getting there," the therapist said. "Can you feel it?"

"I think so." Levi honked into a tissue. "It's a different kind of hurt. But hey, it only took 20 years, right?"

"Can I ask what it feels like? Or is that too much of a shrink question?"

Levi sniffed. "It feels like Julianne was simply in the wrong place at the wrong time. After two decades, I'm coming to the conclusion we will never know WHY, because," he sniffed again, "well, there is no WHY."

Gerry nodded for him to continue.

"Well, we know WHAT and WHERE and WHEN. She was killed by the beach while parked in her car on the worst day of my life. There is a HOW. She was shot at close range with a pistol. There is a WHO, but we will probably never find the murderer. And if we never know WHO, we will never know WHY. Does that make sense?"

"Perfectly."

"Lately, I guess I've been thinking how pissed off Julianne would be if she knew how much of my life I've spent stuck in the Why-Zone, spinning my wheels, and feeling . . ." Levi grabbed another tissue.

"Guilty?" the therapist said.

"Aren't you supposed to let me come to my own catharsis?" Levi laughed.

"You were already there, and we're running low on time."

"Those 45-minute hours run down fast," the client agreed.

"I've got an open session. You can stay if you like."

"No, no," Levi said, fumbling for his courier bag and coat. "People to see, buses to catch. Onward and upward."

The therapist motioned for him to sit back down. "Two more questions, if I may?"

"Be my guest." He settled back down.

"You've told me again and again that Claire, and I quote—Saved your life. Can we agree, if you'll pardon the cliche, that she proved you had the capacity to love another person, someone other than Julianne?"

"Yes, sure." Levi shrugged. "She and I even talked about that. I guess you could say I was half-fixed. I was in love again, but that affection came with a shitload of new fears. It was like I was no longer going to jump off a cliff, but I was paranoid that Claire would fall off the same cliff—and this time it would really be my fault."

"For not saving her?"

"Exactly," Levi confirmed.

"Claire was then in her early 30s, would you say?"

Levi nodded.

"Full of energy and ready to start a family?"

"That's what did us in," Levi agreed.

"Your reluctance?"

"Pretty much. She once said, if we ever had kids together, I would package them in bubble wrap and stick them in the closet until they were full-grown."

"And would you?"

"Probably," Levi said.

"But not Heather?"

Levi cocked his head, processing the thought.

"No," he agreed again. "She's, she's different. She's— this sounds weird—but Heather is . . . not mine, if that makes any sense."

"It does," Gerry said.

'There's enough distance. It's a bond, for sure. I love the little monster, but . . . It's hard to explain."

"Try," Gerry probed.

"It's like, I'm me and Heather is Heather. We know we're connected somehow, but we also know we're separate people. We're like friends from different planets, I guess." Levi paused. "Okay, that sounds stupid."

"It sounds like a great relationship to me," Gerry the therapist said. "And on that note, our time is up."

He stood and walked Levi to the office door and opened it to an empty waiting room.

"Sure you don't want to keep going?"

"I think my brain is small enough for one day," Levi said.

"You're doing good work," Gerry said again, one hand on Levi's shoulder. "I wish you well with this new female friend of yours."

"And she's how old, did you say?"

Levi zipped up his coat and tugged on his favorite baseball cap. "Message received, doc," he said.

Chapter 35

Bill Wiggin squinted into a ring of hot lights trained on him. The producer, a tall, 50-ish man, had the rugged bearing and leathery skin of an aging surfer. His colorful Hawaiian shirt screamed—"I am not from here!"—and made everything in the museum seem older and duller than it had been before he entered the room. His two assistants went about their business with silent military efficiency. An Asian woman dressed in black set up the glaring lights atop expandable metal poles. The sound engineer, wearing headphones, twisted dials inside a metal case that looked like it had traveled the world. A colorful sticker on the side read: Property of Travwell Productions.

"Nothing personal," the sound guy joked as he threaded a thin wire up the inside of Bill's cherry-red sweater. He clipped a tiny microphone to the curator's button-down shirt collar and attached a small plastic box with an antenna to his belt. Bill noticed what he had thought was a turtleneck was actually the young man's elaborate tattoo.

"That sweater is going to pop," the engineer said to the woman who was also the cameraperson.

"No kidding," she replied. "Does he have a backup?"

"No, I like it," said the producer in the Hawaiian shirt,

who was also the director, and whose name was Travis.

The crew continued to buzz around Bill for another 15 minutes, speaking about him, and through him, but never to him directly. Finally, he was asked to recite something into the microphone for a sound level. Bill chose the Gettysburg Address he had memorized as a child. Then the camera operator swooped in to dab a few beads of sweat from his forehead and apply a little powder to his nose and cheeks.

"You'll be great," she said and disappeared behind the glare.

Travis had elected to spend that morning shooting B-roll first. That included exteriors of the museum buildings, Bill walking around campus, Bill standing next to Lucy's dresser, opening the drawers, revealing the hidden space, holding the reproduction Lucy diary, pretending to speak on the phone in his office, and talking to a few museum visitors who happily signed model releases. The California crew then disappeared for a contracted hour-long lunch. Early afternoon was reserved for close-ups featuring the polar bear, the man-eating clam, Lincoln's saddle, and the rest of the museum's greatest hits.

Bill's interview, at last, was being shot in the research area, free from wandering visitors. The final session was planned for tabletop shots of old photographs and documents from the museum archives.

"Ready to become a movie star?" Travis asked as he settled into a chair facing the curator, but off-camera. "We've got an hour before shooting the archive stuff," the director said. "Plenty of time. You want to start, Bill, by giving us a quick overview of the relationship between Lucy and John Wilkes."

"Excellent summary," Travis said when Bill was done. "Now I'm going to toss you a few hypotheticals."

"Okay," Bill said glumly. Beyond the circle of lights, he saw Claire Caswell. She waved and, like a man spotting a friend from the gallows, Bill smiled and waved back.

"Mr. Wiggin, you need to look directly at me. The camera is right over my shoulder, okay?"

"Okay," he repeated. "Sorry."

"So tell us, do you believe Lucy and John Wilkes Booth were actually engaged to be married?"

"Probably."

"Remember, this is TV. We need you to include the question in your answer. As if you were on Jeopardy."

"Oh, right . . . um." He cleared his throat. "Historians generally agree that Miss Hale and Mr. Booth were secretly engaged. Whether Booth's intentions were honest or honorable is up for debate."

"Good, good," the director said. "A nice clean sound bite." In the dark distance, Claire gave him two thumbs up. "And what do you say to rumors that Lucy Hale knew about her boyfriend's assassination plot?"

"Ridiculous!" Bill blurted. He paused to collect himself. "There is no reason, based on the evidence we have, to presume Lucy was anything but a victim and a bystander in Booth's treachery."

"But what about the evidence you found in Lucy's secret diary?" Travis nodded with encouragement.

Disoriented at first, the curator quickly recovered. "The notion of a secret diary is pure speculation. And while I, myself, have considered the possibility, we have only an empty dresser drawer. We have no diary. And if we did,

I'm certain nothing would indicate Lucy was an unindicted co-conspirator. The notion is entirely without foundation."

The director pressed on. "But what about Lucy's belief that John Wilkes was not killed in Virginia, but lived on for decades under a new identity?"

Bill Wiggin sniggered at the thought. "Pardon me for laughing, but the conspiracy theory about Booth's escape and survival is pure fiction. No serious student of history gives it any credence."

"But Lucy believed it, didn't she?" Travis pushed.

"We have no way of knowing what Lucy believed. She never recorded her feelings about the assassination, or Booth, or her time in Spain, or her father's illness, or her marriage to William Chandler. Nothing. Nada. Everything you'll find in books is based on hearsay, speculation, or fiction. Case closed."

"Except for the secret diary," Travis said, as if he hadn't been listening.

"What's going on here? There is no secret diary!" Bill could feel the perspiration beading on his brow and his face reddening.

The director, who had been off-camera, now stood and moved into the circle of light. He handed the curator a folder.

"Isn't it true that you received photographic proof of a missing Lucy Hale diary only a week ago? Copies exactly like these?"

The curator opened the folder and recognized the same three pictures he had received anonymously.

"Where did you get these?" he demanded.

"Have you not seen these photos of Lucy Hale's lost

diary? Our viewers want to know your answer."

Travis was now facing the camera as it pulled back for a wider shot of the room. The sound engineer seated at a table and Claire Caswell were visible in the background. Bill Wiggin rose abruptly to face his accuser as the camera zoomed back in for a two-shot.

"This is bullshit!" he shouted. "We don't know if these photos are real. We don't know where they came from."

Travis moved his face closer to Bill's and the camera operator tightened the frame. "Do you deny having seen these pages, Mr. Wiggin?"

"What is this, Dateline? I think you're on the wrong TV show." Bill's face was now the color of his sweater. "Okay, you got me. Booth is alive. Elvis is alive! And Lucy Hale shot Lincoln!. Satisfied? I'm out of here!"

Bill Wiggin unclipped his microphone, stripped off the wireless receiver box, and stalked out of the room, swearing all the way. Claire followed him.

"Did you get all that?" Travis asked his teammates.

"Every frame," the camera operator said.

"Every syllable," the sound man confirmed.

"Nice work," Travis said. "Drinks on me."

Chapter 36

REPORTER'S NOTEBOOK
FILM CREW SEEKS DOVER "PARA-HISTORY"
BY CLAIRE CASWELL
SPECIAL TO THE *PORTSMOUTH JOURNAL*

PORTSMOUTH—"We were only doing our job as journalists," says Travis Welnick of Travwell Productions. "If we don't ask the serious questions, who will?"

William Wiggin, longtime curator of the Woodman Museum in Dover wasn't convinced. "I suspended the interview yesterday because it was anything but serious," Wiggin says. "My job is to teach history, not promote crazy conspiracy theories."

Welnick says he flew his film crew in from California after reading this reporter's recent interview with Mr. Wiggin in the online version of the *Portsmouth Journal*. That story focused on a Civil War-era dresser that once belonged to Lucy Hale, daughter of a New Hampshire senator. The item was recently donated to the Woodman Museum.

"We were intrigued by Mr. Wiggin's reference to a lost diary hidden in the dresser that linked Miss Hale to the Lincoln assassination," Welnick says. "We wanted to jump on the story before anyone else. It ties into a production we've been working on."

That film, Welnick explains, is based on a century-old

theory that claims presidential assassin John Wilkes Booth was not killed in 1865. A companion theory suggests President Andrew Johnson and Lincoln's Secretary of State, William Seward, were part of the Booth murder plot.

"We've been collecting the evidence and it is compelling. Lucy Hale's diary may be the smoking gun we're looking for," the producer says. His previous television documentaries have focused on alien civilizations on Earth, Bigfoot, haunted mansions, the Loch Ness monster, and the theory that the American moon landing was faked.

Wiggin says he was told the interview was for the History Channel. Welnick says he has done work that appeared on the well-known network and may have mentioned this when he contacted Wiggin.

"But I definitely never told him this particular project was connected to the History Channel," Welnick insists. "Our focus is on what we call para-historical events, ones the traditional history community has ignored or covered up."

It was during filming of the interview at the museum, Wiggin says, he was accused of covering up evidence of Lucy Hale's relationship to Booth. This so-called evidence was delivered to the curator. It includes two photographs possibly taken from an unknown diary by Lucy Hale. Wiggin says the photos are heavily redacted and unconvincing, which is why he did not mention them during the interview.

"We don't know where these images came from, what they say, or who wrote them," Wiggin says. "To consider them seriously, we would need to subject the original pages to a battery of forensic tests. And why were they sent anonymously? And why did Mr. Welnick have copies of the same documents that were sent to me? It's all very fishy."

Asked for his response, Welnick stated: "What's really fishy is why Mr. Wiggin chose to stomp out of our interview rather than face up to my questions. This is the kind of behavior we frequently encounter when trying to expose the truth."

Wiggin says there is, as yet, no evidence that a "lost" Hale diary exists at all, and the idea is "pure speculation." Wiggin says none of the many conspiracy theories related to Lincoln's assassination hold up to careful analysis.

"I've read them all," Wiggin says, "and like the current project, their motivation all seems to be profit, not truth. As to the pages from the alleged Hale diary, I'll release the results after the experts get a look at them. That's how genuine history gets written."

Chapter 37

"Well?" Claire prompted as she faced the three-man panel across the Caswell kitchen table. Corey spoke first.

"Your story scored with the history geeks," he said. "I did a flash poll with the Athenaeum membership. Results are trickling in, but so far, your plan to hit back hard and fast with the facts gets rave reviews."

"You smoked those West Coast conspiracy mongers! I vote YEA." Levi banged an imaginary voter button on the table.

"Sunlight is the best disinfectant," Corey added.

"Hear, hear! When do we eat?" Levi agreed.

"Not so fast, boys," the reporter said. "We haven't heard from the defendant himself. Billy, you look kinda glum."

Bill Wiggin sipped his tea. "You did a great job, again, Claire," he said. "Don't get me wrong. But I'm not sure about the sunlight metaphor."

"How so?" She was concerned.

"Your article was balanced," Bill agreed, "but that may be the problem. I think we forget how many people live in a world very different from ours. They aren't burdened by what we see as facts. What we call conspiracy theories, they call reality."

"And we call them the lunatic fringe," Levi offered.

"Except it's not exactly a fringe, and I'm not sure it ever has been," the curator continued. "For example, how many among us eggheads here believe in ghosts?"

No one replied. "And yet, surveys show at least 40 percent of Americans believe spirits of the dead walk the Earth. Women, statistically, are more likely to believe in ghosts, while men are more likely to believe aliens from other planets live among us. Half of those people claim to have seen either a ghost or a spaceman."

"Spaceperson," Claire corrected.

"Mom?" a voice came from beneath the kitchen table.

"How long have you been under there?" Claire bent down and scolded.

"I'm coloring quiet like you said," Heather argued.

"I meant in your room," but already Claire was smiling.

"This is one of my rooms," the voice protested. "It's my kitchen room."

Levi lifted the little spy with the coloring book into his lap. "We'll go color while you adults save the planet." Heather clung around his shoulders like a backpack and they headed for the door.

"Mom," she said as Levi turned to leave the kitchen.

"Yes, peanut," Claire said.

"I believe in goats. I like goats." And away they went.

"But seriously, folks," Corey revived the conversation, "Bill has a valid point. You guys know how I'm always complaining about the wacky inquiries we get. It's far from 40 percent fringe, but we're trending that way. Six people attended our visiting scholar lecture on Hawthorne, while the public library was packed to the gills for a talk on how to tell if your old house is haunted."

"Ouch," Bill said. "Thank heavens we have a polar bear."

Now Claire was the glum one. "So you're saying that, by offering both sides of the Lucy Hale story, we may be adding recruits to the conspiracy camp?"

Bill had come to this informal meeting prepared. Following one more sip of tea, he let fly.

"Scientists know quite a lot about people who traffic in conspiracies these days. I've been reading up. There have been tons of academic studies. But, of course, the conspiracy people don't believe in scientists—or in any other traditional authority figure. They feel threatened by powerful outside forces that want to harm them. They rely on intuition over facts, are prone to magical thinking, and trust only the people who believe what they believe. It's a closed loop."

"Didn't those people come over here on the Mayflower?" Corey's attempt at levity fell flat.

"The one thing we know for sure," Bill Wiggin continued, "is that people who believe in one conspiracy are very likely to believe in the next, and the next, and the next."

Claire stood and moved to the stove where she was warming two large loaded pizzas. The trio sucked in the intoxicating fumes.

"Another minute," she said, turning back to Bill. "You're saying that for every ten people who read my story, you think four of them thought you were some authority figure trying to hush-up the truth?"

"I'm not saying that everyone who believes in ghosts believes in conspiracies."

"You mean goats," Corey interjected, and this time he got a laugh. "Back in the 1600s, pretty much every English colonizer believed the devil was a flesh and blood creature. If you said there was no devil, back then, you'd be the crazy person."

"That was before the internet and social media." Claire added, slipping one hand into a "World's Best Mom" oven mitt. Corey swooped in to assist.

"I'm not too worried about the locals," the curator said. "But once that video footage gets edited and circulated, I may need to hire a lawyer—or a bodyguard."

Chapter 38

Ten miles away, the Dover Pioneers were having a parallel debate. They were gathered, this time, in the spacious home of Wagner Hilton. Once the wealthiest man in the seacoast, he had been knocked down the list by more than a dozen recent "come-from-aways" who had moved to the region in recent years.

It had been two decades since Wagner had a vision of the future. He converted acres of inherited family farmland into what his colorful brochure called "the ultimate retirement community." Lured by waterfront scenery, flourishing arts and culture, boundless shopping, gourmet dining, and no state sales tax, Baby Boomers had rushed to lease all 200 luxury units. As residents aged, they moved seamlessly from "independent living" apartments to smaller, more costly spaces with round-the-clock care, and into the grave.

That was a generation ago. Wagner and his wife Agnes now lived nearby in a spectacular 7,500 square-foot house. Three families, Jenna Labreche was thinking, could live comfortably in the Hilton home, sharing only a kitchen that was bigger than the split-level she shared with her aging mother. But Jenna restored old books and documents for a living, a craft she both loved and excelled at. Despite her

MFA in Fine Arts, she knew this was not her world. As the token historian, she was there to drink tea, contribute her two cents, then drive down the long and winding Hilton driveway and go home.

"Are we all decided?" Bethany Walford-James, the former city councilor and self-appointed Pioneer chairperson said. The living room, ringed with leather couches and palladium windows, boasted a cathedral ceiling that forced the speaker to shout.

"I volunteer to draft the letter to the Woodman Museum trustees," Rusty North, the auto dealer, said. "My secretary will circulate a copy for your approval before it goes out."

"Be sure to have her use the Pioneer stationery," Wagner noted. "We don't want to include any business affiliations. We are a group of concerned citizens, nothing more on this issue. And don't forget to include a copy to the newspaper. Did everyone get enough cake?"

Heart pounding, Jenna raised her hand to speak.

"Are we certain that requesting Mr. Wiggin's dismissal as curator is necessary? Wouldn't a warning be more in line?"

Bethany shook her head. "We understand your concern, Jenna. But we really need to nip this crisis in the bud. You saw the pictures Wagner got from the filmmaker. Didn't you authenticate the handwriting?"

"I only said it looked like Lucy Hale," she stammered. "There's a whole battery of tests we need to do once we get the originals."

"Steady on," Wagner said, sliding in her direction. "We all know you care about Mr. Wiggin. But a deal is a deal. Mr. Welnick's promise to shut down his little film is, so far, only an oral agreement. We need to get it in writing. Rusty and I will cover his fee for turning over the footage he shot the other day, and that should be the end of this nonsense."

"And don't forget the little bonus," Rusty interjected, pointing a finger at his host.

"Oh, yes," he said. "The film crew also shot a day's worth of footage around Dover. We've hired them to use those shots to produce a short PSA about our historic city."

"PSA?" Bethany asked.

"Public Service Announcement," Rusty said. "It's an upbeat little holiday piece that will run on social media."

"That's lovely." Bethany was so delighted with the news, she took a third piece of orange sponge cake, the pieces being rather small.

Jenna frowned. "But what about Mr. Wiggin? Why bring him into this at all?"

Bethany dabbed her lips with a linen napkin. "It's for the best, dear. His time has come."

"But he knows more about the city's history than anyone," Jenna protested.

Mrs. Dawes, who rarely said anything, gave Jenna a sympathetic look—and said nothing.

"I'm sure there are plenty of young History majors more than willing to fill his post," the car dealer said. "Someone with a more pragmatic approach to how much it costs to run a museum in a small New England town. And besides, we're suggesting that a room in the museum be named in his honor."

Jenna managed to restrain her tears, but not her anger. "And how is that going to change the past? People are still going to want to examine Lucy's dresser and dig into her story and authenticate the lost diary." She shot a plaintive look at Wagner Hilton.

"Well, I guess we'll have to cross those bridges when we come to them, Jenna," he said calmly. "Won't we?"

Chapter 39

Around of applause rippled through the room as a woman in a red and green outfit delivered Levi's second beer.

"Isn't she great?" the server asked rhetorically, leaning in to be heard above the fray. "Everybody loves her."

"Totally," Levi called back.

His designer beer was huge and so was the price tag. While it certainly had hints of grapefruit and walnut as advertised, he would have preferred Bud Light at a dollar a can. Corey was the beer aficionado, but his efforts to train Levi's palate had made little progress over the years.

"My palate is connected to my wallet," Levi always told his oldest friend. It was painfully true. While the caretaker job included his little apartment, his actual salary barely covered the essentials. Levi was, to the ever-changing cast of historic house staff and trustees, part of the museum itself. Now and again someone would suggest renting the carriage house at the going Portsmouth rate would bring in much needed cash. Then someone else would note how the cost of hiring professionals to do all the things Levi did would far outweigh the benefits. So as long as he accepted his nominal salary without complaint, life carried on. The costs of eating, drinking, and dating, however, were on the rise.

Dating? A wave of doubt washed over Levi. What the hell was he thinking here? He was a middle-aged museum caretaker with crappy eyesight. He didn't own a house or even a car. He didn't have an IRA. Heck, he didn't even own a decent bed.

Another wave of laughter crashed against his rocky thoughts and he joined the applause.

"Thanks so much," Emily said, gripping the microphone stand with both hands. "You've been a great audience, but it's time, once again, for our closing riddle, a joke so bad you can't stop thinking about it. Ready?"

"Ready!" the audience thundered.

"Okay. Why can't you hear a pterodactyl taking a leak?"

"Why?" The crowd responded en masse.

"Because the P is silent."

A collective groan was followed by more applause as the Open Mic host reappeared.

"Give it up for Emily Smyth, ladies and gentlemen," he announced. "And don't forget to thank your server."

Five seconds later, Emily was sitting across from Levi, flushed, smiling, and pretty as a picture.

"Well? How was I?" she asked. "No, no, don't tell me. I can't take it."

She signaled for a drink. "Let's just pretend it was great. Yes. You're a reporter from *The New York Times*. You're doing an interview after my HBO special. Ask me a question."

"Um," Levi improvised. "Is it true that you always close with a really dumb joke?"

"Yes. I get them from my fourth graders," she deadpanned. "It's become one of my signature moves. And it's cheaper than hiring a team of comedy writers." The comedian took a long slow breath. "That was good. Ask me another."

Levi spoke into a salt shaker, then pointed it toward the comedian. "Have you always been funny?"

"Since birth," she said. "As a kid, I was always getting in trouble for telling jokes in class. I couldn't help myself. In junior high, they called me Emily Punchline, and I didn't hate it."

"Another!" she commanded.

"Errr, Ms. Smyth," Levi had an idea. "Now that you're at the pinnacle of your career, how do you find time for family life?"

Emily's eyes popped. "Wait a darned minute! You're not really from *The New York Times!*"

"Sure, sure I am," he fumbled.

They were interrupted by the server who delivered Emily's drink. "Loved your set," she said.

"Thanks, Marcy." Emily sat up straight and wiggled her shoulders. "It's the new bra."

Marcy gave a hearty laugh and put her hand on Emily's shoulder. "You on the calendar for next month?"

"You betcha!" Emily said and immediately focused her gaze back on Levi.

"What?" He feigned innocence.

"You know what." She locked her gaze on him. "That was the old biological clock question. You want to know what I think about babies."

"It wasn't my idea," he protested. "My therapist said I should . . ."

Emily gave a small squeak and her eyes grew even larger. Or maybe she was just moving closer, Levi wasn't sure.

"You talked about me to Gerry?" Her face was fully within his vision now and she was . . . she was smiling, definitely smiling. "Mr. Woodbury!" A fleck of her hair brushed against his face. "I think you like me. You're worried. You're nervous. But you like me."

"Yeah," he admitted. "You're pretty neat."

Chapter 40

"Pretty neat?" Corey repeated as they headed out. "That's the best you could do?"

"She put me on the spot. I couldn't think straight."

"She saw right through you, man. I don't know how they do it. I never know what's going on."

The Caswells had one car, a not terribly old green Subaru. Claire needed it most of the time. Their home in "The Heights" was two miles from downtown Portsmouth. Corey liked to walk to work, or his wife would drop him at the Athenaeum if he was loaded down with books or the weather was bad. There was also a public bus that he rarely took, for a dollar and fifty cents, the same one Levi was trying to learn to use.

But today, Claire was doing interviews from home, something she did more often lately, and the boys were on the road. Levi liked riding shotgun. Corey was the most conscientious driver he knew. There was no agenda when he was at the wheel. With everyone else, Levi felt like a passenger, or a burden, or a customer, or some damaged person who needed help. He owed them for the ride. He was in their debt. With Corey, they were just two dudes in a bubble floating safely through the world.

"Did you solve the she's-younger-and-might-want-to-have-a-baby crisis? You don't want a thing like that to fester after two dates," Corey snickered.

"You mock me, sir," Levi said.

And it was true. They had been mocking each other for decades. It began at recess in third grade when two nerdy boys discovered one another. Both had embarrassing names, inherited from long-dead and locally famous ancestors. Both boys preferred books to video games, solitude to sports, and long walks to hot cars.

Emily, Levi now explained to Corey, had almost married her college sweetheart. The couple was within spitting distance of the altar when her fiancé revealed his plans for a big family. She was teaching kids all day with no immediate interest in becoming a mom. He asked—when? She said—who knows? He said—be serious, for once. And that's the way the cookie crumbled.

"And get this," Levi continued. "She used to go to the same therapy guy that I have."

"Pull the other one," Corey said. "You two are shrink-mates."

"Emily says Gerry helped her a lot. Rather than tone down her sense of humor, he suggested she try stand-up comedy. She worked up the courage to end the engagement. Now she's much happier."

"Well, she'll be back in therapy if she starts dating you. Maybe you can get a couple's discount."

Having passed the Miracle Mile of franchise stores and restaurants, fading malls, and gas stations, Corey connected with a scenic spot on the Spaulding Turnpike. Here the Piscataqua River meets Great Bay and Little Bay. Despite the view, the boys knew from experience that the current could grow ferocious as the fast-flowing tide met the bay in a violent marriage of fresh and saltwater.

"Remember when we almost died here in your cousin's two-seat kayak?"

"Like I could forget it," Levi said. "We were spinning like a top and almost crashed into the General Sullivan Bridge."

"What did that guy with the fishing pole say when we struggled onto the boat ramp at Hilton Point?"

"Thought you two was a goner," Levi recited in a passable Yankee accent. "You boys looked like a toothpick in a toilet."

Even told a hundred times, they still found the story hilarious. "We were pretty stupid back then," the driver said, honking his horn for emphasis. "No wonder the girls wouldn't go out with us."

"Good thing we got over being dicks," the passenger replied.

"Ayup, we're cool now," Corey said as they exited the Spaulding Turnpike towards Old Dover Road.

They were about seven miles from the Woodman Museum. The meeting with Billy Wiggin was more like a mission of mercy for a wounded comrade. The curator had not taken his notice of dismissal well. He knew what strings were being pulled and his initial reaction was to pull back hard. That had only made things worse.

In two weeks, Bill was informed by email, he must turn in his ring of keys. Retirement was not a punishment, but an opportunity, the letter said. He should write a book, one museum trustee suggested, or take his wife somewhere warm for the winter. The brouhaha over Lucy's lost diary had nothing to do with the board's decision, he was told. It was just time for a change. But he didn't buy it.

"Bill is racking his brain to find a Chandler connection to the whole mess," Corey said. "The family has always been a friend of the museum. They even helped fund a memorial for Lucy at Pine Hill Cemetery. We'll be passing right by it in a couple of minutes."

"Isn't her hubby buried next to his first wife in Concord? How weird is that?" Levi asked.

"I guess it's pretty clear who he wanted to spend eternity with." Levi did a quick calculation. "Lucy and William were married for 40 years."

The two old friends lapsed into silence.

"In 40 years Heather will be our age," Corey said, at last. They were passing the first of two expansive Dover cemeteries. The Tuttle farm, established in the 1600s, was also on their left.

"We'll probably be pushing up daisies," the passenger added after another pause.

"Not me," the driver said. "I'm having my ashes sprinkled out by the Isles of Shoals where my ancestors fished for cod."

"So Heather gets to feed you to the fishes. Nice symmetry," Levi said.

"And you?" Corey asked. "Any funeral plans?"

"Yes. I think it's time I asked Emily if she wants to take in a movie."

Chapter 41

A PORTSMOUTH NEWSPAPER
JANUARY 1875
WEDDING CEREMONIES AT DOVER

PORTSMOUTH—The wedding of the Hon. William E. Chandler of Washington to Miss Lucy L. Hale, youngest daughter of the late honorable John P. Hale, took place at the family residence in Dover on the 23rd of December, 1874. it was a private wedding in the strictest sense, for there were not 40 persons present. The Rev. Dr. Lambert of Charlestown, Massachusetts, an uncle of the bride, assisted by the Rev. Mr. Brown of Dover officiated using the Episcopal form.

The bride was elegantly attired in a rich white silk gown trimmed with satin and lace, and wore a long tulle veil. The parlors in which the ceremony was performed were beautifully trimmed with evergreens and flowers. At the conclusion of the ceremony, a wedding breakfast was served, after which the guests resident in town retired.

The bride's presents were numerous and valuable. From the bridegroom she received a set of diamond jewelry, the only ornaments worn by her at the altar. A brother of the bridegroom presented a handsome case of spoons, the handles of which were procured in Japan. Other table silver of great value was received from various relatives and friends. Taken all in all it was one of the pleasantest weddings ever known there. Mr. and Mrs. Chandler left Dover in the afternoon for Washington, accompanied by Mr. Chandler's mother and brother.

Chapter 42

They found the curator in the research room, the scene of his spectacular exit during the recent filming. Following the obligatory greetings, Bill, who looked like he hadn't slept in days, dropped a giant book in front of his guests. It hit the table with a thud. The title said it all—*William E. Chandler: Republican*.

"That's some heavy reading," Corey joked, but no one laughed.

"Seven hundred and fifty-two pages," Bill said wearily. "May I summarize?" Both men nodded.

"To be honest, I've always seen Lucy and William as a couple of odd ducks. Despite frequent newspaper descriptions of her as a raving beauty, to be frank, Lucy wasn't, at least not in the movie star stereotype. There's a made-for-TV film about the assassination. The actress who played Lucy Hale was drop-dead gorgeous with the body of a supermodel. In the film, Lucy and Booth actually, um, you know, get it on, if you know what I mean."

"I think we do," Corey said.

"The historic Lucy, the one we see in photographs, was voluptuous, curvy, but without the fashionable tiny waist. The owner of Ford's Theatre described her simply as 'stout'.

Another witness called her 'matronly'. None of that matters except to point out how the press exaggerated their romance from the start."

Bill opened the thick biography and pointed to a rare photo of the Chandlers in middle age. Both stared directly into the camera lens. William, with his neatly trimmed haircut and beard, had a forgettable face. He wore pince-nez spectacles and sometimes sported a monocle on a string. While William appeared bored, possibly irritated, Lucy offered a slight, even impish, Mona Lisa smile.

The curator continued his analysis.

"Lucy often wore black, according to people who knew her. At public events, even in her own home, she tended to stay at the back of the room or in the hall. She observed and hosted, but rarely participated. This wasn't uncommon for wives of the era, of course. But for someone who was once the life of the party, intriguing, and adventurous, she found herself, like her mother, tied to a controversial politician with a lot of enemies."

"No mention of John Wilkes Booth in the index," Corey said, flipping to the back of the Chandler biography. Despite himself, this made the curator laugh.

"I'm guessing that name was never spoken in the Chandler household. I wouldn't be surprised if William, like Lucy's father, was in denial over the whole engagement story."

"And yet the media kept dredging it up," Levi interjected. He couldn't help thinking about the tragedy in his own life. Even 20 years gone, Julianne was never far from his mind. Corey knew, instinctively, what his friend was thinking.

"That's true," Bill agreed, "but denial is a powerful drug.

And let's not forget this man had one hell of a busy career." He lifted the book from the table for emphasis.

"William Chandler practically grew up in the Capitol building in Concord. He was a lawyer before he was old enough to vote. A political operative and congressman in his twenties, he was active from the Civil War to World War I—under a dozen presidents."

"That's a lot of presidents," Levi said.

The conversation turned to politics. Levi had seen a sign naming the nearby town of Exeter as "the birthplace of the Republican Party." Amos Tuck, a teacher from Hampton, according to local legend, had been ejected from the Democrat Party, back when the Democrats were pro-slavery. Tuck threw his hat in with JP Hale, the abolitionist, during a secret meeting at Exeter in 1853. Apparently, Tuck suggested they form a new political group called Republicans. Unfortunately for New Hampshire, nothing came of the meeting except a historic marker. Wisconsin now claims bragging rights for kickstarting the party a year later.

As the two historians probed deeper into William Chandler's career, Levi grew restless. He wandered the shelves of the research room, glancing at documents through the small magnifying glass he always carried. He was drawn to an area devoted to generations of old recordings. There were CDs, DVDs, VHS tapes, floppy discs, audio cassettes, round metal film canisters, vinyl records dating to 78 RPM, and even a few wax cylinders.

"Here's another project I'll never get to," Bill Wiggin said, startling his guest and apologizing. He opened a wooden cabinet that contained all manner of electronic playing devices, from an iPod to a gramophone.

"Even the digital copies I've been making will someday be useless if there's nothing to play them on," the curator said.

"I'm a bit of a Luddite," Levi confessed, "although Corey keeps bugging me to modernize."

"Speak of the devil," Bill said as Corey appeared chugging a can of soda.

"Thanks for this," he said, holding up the can. Anyone for lunch?"

"Always," Levi said, but the look on Bill's face gave him pause. "I'm afraid we haven't been any help."

"Simply letting me vent is helpful," the curator said. "I can't convince myself the loan of Lucy's dresser from the Chandlers and the appearance of the lost diary pages is a coincidence."

"Maybe, instead of looking for the answer in the past, we should check out Exhibit A." Corey was pointing to the door as he spoke.

"That's right!" Bill reached for his coat. "I forgot you two haven't seen the furniture from Hell."

Chapter 43

A fresh inch of snow greeted the trio as they trekked from the research office in the Keefe House across the Woodman property towards the Hale House. Ever the tour guide, Billy Wiggin paused at the large black cannon that marked the center of the museum campus, now frosted white.

"Bet you two historians don't know this story," he taunted. They didn't.

"This cannon was captured from the British during the War of 1812 and stored at the Portsmouth Naval Shipyard. A group of Democrats bought it in the 1850s. They planned to fire off a salute in honor of the newly elected President James Buchanan."

"My hero," Levi said. "Our only bachelor president."

"Not to mention a man high on the Ten Worst Presidents list," Corey added.

"Those Democrats floated this baby up the river to Dover on a gundalow and hauled it up Garrison Hill by oxen. Quite a feat. It was going to be a big party. Two young shoemakers set up the honorary salute. They were ramming in a cartridge when the gun went off. Both men were killed."

"Jeez," Levi said. "I didn't see that coming."

"Neither did they," Bill deadpanned. "John Foss was blown to the bottom of the hill. George Clark, although he didn't appear wounded, died that night."

Bill leaned sideways and rested his head against the cold muzzle of the great heavy weapon. "You try to do something nice for people—and it all blows up in your face."

Once inside the exhibition hall at the Hale House, Levi disappeared. The sprawling annex was a candy shop for history buffs. He pressed his nose against one glass case full of artifacts after another, reading the identification cards with his portable magnifier. Corey had to physically drag his friend away from a medieval Japanese warrior uniform to examine Lucy Hale's dresser.

"It's authentic all right," said Levi, who was an expert carpenter. "Such amazing craftsmanship. May I touch?"

"Okay," the curator hesitated. He watched nervously as Levi ran his hands over the wooden surface. He tapped gently here and there, leaning in so close that Bill feared he might lick the polished surface.

"The hidden panel is in the bottom drawer?"

"Yes," Bill said and showed his guest how to trigger the false bottom.

"Cool," Corey whispered, leaning just above Levi's ear.

The curator gasped as Levi pulled up his shirt sleeve and slid his hand into the empty space. "There's something here," he said.

"Don't . . ." Bill began, but it was too late. Levi gently withdrew his hand, palm up. In it was a small square of paper.

"It . . . it . . . it," Levi stuttered. "It must have been stuck to the top of the panel."

He stood slowly, holding the note like a butterfly wing. He let it slide onto the top of Lucy's dresser. A four-word message was easy to read: I'M SORRY. PLAY LAMBERT.

Bill Wiggin had one hand pressed against his heart. "That's Lucy's handwriting," he gushed. "I'd know it anywhere."

"Lambert was her middle name," Corey said, revealing nothing new.

"And her mother's maiden name," Bill confirmed. "The Lamberts were from a little riverside town nearby."

"Perhaps we've been barking up the wrong family tree," Corey suggested. "Assuming this note is authentic."

But the curator was in a trance. He stared wordlessly at the note. Then, donning a pair of white cotton gloves, he placed it lovingly in an acid-free envelope.

"I think," his voice cracked with emotion, "Lucy went looking for her 1865 diary. She had poured her heart and soul into that book. But years later, maybe after the death of her father, or her marriage to William, or the birth of her son, she remembered it. She knew it was a time bomb that could destroy her family's reputation. When she opened the hidden compartment, the diary was gone. Maybe an analysis of this note will give us a clue when she wrote it."

Levi was shaking his head. "It's a pretty obscure note left in a pretty obscure place," he said. "I'm sorry. Play Lambert. What the heck? It sounds like a very personal apology to someone she knew."

"Well, she couldn't exactly say—To whom it may concern: Please return my bombshell secret journal," Corey said.

"If there ever was a secret journal," Levi argued.

"I'm totally convinced there was," Bill said. "I think Lucy was sending a coded request for help. Her note was like a message in a bottle tossed into the sea, a plea for someone from the future. You guys are going to think I'm nuts, but it feels like she was writing to me. She wants me to find her diary and destroy it."

All three men jumped when Corey's cell phone rang. "Ya, babe," he said.

Chapter 44

The last thing Claire wanted was a telephone call from her boss. It just wasn't done anymore. Bosses sent texts. She couldn't remember the last time she had heard her editor's voice, or been in the same room with the guy. Which was probably a good thing, since she had a lot to say about the direction the newspaper was heading and no one wanted to hear it. Better to keep her head down and her opinions to herself. So this call couldn't be good, Claire thought. And it wasn't. Five minutes later, she was on the phone to her husband.

"Ya, babe," Corey said, his tone almost buoyant. "We just made an exciting new . . ."

"No time," she snapped. "I need the car, pronto. Where are you?"

"At the Woodman with Billy and Lee. Is Heather all right?"

"She's fine, sorry," Claire said, reading his fear. "It's a work thing. I was planning on going to Dover. Maybe you can help, since you're already there. Please, put me on speaker."

Ten minutes later, the three men were gathered around a sizable computer monitor in the soon-to-be-ex-curator's office back in the Keefe House. Levi nosed in close to the screen as Bill clicked on the internet link Claire had sent.

An ominous undercurrent of music began as portraits of two familiar figures appeared on the screen. A male narrator with a booming voice began to speak.

"In 1865, John Wilkes Booth, the infamous assassin, was secretly engaged to marry Lucy Hale. Lucy was the daughter of a senator from New Hampshire. Her secret diary was recently discovered."

The photographs of Booth and Lucy dissolved into pictures of Claire Caswell and William Wiggin. Three men gasped as one. The narrator continued.

"But not everyone wants you to know the truth."

The scene cut from shots of Bill Wiggin walking across the Woodman campus, displaying Lucy's dresser, and showing the hidden bottom drawer. It morphed to footage of the curator being interviewed as the narrator said, "This museum curator believes Lucy Hale kept a lost diary hidden in this recently discovered dresser. But here's what happened when we interviewed him for our forthcoming documentary."

A close-up of Bill Wiggin in a bright red sweater staring angrily filled the screen. He shouted, "What's going on here? There is no secret diary!" A quick jump cut found Bill, now yelling, "Okay, you got me. Booth is alive. (Cut) and Lucy Hale shot Lincoln."

The video cut to a photo of Lucy Hale's diary. The camera zoomed in on two pages of Lucy's handwriting. Bill reappeared, ripping off his microphone and stalking out of the room shouting, "This is bullshit!" A shaky hand-held camera zoomed onto the startled face of Claire Caswell, who followed the curator out. Bill's voice echoed, "This is bullshit! This is bullshit!"

"That's merely a taste of the exciting story to come," the narrator said as the screen showed an illustration of Booth shooting Lincoln. A gunshot sounds. "Stay tuned for more sneak preview clips from our explosive independent documentary: LUCY'S VOICE: The Assassin's Lover Speaks."

Bill tapped the keyboard and the screen went blank. No one spoke. Corey's phone rang. He placed it on the table and activated the speaker.

"We're all here, babe," he said.

"What the hell do we do now?" Claire's disembodied voice filled the room. "My editor wants me to respond right away."

"Is he pissed at you?" Corey asked with concern.

"Are you kidding?" Claire boomed. "He loves this kind of thing—conspiracy theorist accuses staff reporter of hiding secret documents about a dead president. What could be better? Sure beats a feature story about the latest pizza toppings."

"But are you okay?" Levi said, leaning in towards Corey's phone.

"I'll be okay as soon as you guys give me the ammunition to fight back."After a pause, Claire added, "Thanks for asking, Lee."

Bill, who had been cradling his head in his hands, spoke next. "Why can't we just sue the bastard for libel or slander or whatever that was?"

"Because it was neither," Claire said. "Sorry, Billy, but the video guy built a trap and you stepped right in it." The curator's head fell back into his hands.

"Maybe our best move is to do nothing," Corey suggested. "How many people actually see this garbage?"

"You don't wanna know, babe," Claire said. From her computer in Portsmouth, she could tell the clip had already been "liked" by over 4,000 viewers in a matter of hours. A few of the comments were downright offensive.

"Why don't you boys put your heads together and get back to me," she said. "I need to file a response to my editor in time for the Sunday paper. And Corey, I'll find a way to pick up the rugrat while you do your thing."

"She sure is taking this better than I am," Bill said as soon as Claire had clicked off.

Levi and Corey shared a smile. "Not really," Levi said.

"When she's that calm," Corey explained, "it means she's moving into warrior mode."

"In fact," he added, "this may be exactly the kind of battle she's been looking for."

"Which means?" Bill asked.

"Which means, we better get busy making her a stockpile of arrows."

Chapter 45

"Billy!"

Jenna Labreche was only half surprised to find him at her front door. "Please, come in from the cold."

The curator spoke without moving.

"I need . . ."

"I know what you need," she said. "You want me to tell you whether those new Lucy pages are real."

Minutes later, his heavy winter coat now tossed over the back of a worn and comfortable chair in the modest living room, Bill Wiggin was waiting for Jenna to bring tea from the kitchen. He cast his eyes around the room. Nothing, he thought, had changed in the decades he had known this talented woman.

The living room was lined with books, but it was nothing compared to her workshop, a former den, nearby. He had been there often, watching with admiration as she worked her magic with aging books. The room was packed floor to ceiling with shelves and drawers stacked with cuts of leather, layers of fine paper, fabrics, cardboard, matte board, tissue paper, delicate sheets of gold leaf, and every other element of the bookbinder's trade. A sturdy workbench was surrounded by an array of cutting tools, glues, awls, needles, clips, scissors, binding bone, metal rulers, waxed thread, metal stamping tools, and more. Jenna's prized possession was a vintage, 80-pound, jet-black, cast-iron book press, topped with what looked like a steering wheel. Embossed lettering on the side read: Demonstration Model, Chicago World's Fair, 1893.

Jenna had restored dozens of books for the museum over the years, but despite her reasonable rates, not as many as Bill had wished. Her reproduction of one of Lucy Hale's diaries for the Woodman had been a special treat, funded by an anonymous donor. No one knew Lucy better. But, so far, Jenna's analysis of the redacted pages had been disheartening.

"Sorry," she said, coming from the kitchen, a bamboo tray held in both hands. "I had to check on Mother."

"How's she doing?" Bill asked, scolding himself for not asking sooner. His eye now caught the wheeled aluminum walker folded up by the stairway. For the first time, he noticed the electric-powered chair that followed a track to the second floor.

"We had hoped to add a downstairs bathroom," Jenna said, following Bill's gaze. She set the tray of cups and cookies on a coffee table between them. "But you can imagine what that costs. Mom's half-napping in the little sunroom now. She says hello."

Another faux pas, he thought. "And don't forget to invoice this meeting," he said clumsily. "You better send it directly to me, now that I'm . . ."

Now it was Jenna's turn to squirm.

"I'm so, so sorry about your job. I meant to call, but . . . I have no excuse. And don't worry about the fee. The Pioneers have already agreed to pay for any further analysis."

The awkwardness over, Jenna continued. "But like I was saying, there's still not much to go on, working from those photos. Unless we get our hands on the original and can analyze the paper and the ink, it's just guesswork."

Bill sipped his tea and, despite himself, could not resist a peanut butter cookie.

"Mom made those," Jenna said. "She goes in and out. But when she's in the pink, she loves to bake, not that I need the pounds."

"Tell me about it," Bill said, patting his stomach.

"Do you have plans?" she asked. "If that's not too painful a question. Finally writing that town history you've been promising us for years?"

"I guess," Bill said. "I don't think the whole retirement thing has sunk in yet. To be honest, there's a sort of crisis going on, which is why I'm here. It's about Lucy."

Jenna's face fell as the curator told her about the *Lucy's Voice* video. When he finished, she was weeping.

"Jenna," he said, moving from his chair to the couch where she was sitting, her hands in her lap, head bowed. "It's not that bad."

"But it is!" she sobbed. "You asked me to keep an eye on those people and I failed. You lost your job. It's all my fault."

It took a while, but Jenna regained her composure. Bill had her smiling, then laughing at his flawless impersonation of Bethany Waldron-James.

"She really does think her ancestors walked on water," Jenna giggled.

"Hell of a long walk from England," Bill said. "Can you imagine if she actually met one of the founding fishermen she worships—no teeth, reeking of rum, tobacco, and fish guts?"

"She wouldn't understand a word they said!"

"And vice versa. They'd probably accuse her of being a witch!"

"Who's to say she isn't?"

The two historians were on a roll. Eventually, however, the curator got around to the question he had come for.

"Yes. It does look like Lucy's writing," Jenna said slowly, her voice choked with emotion.

"That's what I was afraid of," Bill said, reaching for his coat.

Chapter 46

"Heather?" her mother asked casually. "Why are you wearing underpants on your head at breakfast?"

"Dad's sad. I'm going to make him laugh," Heather replied, digging into her peanut butter-flavored cereal. Her carved wooden hamster, the birthday gift from Uncle Lee, stood sentry by the edge of her bowl.

"And how do you know he's a sad dad?" Claire asked.

"I heard him talking to Mr. Wiggly on the phone. Mr. Wiggly is sad about Lucy and Dad said so too."

"I see," Claire said, resisting the urge to run upstairs and interrogate Corey. Heather was headed off to daycare with a friend and her mother before Claire confronted Corey. He was taking his bite of breakfast when she snapped.

"So what the hell is the bad news you're not telling me about Lucy?" she demanded. Her husband looked up wide-eyed from his French toast.

"How the heck . . ." he said, then smacked himself in the head. "That explains the underpants hat."

"Out with it!" Claire demanded. Corey quickly filled in the details of the curator's visit with Jenna.

"Just a blip," he said, but without conviction. "You know what's going on with Billy. Getting dumped at the museum.

182

That awful video. Now Jenna. He's struggling."

"But what if Jenna is correct," Claire posited, "and Lucy did write those pages?"

Corey hedged, deflected, avoided, and eventually carried his plate to the sink. He poured himself a second cup of coffee. "Jenna only said she couldn't be certain. It's not a verdict, dear."

"But even you have admitted there were unexplained details about Lucy and Booth. Wasn't there a witness who saw a woman in the alley behind Ford's Theatre that night? And another mysterious woman in black was seen at Booth's autopsy?"

"Rumors and hearsay," Corey said.

"What about Lucy getting Booth a ticket to Lincoln's inauguration? And their engagement? Or the way she was never questioned about the murder and then rushed conveniently off to Spain for years?"

"You're connecting random dots, babe. And none of it proves Lucy was somehow in league with Booth, or that he survived being killed."

"At what point," Claire said, her voice rising, "does connecting random dots become circumstantial evidence? I mean, we've been acting like Lucy was some airhead social butterfly. Maybe we've been treating this case like Romeo and Juliet when it should be Bonnie and Clyde."

Corey raised his hand in protest. "Whoa, whoa, hold your horses, Geraldo."

"Don't whoa-Geraldo me!" she snapped. "I'm not a historian. I don't have a whole lifetime to come up with the facts. We journalists have deadlines."

"I know, but . . ."

She cut him off. "Look, you got me into this thing. And it was my face, my name, and my career being pissed on in that freaking video!"

Corey swallowed his defense and pivoted. "Sorry, dear," he said. "How can I help? I mean, more than I'm already helping?"

"For starters, you can get me Jenna's phone number," she said.

Corey's hands were back up, urging delay, but he said nothing.

"She's the expert," Claire countered. "She needs to go on the record."

"On the record with what?" he said. "She told Billy the handwriting looked like Lucy's. But without forensic testing, she has no way to tell if the diary pages are real or fake."

"Somebody goddam knows! And I'm going to track the bastard down and John-Wilkes-Booth his ass all over the front page!"

Claire's threat would have been more frightening, Corey thought, if not for her attire. Her flannel pajama top was decorated with smiling snowmen and cuddly baby reindeer. The leggings were candy cane striped in red and white. She was half ninja warrior, half Doris Day in the *Pajama Game* and 100 percent the most alluring figure he had ever seen.

"What?" she said, responding to his stare.

"You're beautiful," he said.

An hour later, Claire was running a brush through her freshly washed hair in the bathroom mirror. She was examining a strand of gray when Corey tapped on the half-opened door.

"Are you going to be late?" she asked, responding to his

air of urgency. He was still wearing a T-shirt and boxers.

"No, no, I'm covered. Just had an idea."

"Shoot," she said.

"Well, you know how I humbly advised against your interviewing Jenna at this point?" he said.

"I remember a similar discussion," she teased. "Then suddenly you thought I was beautiful."

"We both know you will probably do it anyway."

"Uh-huh," Claire said, nodding in agreement.

"But you know what we really need is for Jenna and Bill and your brilliant husband to get their hands on more of this alleged secret diary—and to figure out where the hell it is coming from."

"Uh-huh."

"So I was thinking, you know how you sometimes ghost write an editorial when your boss is overworked or on vacation?"

"Uh-huh."

"Maybe the poor guy could use a little help on this week's opinion page from Portsmouth's sexiest reporter."

"Go on," Claire said, but the seed of Corey's idea was already planted in her mind and growing.

Chapter 47

OPINION PAGE
PORTSMOUTH SUNDAY JOURNAL
DECEMBER
MR. FILMMAKER, SHOW US THE EVIDENCE!

PORTSMOUTH—A California film company has impugned the honesty of one of our top reporters. We are offended. *The Portsmouth Journal* has been here, digging into local news, for almost 200 years. Travis Welnick of Travwell Productions has been creating programs about space aliens, Bigfoot, haunted houses, and other paranormal topics for the last 15 years. Facts are facts.

In a recent video posted on social media, Welnick claimed, without evidence, that award-winning journalist Claire Caswell and veteran seacoast museum curator William Wiggin have conspired to hush up the details of an alleged diary written in 1865.

Fact One: There is, as yet, no definitive evidence that the "lost diary" of Lucy Lambert Hale Chandler exists. The filmmaker based his accusation on photographs reportedly showing two heavily redacted pages from the alleged journal.

Fact Two: An independent expert has suggested that the handwriting in the samples is similar to that seen in other diaries by a young Lucy Hale of Dover, NH. The same expert noted, however, that no analysis based on two handwritten sentences seen only in a photograph is proof of anything.

Fact Three: The owner and whereabouts of the alleged diary remain unknown.

Based on copies of two largely obscured pages from a possibly fraudulent document, the filmmaker has jumped to the conspiratorial conclusion that Lucy Hale may have played a role in the assassination of Abraham Lincoln and that Lincoln's assassin, John Wilkes Booth, may have escaped being captured and killed in 1865. The filmmaker further implies that two highly reliable and educated professionals are attempting to block these wild theories from reaching the public.

Libel, for the record, is a published false statement that is damaging to a person's reputation. In this case, we assume Travwell Productions merely hopes to spice up its next paranormal video with a little controversy rather than incite a lawsuit.

People have been intrigued by the relationship between Lucy Hale, the daughter of a New Hampshire senator, and actor John Wilkes Booth since the day after Lincoln's murder. The recent rediscovery of a dresser once owned by Lucy Hale has reinvigorated that controversy. That is true.

The antique dresser, now on display at the Woodman Museum, is real. It appears, barring further analysis, to have belonged to Lucy Hale. The lowest drawer of the dresser does contain a false bottom, a possible hiding place. Lucy Hale was in the habit of keeping a diary or journal, and no authenticated volume for 1865 has yet surfaced. Lucy Hale, it appears, was engaged to Booth. Booth killed Lincoln. These are things we know, things that responsible historians like Bill Wiggin have studied and responsible journalists like Claire Caswell have reported.

If Travwell Productions wants to be taken seriously, it should cease the name calling. If Travis Welnick has access to the unredacted pages in the alleged diary, he should release them and allow others to judge whether they may be authentic. The hurtful video should be removed from the internet and an apology issued to Ms. Caswell and Mr. Wiggin. The *Portsmouth Journal* calls on him to do exactly that.

Chapter 48

"Impressive," Emily said after reading the Sunday editorial aloud to Levi.

They were appropriately seated in matching leather chairs in the ancient Reading Room on the ground floor of the Portsmouth Athenaeum. Two centuries earlier, it had been the go-to gathering place for the port city's prominent merchants, ship captains, and clerics. Today it was one of the most beautiful and least-known spots downtown. Emily, despite having lived her entire life in the region, had never been inside the ornate doors of the stately brick building in the heart of Market Square. And she had been wholly impressed when Levi used his digital key to enter the hallowed space.

"The newspaper totally came to the defense of your friend Claire with guns blazing," she said, setting the paper aside near a Tiffany lamp and studying his face.

"What?" he protested.

"You're grinning like that cat from Alice in Wonderland," she said.

"I shouldn't," he said.

"Shouldn't what?"

"That editorial," he hesitated, "about Claire. . . . She wrote it."

"Reporters can do that?" Emily was stunned.

"Claire can," he replied. "She's a force of nature."

"I'll say! And you two were a couple . . . ?"

"Briefly," Levi filled in.

"Right," Emily teased. "So, clearly you are attracted to strong women." She struck a comical weightlifter pose.

"If you say so, mistress," he mugged. "Now, how about a tour of my favorite place on Earth?"

The giant full-length portraits that dominate the Reading Room, Levi explained, were two dudes from the Siege of Louisbourg, Nova Scotia. Emily had not known that 3,000 New Englanders invaded Canada in 1745.

"No reason you should," he said, extricating himself from what might have been a lengthy history lecture. They moved on to the story of leather fire buckets and three devastating blazes that had flattened the city. They examined wooden models of ships lost at sea. Halfway up a curving wooden staircase, Levi revealed a collection of oddities, including a stuffed armadillo and an ax from a double homicide. The entire building was festooned with red bows and bits of greenery left over from a recent holiday party. But today, the place was vacant.

Leaning against an ancient table on the second floor, amid shelves of brittle leather-bound books, Emily dragged the conversation back to the 21st century.

"I love everything on this tour, but it feels like," she hesitated, "like we're not talking about the two elephants in the room."

"I thought only one elephant could fit in a room?" he said.

"That's true for most people," Emily agreed. "But you seem to have either a bigger room than most of us, or smaller elephants. There might even be three."

"Okay," he sighed. "Hit me with elephant number one. But you know I already have a shrink."

"I don't want to shrink you. I want to help with Lucy," she said. "I think we like each other and you're clearly worried about Claire. What's going on?"

They migrated from the dark, moody book room to a modern research space next door. Levi flicked on the lights to reveal study desks, more books, filing cabinets, and computers. He gestured towards a long wooden table and they settled in. Levi did his best to bring Emily up to speed on the Lucy affair, The Sunday editorial, he finally explained, was an attempt to lure the film company into releasing more of the alleged 1865 diary.

"How do you know if they have more pages?" she asked.

"We don't," he said. "But whoever sent copies to Bill Wiggin and the film crew must be behind all this."

"But to what end?" she opened her arms in a gesture of supplication. "Where's the payoff for the filmmaker?"

Levi shrugged. "Fame? Glory? Money? I don't know what drives these conspiracy theory types. We're hoping more pages will offer a clue as to whether this blasted thing is authentic or not," he continued in frustration. "So far we've been getting all bent out of shape from a couple of sentences. The rest of the pages were covered up, probably to make the whole thing seem more mysterious. The problem now . . ."

Levi suddenly perked up, eyes wide, head cocked. "Did you hear that?"

"Hear what?" Emily said.

Since his sudden decrease in vision 20 years ago, right after Julianne's death, Levi had felt his other senses sharpen. His ears, nose, taste buds, and fingertips were more alert. It wasn't something he talked about—this comic "spider sense"—and not a full-blown superpower. His body, he reckoned, was merely protecting itself from loss. He only noticed the difference when others failed to react to a suspicious sound or scent, or texture. This time it was a beep, a click, and a distant murmur.

"Nothing much," Levi said. "Probably someone coming in to use the bathroom downstairs. It's a benefit of membership."

"You were talking about a problem," Emily coaxed.

"Right, right," he continued. "Well, Bill Wiggin met with an expert who says, based on the little information we have, the handwriting looks authentic. The idea that it might be real has got Bill rattled."

"You too?"

"A little," he admitted, rubbing his eyes. "If this isn't a hoax, then it could change history as we know it. Not to mention how it makes Billy and Claire look."

An audible click was followed by a whirring sound. This time Emily responded. "Elevator?"

"We added it to the outside of the building a decade ago," he nodded toward the back wall facing an alley. "It was part of a huge capital campaign. It's not like the people who come here are getting any younger."

The electrical whining stopped. A bell sounded. They

heard a sliding mechanical door. Emily had not noticed the curtain at the end of the room until a hand whisked it aside to reveal the entire Caswell family, each wearing a red and white Santa Claus hat.

"Well, well," Corey said, smiling broadly.

"EMMA-LEEE!" Heather screamed and rushed into the teacher's arms.

Claire set down a colorful shopping bag, pulled off a leather glove, and stepped forward. She thrust her bare hand towards Emily.

"We meet at last," she said.

Chapter 49

From its highest point, South Cemetery stretched as far as the eye could see. It was at this point, Levi knew, that Ruth Blay had been hanged in December 1768. The story was never far from his mind. Two other young women, Sarah Simpson and Penelope Kenny, had previously been executed here for the crime of infanticide. But Ruth's baby, most researchers agreed, was stillborn. Innocent of murder, she was hanged for concealing the death of an illegitimate child. Life was so unfair.

"Penny for your thoughts," Emily said as they wandered among the faded stones.

"I guess I can't believe I agreed to come here," he said thoughtfully. "Can we go now?"

Emily laughed and they linked arms. "It's this way, right?"

He steered her without speaking down a gentle slope to a paved path and a clump of cypress trees by a little pond. It was early afternoon. Q-tip-sized flakes began floating by.

"This is actually five conjoined cemeteries," he said at last. "I loved coming here as a kid. Reading the inscriptions, looking up the people and imagining their lives."

"She hates me, you know," Emily said, shifting the topic.

"Who hates you?"

"Elephant number one," Emily quipped. "Did you see the way she shook my hand? I thought she was going to challenge me to a duel."

"Aw, Claire's just jealous because Heather thinks you're cool," Levi said.

"I guess," Emily replied, and let the matter drop.

A minute later, he halted their pilgrimage in front of a granite obelisk. "This section is called Harmony Grove," he said.

Emily waited for the punchline, but Levi was mute. It took a moment before she spotted the inscription.

"Oh, my God!" she shouted, breaking the funereal stillness. "It's you!"

"I hope to hell not," he laughed. "Get a look at this guy."

Emily stepped up to the rocket-shaped memorial that shot a dozen feet into the snowy sky. A life-sized three-dimensional portrait of Judge Levi Woodbury, carved in stone, protruded from the tomb at waist height.

"It's creepy," Emily said, tracing her finger around the stern, balding head. His sculpted mutton chops felt like cold stone worms. Emily licked her finger and stuck it in the judge's granite ear.

"Eww, gross," she said and stepped away.

"That's my namesake you're messing with," Levi said with mock pride. "New Hampshire senator, governor, Supreme Court justice. He even ran for president in 1848. He died three years later. My father never stopped talking about the great Judge Woodbury when I was little. It was a lot to process. Dad is buried right over there beneath the big shiny WOODBURY stone."

"And your mother?" Emily asked, linking arms again.

"Right next to him, as always. She died when I was in high school."

"So they never met Julianne?"

It was only a hollow question; the answer was obvious. But Emily couldn't think of anything else to say. She felt herself being submerged in his loss.

"They never did," Levi agreed. He, too, felt the weight of the land of the dead. Its gravity pulled on them both.

"Look, maybe this isn't such a great idea," he said.

"Trust me," she said. "How far is it?"

"All the way to the end of the cemetery," he said. "She's on the left, down near Little Harbor."

"See you there, old man," Emily shouted over her shoulder as she jogged down the paved path that cut between rows of white markers.

The woman sure could run. Levi was panting by the time he caught up. The melting snow and rising steam that fogged his glasses made Emily almost invisible to his already limited vision.

Somehow, amid all the dying, Emily had found Julianne's grave. It was in the newest section of South Cemetery, a fallow former field, set aside for the planting of Portsmouth's next generation.

Julianne, as the dates on her gravestone revealed, had arrived here way too soon. She was barely out of college when the "accident" occurred. The facts of her passing had been too much for Levi to say aloud. Which was why, in the two decades since, he had only recently found the strength to visit this spot, the saddest spot on Earth. He had never in all those years been here with anyone else.

"We were afraid you wouldn't make it," Emily said, her voice determinedly upbeat.

The snowfall was picking up, the white dusting beginning to thicken on the last bits of grass, leaves, flower baskets, and stones. Despite the chill, Levi thought, it was beautiful here. He gestured to Emily that it might be time to go, but she shook her head.

"I have something to say," she announced. And taking a deep breath, she began.

"Hello Julianne. My name is Emily. I know you're not here, and I know you can't hear me, but I wanted to stop by to report on how your old friend Levi is doing. He's still messed up, of course. But that's not your fault, nor his. Excuse the cliché, but bad things happen to good people. I guess you know that."

Levi tried to cover his emotions with a laugh that came out more like a snort. Emily shook off a coating of snow, smiled in his direction, and continued.

"He's seeing a therapist, which is a good sign. He's also seeing me, which is a good move. I'm 35. My hormones are raging. I was brought up Catholic. I teach school. I'm a pretty happy person. People think I'm funny. But between us girls, I don't know what the hell I want out of life. Okay, back to Levi."

Emily cleared her throat and addressed Julianne's tombstone directly. "He's cute, in a rugged handyman sort of way. He's sensitive and smart. Of course, you know all this. Well . . . ." Emily leaned down and lowered her voice conspiratorially. "This is a little embarrassing. We kinda made-out a couple of times. That's all, so far. But . . . it's as if he's . . . afraid of me, you know. Or maybe he's afraid he likes me. And, if he likes me, something bad might happen."

Levi, looking increasingly like an Arctic explorer caught in a blizzard, moved towards her until they were both standing on Julianne's grave.

"I'm so sorry about what happened to you," Emily said, still staring downward.

"It's okay," Levi said at last, inching in. "It happened a long time ago."

"No," Emily said, unable to hold back any longer. "It's still happening. Look at me. I'm talking to dead people."

Levi pulled her close and laughed. "No," he corrected. "You're talking THROUGH dead people. And I hear you."

"I want to promise you bad things won't happen ever again," she said, looking up at him through tears and swirling flakes. "But I can't."

"I know," he said, holding on for dear life. "I know."

Chapter 50

"Thank God for snow days," Emily said the next morning. She leaned her head, wet hair dangling, into the main room of the cozy carriage house.

"Shower all right?" Levi called back. He was collapsing the bed back into a couch. He smiled up at her distant shape, half hidden behind the door frame.

"Top notch," she replied. "I can't believe you built this whole apartment yourself."

"A carpenter's gotta do what a carpenter's gotta do."

"Well, Mr. Carpenter," she said, shivering slightly, "could you toss me a few of those bits of apparel?"

"Like this?" he asked, swirling a small item in the air.

The storm, though mild by New England standards, had left the world a smooth undulating blanket of sameness. Minutes later, gazing out onto the empty museum grounds, Emily felt a moment of utter peace. Lovely, but she was starving. She could see Levi in his micro-kitchen making tea.

"Does this little hideaway come with breakfast?" she ventured.

"Depends on whether you fancy expired eggs with greenish toast." He sniffed a small carton of milk, seemed satisfied, and added a dollop to each cup of tea.

"You really are a card-carrying bachelor," she said, accepting the warm mug. They kissed.

Levi cranked up the dial on a small electric heater. They would go to the Bow Street Eatery, he promised. It was open in all weather. He pulled on his jacket and disappeared briefly. She watched out the window as he shoveled a quick path from the carriage house door to the street. The peaceful feeling returned.

"Before we go," Levi called up from the bottom of the stairs while removing his boots, "I'd like to make sure I have this elephant thing straight."

"All right," Emily said tentatively.

Elephant number one, they agreed, revolved around Claire. The whole "Lucy Thing," Levi admitted, was eating at him. When Claire was upset, he was upset. Yes, he admitted, there was some vestigial affection between them. It was only natural, Emily agreed, as long as they had a handle on it.

"We're cool," Levi confirmed, deciding not to mention the drunken one-kiss-per-year agreement Claire had proposed only a week ago.

"Claire's really unhappy at work," he offered. "Corey says she keeps threatening to quit and go freelance, maybe try to write a book."

"Is that a bad thing?" Emily asked.

"It is if you want to make a living. Corey says the publishing industry is in free-fall. He's afraid the Lucy mess might push Claire over the edge."

Elephant number two, of course, was Julianne. "Do you think," Emily asked boldly, "it would help if the case was solved and the killer was caught?"

Levi swallowed hard. "I don't know, Emily. There are

days when I'm glad the only thing I remember is that she never came home for dinner."

"I get it," she said, clinging to his arm for a silent moment. "And to wrap up before I starve—I am elephant number three."

"You mean, my fear that something bad might happen to you if we get involved, right?"

"And the baby thing. And my being in the bloom of youth, while you're withering on the vine."

Emily took her coat from a wooden peg on the wall. She pulled it on and spun around, grabbing Levi by the collar with both hands.

"FOOD!" she screamed and kissed him.

"You know," she said as they struggled into their boots in the tiny space at the bottom of the stairs, "the elephant thing is now over."

"What?" Levi was visibly disappointed.

"Elephants in rooms are the things we don't talk about," she explained in her best teacherly tone. "When you talk about them, they go poof."

"But I like the elephants," Levi said, pulling open the door to reveal a foot-deep path through the brilliantly sunlit snow.

Emily wrapped a scarf around her neck. "POOF!" she shouted.

Levi had closed the door behind them when he heard a distant phone ringing.

Emily whined as he opened the door and bolted back upstairs. In his absence, she packed a few snowballs and expertly knocked down four icicles hanging from the carriage house roof. She was going for five-in-a-row when

Levi reappeared, his mouth and eyes wide open.

"You, okay?" she said before he could speak. "What happened?"

"It's elephant number one!" he said.

Chapter 51

"What did the boys say?" Claire asked. She hadn't been this hopeful in days.

"Levi said you're a genius," Corey cheered, cell phone in hand. "Billy is thrilled. He's going to take the new pages to Jenna for analysis as soon as the plow clears his driveway."

The news from Claire's boss had them quivering with excitement. The editorial had worked. His call was followed by an email. Attached was a file containing photos of four handwritten pages from the so-called secret Lucy diary. The filmmaker, chastened by the newspaper editorial, had decided to meet the challenge.

Corey caught his wife in the hallway and spun her around. Their five lessons in ballroom dancing, a wedding present from years ago, kicked back in. Although it was nearly noon on a weekday, neither had dressed for work.

"I still can't believe that Travis guy fell for it," Claire said, moving with the imaginary music.

"Hey, you're a genius," Corey said.

"And you're still a pretty good dancer," Claire admitted. Heather, who had never seen her parents dancing in holiday-themed pajamas, came flying out of nowhere to join the snow day celebration.

"I want to talk to Jenna too," Claire said later. She was sitting at the kitchen counter watching her husband make three perfectly toasted cheese-tomato-and-avocado sandwiches.

"You definitely should," Corey agreed as he carved each sandwich into matching triangles." But don't expect much. Even though we now have a few unredacted pages, Jenna is still working from photographs. The results won't be conclusive until she gets her hands on the originals, if ever."

"I know," Claire said. She hollered for Heather to come to lunch. "But I need an expert on the record who isn't a recently fired museum curator, and who isn't married to me. I understand she's a member of that town history group that went after Bill's job."

"Dover Pioneers," Corey filled in. He dabbed a little homemade raspberry preserves on each sandwich.

"They're a conservative bunch left over from the Colonial Revival days when all things perfect came from the past. They'd bring back horse carts and chamber pots, as long as they didn't have to use them."

"And Jenna is a Pioneer? I don't get it."

"She's been sort of spying on the committee for Billy. She's done a number of bookbinding jobs for me over the years. I like her," Corey added as Heather bounded in and climbed into her chair.

"More red jam!" she demanded.

Claire slid the five-year-old's plate out of her reach.

"So you've got her number? Claire said, ignoring the daughter who glowered at her, arms crossed.

"I'll get it for you right after I give those new pages a hard look," he said and bit into his toasted creation.

"Yum," he said.

"Delicious," his wife agreed.

"Daddy?" Heather was learning when to quit.

"Yes, my precious ray of sunshine."

"Can I please have more red jam on my excellent sammich?"

"Indubitably," her father replied.

"Doo-Billy you too," Heather giggled as Claire slid the girl's plate back within her daughter's reach. Corey added a spoonful of jam.

"And?" her mother scolded.

"Thank you, Daddy," Heather recited, and dived in.

No one in The Heights seemed in a hurry to return to the hurly-burly of daily life. From her makeshift office in the family room, Claire could hear kids playing, dogs barking, the scrape of plastic shovels against pavement, plus the occasional roar of the city plow. Around the time Levi and Emily were leaving The Eatery, and Bill Wiggin was pulling out of his driveway to visit Jenna, Corey knocked on his wife's door.

"On deadline!" Claire shouted.

"Christmas cookies!" he called back through a narrow opening.

"Enter!" she announced.

Corey set a tray of baked holiday shapes and a cup of cocoa on her makeshift desk. He winced reading the head-line on her laptop: Top 10 Seacoast Holiday Events. His reaction made her slam the computer shut. She growled and bit the head off a sugary elf.

"Where's the rugrat?" she asked, reaching for the hot chocolate.

"I cracked and let her open one holiday present early. She's building the Toy Story puzzle."

"You're a good dad," Claire said, nibbling the elf. "I know I don't say that enough."

"And a marvelous dancer," he reminded her.

"That too," Claire admitted. Then, standing behind her chair, he began massaging her rigid shoulders.

"Well," he whispered in her ear. "Dancing Daddy may have a little present for Mommy too."

"Coreeeey," she groaned.

"I'm not kidding." He stepped back, pulled a folded copy of the new Lucy pages from his back pocket, and flattened them on the desk. "I don't want to give you false hope . . ." He paused.

"Got it," she said. "No false hope. Now, show me."

"Right here." Corey pointed to an underlined passage.

Claire took another chocolate sip and leaned in. It took a moment to adjust her brain to the 19th-century cursive entry. Squinting, she was able to decipher the passage.

"W has a most jealous temperament," she read aloud from Lucy's alleged diary. "It was on display at the hop in the ballroom last night. W grew quite mad when I accepted a waltz from R."

"R?" Claire looked up.

"It has to be Robert Todd Lincoln," Corey said. "The president's son."

"I think Billy mentioned him at our first interview," Claire was nodding. "Robert had a crush on Lucy, right?" She flipped open her laptop and began tapping through files.

"Here it is. Robert Todd Lincoln is the one you said went to Phillips Exeter Academy. That's why Lincoln visited

Dover that one time, to see his son. Robert then went to Harvard and joined the Union Army."

"Good notes, babe," Corey said.

"So when did he get time to go ballroom dancing?"

"He didn't, as far as we know, at least not with Lucy Hale at the National Hotel in Washington, where she was staying according to this entry. It's dated only two weeks before the assassination. Some say Robert sent Lucy a bouquet of fresh flowers every day while courting her."

"From the battlefield?" Claire said. "Not likely."

"And what's this?" She pointed to where Corey had circled a few words with a bold marker.

"According to many historians," he said, "Booth referred to his fiancée as Bessie. See here . . ." This time Corey read the line. "W called me his beautiful Bessie, and asks if he can trust me utterly."

Claire's face registered confusion, but she chose not to interrupt.

"There's more," Corey said and flipped the page to another underlined passage. This one was dated a week after the assassination. Haltingly, running her finger along the line, Claire read on.

"Mrs. T did her best to calm me. She helped me compose a letter to my beloved W, though where he may be, no one knows. I promised to marry him even at the foot of the scaffold."

"Holy crap!" she said. "Mrs. T?"

"Mrs. Temple, I presume."

"I'm losing you," Claire had to admit. "Who the bejesus is this Mrs. Temple?"

"Exactly," her husband laughed. "These passages

follow almost word for word from a story written by a guy named Alexander Hunter. It appeared in newspapers across the country in 1878, long after the assassination. Hunter suggested that Booth murdered Lincoln, in part, to avenge Robert Todd's attempt to steal his girlfriend."

"That's ridiculous," Claire squealed. "Give me more."

"Well, Hunter claimed Mrs. Temple was a resident of the National Hotel while Booth and the Hale family were living there during the Civil War. But there was no Mrs. Temple. Hunter later admitted he used an alias to protect his source."

Claire had pulled up an empty computer file and was typing at light speed. Corey, a two-finger typist, watched in envy while eating a sugary reindeer.

"So there's no Mrs. Temple," Claire summarized. "Robert Todd was not in love with Lucy. And there is no evidence that Booth, or anyone, ever called Senator Hale's daughter BESSIE. I'm beginning to think Hunter made this whole story up."

"If there's no Bessie and no Mrs. Temple . . ." Corey paused to let the facts sink in, "then these diary pages couldn't have been written in 1865."

"Because Bessie didn't exist until Hunter invented her years later!" Claire punched her husband on the shoulder.

"Who's the genius now?" he teased.

Chapter 52

"BOOTH AND BOB LINCOLN"
Excerpted from *The Chicago Daily Inter-Ocean*
JUNE 18, 1878
BY ALEXANDER HUNTER

(1878 Editor's Note: The story is given as told to the author by Mrs. Temple, one of the circle of friends at the National Hotel in Washington during the last years of the Civil War.)

Among all of Bessie Hale's admirers, Booth was the most ardent and devoted, distancing all competitors except one, and that was the president's eldest son, Robert Lincoln, who was madly in love with Bessie. He courted her again and again, and wouldn't take no for his answer. She would have given in, I am confident, but for Booth, who, with his charm of person, manner, and intellect, carried the day, and won her heart but not her hand; for her parents frowned down and most emphatically vetoed the intimacy between their daughter and the actor.

How much Bessie Hale cared for Booth none of us know; probably not even [Booth] himself could tell. No one was aware of the absorbing, true, devoted affection that Bessie had for him—a love great in its purity and singleness, firm in its attachment, as true as death itself, and stronger than life and death combined.

Booth's was the most jealous temperament I ever knew; he was insane, sometimes, it seemed to me, and when Bessie accepted any attribution from any other man, Booth would act like a patient just out of Bedlam.

One night—I can never forget it—there was a large hop at our hotel, and the salons were crowded. The band had just commenced to play one of Strauss's waltzes, and while I was standing by the door, I turned and saw John Wilkes Booth.

He had but a few moments before he returned from Ford's Theatre, where he had been acting. He came over to me. I noticed that he looked very angry and very much excited, and I asked him the cause. He pointed to a couple circling in the rhythmic measure of a waltz. They seemed to be oblivious of everything in the world. Their movements were perfect—the maiden's head almost rested on the youth's shoulder, and with her eyes half closed, she listened to the earnest, tender words that her companion was pouring into her ear.

It was Bessie Hale and Robert Lincoln. As he witnessed this scene, Booth's white teeth clenched over the mustache and his face grew very white, while his eyes blazed like fire. He caught me by the arm with a grasp that made me wince, and caused me to utter an involuntary cry, and hissed into my ear: "Mrs. Temple, see that damned villain? Oh, I could kill him—AND HIS FATHER TOO; and, by the Lord of Hosts, the sands of his life are fast running out."

"What do you mean?" I asked him, thoroughly startled by his manner and words.

"Oh, nothing," he said, recovering himself. "Only the man had better never been born than come between me and my love. Bessie loves me, I'll swear.

He left us abruptly and went out of the room, and we saw him no more that night.

I told Bessie Hale of this scene, and she was at first distressed about it, and then got mad, as a woman always does when she doesn't know what to do, and flirted openly with Robert Lincoln, much to that young man's delight.

Chapter 53

Claire didn't waste a moment. It was like watching General Patton in snowflake pajamas, Corey thought.

"You," she said to him, "are going to dig into that Bessie thing. Was she, or wasn't she?"

"Aye-aye," he saluted. "I'll need to use the computer at work after I shovel out the car."

"Good. I'll see if the girl next door can take Heather for a few hours."

"Check."

"And no planning dinner," she commanded. "We're ordering takeout tonight."

"Double check."

"Can you text me a link to that 1878 article? It's online somewhere, right?"

"On it." Corey was already fiddling with his phone, tracking down the article.

"I'm going to focus on this Alexander Hunter guy. He doesn't smell right. I'll keep tabs on Billy Wiggin and set up a meeting with Jenna for tomorrow. How about Levi?"

"Er," Corey hesitated, remembering their phone call. "He might be indisposed."

Claire rolled her eyes. "We'll put him on standby."

"Point of order?" Corey said, waving a finger in the air. "Weren't you on deadline for the newspaper?"

Claire swore. She toggled back to her *Portsmouth Journal* story, already overdue. The headline read: Ten Top Holiday Events This Weekend. Claire tapped a few keys until it read: Eight Great Holiday Happenings. She smiled to herself and tapped the SEND key.

"All done," she announced.

The Caswells, in their way, were both trained detectives. Each knew where to look for clues, and when lost, whom to ask for help.

From his office in the Athenaeum, Corey burned through countless old newspapers, all stored in digital files online. Combing the 1800s, he found a few Bessie Hales, but none were the senator's daughter from Dover. Then, digging into the summer of 1878, he struck gold. Newspapers from Rhode Island to Alaska carried the story of Booth and Robert Lincoln, the "deadly rivals" in love with Bessie Hale—as told by the imaginary Mrs. Temple. While a few editors cautioned that Alexander Hunter's story was mere gossip, most treated it as gospel.

Enraged by the 1878 article, Robert Todd Lincoln shot back a reply that appeared in some publications the following day. He was never "madly smitten" by Miss Hale, if he knew her at all. He had been courting another woman at the time, now his wife and the mother of his children. The president's son argued he had not even been in Washington at the time referenced in the false and hurtful article. Furthermore, his mother, Mary Todd Lincoln, had never been friends with anyone named Temple at the National Hotel. And if Mrs. Temple was a bosom friend of Miss Hale, how could she not know Senator Hale's daughter was named Lucy, not Bessie? There it was. Corey did a little solo dance as he ran copies of Robert Todd's response on the office printer. It wasn't exactly a smoking gun, but a solid clue. If Mrs. Temple was fake, wasn't her depiction of Bessie Hale? And so, by extension, were the pages of the lost Lucy diary. But why would Hunter publish such a hurtful story 13 years after the assassination that had rocked the country? It didn't make sense.

By 1878, Corey knew, Robert Lincoln was a working lawyer. He would later serve as Secretary of War, Ambassador to England, and president of the Pullman Company which manufactured railroad cars. Robert would turn down every effort from sponsors to lure him into politics. Lucy, meanwhile, was married to William Chandler. The couple divided their time between the nation's capital and New Hampshire. Why, Corey wondered, did the writer end his account with a vicious attack on Bessie Hale? According to Mrs. Temple, Bessie never recovered after losing Booth. The sweet, radiant, and happy young maiden was transformed into a sad, pale woman. She was, thereafter, Mrs. Temple concluded, like "A DEAD WOMAN."

"Miss Hale did not pine away," Robert Lincoln wrote in his rebuke of Alexander Hunter's article. Neither did she throw herself into a "heartless marriage," as Mrs. Temple claimed.

"She has long been the happy wife of Mr. William E. Chandler," Bob Lincoln wrote. The author of this vile fiction, Lincoln concluded with a verbal slap in the face, should stand up and explain himself.

Many newspapers published Robert's brief rebuttal, but

it was no match for Alexander Hunter's lurid and lengthy conspiracy theory. After all, as one contemporary editor remarked, "Why spoil a good romance with the facts?"

The result, Corey discovered, was that by the 20th century, the Bessie legend invented by Hunter was finding its way into accounts of the real Lucy Hale. Even prominent historians fell for the fictional tidbits in an effort to flesh out the mysterious young woman who had "captured Booth's heart."

Corey grabbed a beer from a hidden mini-fridge known only to members of the Athenaeum's inner sanctum. He was leaning back in his chair for a quick break when the phone rang.

"How we doing?" Claire asked. She's psychic, Corey told himself, before filling her in on his findings.

"So why Bessie?" Claire wondered aloud. "It's bugging me."

"Maybe Hunter just got confused," Corey suggested, discreetly sipping his beer. "Lucy's sister was Elizabeth, better known as Lizzie. And Bessie is another common nickname. Maybe he just glued the two together."

"Maybe he was afraid of being sued?" she suggested. "You said both Robert and Lucy's husband were lawyers. Hunter did cover his ass by giving his source a fake name."

"If there was a genuine source, which I doubt," Corey said. It was late afternoon by now and he was sitting in near darkness. "Remember, William Chandler was also a newspaper editor in the 1870s. Maybe there was some bad blood."

"A YANKEE editor," Claire emphasized.

"Come again?" Corey said.

Claire quickly summarized her research on Alexander

Hunter. He was described in southern newspapers, she noted, as "a brilliant writer from Virginia." He had been a loyal soldier for the Confederacy. He was wounded twice in battle and captured three times during the Civil War—but fought on.

Corey whistled. "I didn't know that," he said.

"Fun fact?" Claire added.

"Shoot," Corey said.

"I'm just spitballing here, but for the record, Alexander Hunter was pardoned after the Civil War by President Andrew Johnson. William Chandler, it turns out, was a witness in Johnson's impeachment trial."

"Ouch," Corey said. "So maybe some bad blood lingered after the war."

"You think?" Claire said. "Chandler was deeply involved in the politics of Reconstruction. He was also an abolitionist, while Hunter, well, let's just say he never forgave the North, not to mention President Lincoln, for destroying what he called—and I quote—'the old plantation race'."

"By the way," Claire added, saving the best for last, "our Mr. Hunter was a fiction writer, not a reporter. He made stuff up for a living."

Corey whistled again. "Like Mrs. Temple and Bessie Hale," he said. "Did I marry Sherlock Holmes, or what?"

"Dig this," she said. "Hunter ended up writing three nostalgic novels about life in the Old South. I downloaded one called *Johnny Reb and Billy Yank*. It's over 700 pages long, so I only had time to give it a quick scan."

The more she read of Hunter's work, the clearer his views became. Before the Civil War, according to Hunter, the "negro" and the "master race" were bound together in an "affectionate relationship"—his exact words. Slavery, he claimed, was a fair and balanced arrangement between the races. There were rules, order, respect, loyalty, and mutual trust under slavery. Everyone was happy. From his perspective, it was the abolition of slavery that destroyed the balance between the races, leading to all the problems that followed in America.

"Babe?" Claire said after a long silence. "Did you get all that?"

"I'm speechless," Corey said at last.

"Can you come home now?" she asked, and he could hear the sadness in her voice.

"On my way," he said.

Chapter 54

"Sugar?" Jenna offered, her hand poised above an ornate little bowl.

"No, thanks. But I will take a shot of that milk," Claire replied.

"It's cream, if that's okay? I can get you milk in the kitchen if you prefer."

"Cream is great."

Claire considered shutting off her tape recorder. But maybe there was some cash prize, she joked to herself, for surviving the most boring interview in the history of journalism.

So far, they had talked about the weather, taken an agonizingly detailed tour of Jenna's workspace, discussed every aspect of the bookbinding trade, chatted about what a nice man Claire's husband was, and met Jenna's elderly mother.

The mother was with them now, sitting in her wheelchair, wrapped in a shawl and smiling. Another 40 years, Claire mused, and Heather might be her caregiver, propping up her pillow and feeding her Jello.

"Mom was a reporter back when newspapers were still printed on actual paper," Heather would say.

"Another cookie?" Jenna asked, breaking the daydream.

Claire held up one hand in protest. The Mrs.-Nice-Guy approach was getting them nowhere.

"Come on, Jenna." The reporter locked eyes with her subject across the coffee table. "Nobody knows more about Lucy's handwriting than you. There has to be something you noticed—an extra large loop, an inconsistent spelling, a strange reference. Something caught your eye."

"As I told Billy yesterday, it all looks like Lucy to me. I'm not a graphologist. I restore old books. The replica volume I did for the Woodman Museum was a copy. I traced it from one of Lucy's earlier journals in the archive in Concord."

"But now that we know these pages are fake . . ."

"Do we?" Jenna set her cup on its saucer with a loud clunk that seemed to rouse her mother.

"You know," Claire said. "That thing we talked about. Any mention of Bessie Hale all but proves the pages are fake."

"It's an interesting theory, I admit." Jenna stood and began clearing the coffee table. "But it doesn't in itself prove the pages are fabricated. Maybe Booth did call Lucy by that pet name. Maybe that reporter, Mr. Hunter, invented Mrs. Temple to protect the identity of a real person. Don't you reporters use unnamed sources all the time? I mean, what's the big deal about this whole stupid thing? It's not like somebody got murdered or anything."

Jenna marched the tea tray into the kitchen.

"I'm sorry," Claire said, following her. "I didn't mean to insult your reputation. I'm just frustrated, you know, over that whole dang video. It made me feel like such a failure. And I know it hurt Billy."

"It's okay." Jenna set down her tray. "I'm just stressed out with the holiday, and my mother, and . . . It's not like the bookbinding business is booming."

Claire laughed. "Tell me about it. You're talking to a writer who married a historian."

"Not exactly what you would call sound financial planning," Jenna said, her mood brightening. She was absently rinsing the teapot and looking out the window at the snow.

The two women were silent until Jenna spoke.

"But you do have that wonderful little daughter. I've seen her at the Athenaeum with your husband. What was her name again?"

"Heather," her mother said prayerfully. "She just turned five."

"That's wonderful," Jenna said, still staring out the window. Claire saw two tears fall towards the sink. She said nothing, pretending not to notice when the other woman wiped her eyes on a dishtowel.

"Again," Claire spoke first, "I apologize if I upset you. But, in a way, we are talking about a murder here. Those pages are red meat for conspiracy theorists. Do you really think Lucy Hale was in on the plot to kill Lincoln? Not to mention that Billy Wiggin and I are being accused of covering up the facts. My whole reputation is based on uncovering the truth, not covering it up."

"But what more can I do?" Jenna's eyes were red.

"Nothing, I guess," Claire said. "If we could only get our hands on those original pages. I'm convinced you could tell us more about the ink and the age of the paper, and stuff."

"Can I read you something," Claire interrupted herself. She walked quickly back into the living room and fumbled through her camera bag. She extracted a copy of a newspaper clipping. Jenna's mother was dozing in her wheelchair.

"Corey found this yesterday. I know it doesn't prove anything. It's from a Kansas newspaper from June 1878. The writer calls Alexander Hunter 'a gorgeous and pyrotechnical liar.' Isn't that great? I wish we could still write like that."

"They did have a way with words," Jenna said, attempting a smile. Claire sensed a glacier beginning to melt.

"Hunter was a sort of Victorian shock-jock, if you think about it, a sensationalist. The media is full of them today, setting off fireworks so bright and loud that they distract readers from the facts. Eventually, people don't know who to listen to or who to trust—or if there is any truth left at all."

"Look at me standing on a soapbox in your living room," Claire said, her cheeks reddening. "I'll get out of your hair."

"I hear you," Jenna said. "Come to think of it, I have something that might help with your article."

The bookbinder disappeared briefly and returned with a large envelope that she handed over.

"What's this?" Claire said.

"The original Lucy pages," Jenna said. "I was afraid to tell anyone I had them here."

Claire was speechless. "But how . . . ?" she managed.

"Give me a few minutes to put my mother to bed for her nap," Jenna said. Her face, the reporter observed, seemed suddenly calm, as if relieved of a great weight. "I promise I'll come back and tell you the whole story."

She gently wheeled her mother, still asleep, toward the door, then turned. "And you're right," she whispered to Claire. "They're fake."

Chapter 55

REPORTER'S NOTEBOOK
LUCY HALE'S "LOST 1865 DIARY" IS A FAKE
BY CLAIRE CASWELL
SPECIAL TO THE *PORTSMOUTH JOURNAL*

PORTSMOUTH—"I'd call the whole thing a tempest in a teapot," says Jenna Labreche, a professional bookbinder from Dover, NH.

Yesterday Labreche revealed how she created four "imaginary" pages of a 19th-century diary attributed to Lucy Hale, also of Dover. Those fabricated pages, mistakenly considered authentic by a California filmmaker, were the bedrock of a Civil War-era documentary in development.

In 1865, Hale was engaged to marry the now infamous John Wilkes Booth, an actor who assassinated President Abraham Lincoln. Lucy's photograph was discovered in Booth's pocket after he was captured and killed 12 days later.

A big mistake

"Lucy Hale has long fascinated me. She is a mysterious and tragic figure," says Labreche. "Her father and husband, both New Hampshire senators, were controversial figures. Both are largely forgotten today. But Lucy is remembered because she fell in love with the most hated man in America. As a footnote to the Lincoln murder, she has become an easy target for conspiracy theorists, but I'm afraid I only made matters worse for her."

Labreche says she learned about Miss Hale while working to preserve documents for the Woodman Museum in Dover. Recent speculation about a "secret Lucy diary" piqued her interest.

"It was probably a dumb move," Labreche admits, "but I couldn't help wondering what that lost journal might reveal. I knew from an existing journal I had worked on, what Lucy's earlier diary writing looked like. My big mistake was showing the made-up pages to a few people, just for fun."

According to Labreche, those fabricated pages found their way onto the desk of Wagner Hilton, owner of Founder's Point Estates retirement community. According to Hilton, an associate spotted the documents.

"He thought they were real," Hilton confirmed in a telephone interview yesterday.

"This was the week after the story about that piece of furniture at the museum came out in your newspaper," Wagner Hilton told this reporter, referring to the *Portsmouth Journal*. "Well, one thing led to another. I was out of town at the time, so I had nothing to do with it."

According to Hilton, his associate, whom he refuses to identify, sent photos of the pages anonymously to the *Portsmouth Journal*, to a filmmaker he had seen online named Travis Welnik, and to Bill Wiggin, curator at the Dover museum.

Official apologies

"It was all very cloak and dagger," Wiggin recalls. "The photos I received were heavily redacted. I was skeptical from the start. But before I could do much research, the film-maker and his crew showed up in Dover for an interview. It turned out to be an ambush. I walked out of the room. The next thing I knew, I was being depicted as a liar in an internet video."

The short video by Travwell Productions appeared on YouTube and was circulated through social media. In it, Mr. Travis Welnick claimed Mr. Wiggin and this reporter were covering up the existence of the lost Lucy Hale diary.

Mr. Welnick declined to be interviewed by telephone for this article. His office has since emailed the following response: "Based on the recent confession by Ms. Labreche about the forged Lucy Hale documents, Travwell Productions has suspended work on its documentary entitled LUCY'S VOICE. We regret any inconvenience our promotional video may have inadvertently caused in our quest to uncover the truth."

At the request of the *Portsmouth Journal*, the controversial video has been removed from the internet. Ms. Labreche has offered her personal apologies to Mr. Wiggin and to this reporter.

"I guess this is a confession," Labreche said in response to the film company's statement. "I reject the notion, however, that this was some sort of forgery. It was more like an experiment that went wrong."

A finely crafted wooden dresser recently donated to the museum, has been authenticated as belonging to Ms. Hale. But according to curator Wiggin, the jury is still out on whether Lucy Hale ever recorded her impressions of the historic events of 1865.

Following the assassination, the Hale family lived in

Spain where JP Hale served as ambassador. Upon their return, Lucy Hale served as her father's caretaker at their Dover home until he died in 1873.

The Hale House is part of the Woodman Museum, open to the public at 182 Central Avenue in Dover. Lucy Hale Chandler, her father, mother, and sister, are buried in nearby Pine Hill Cemetery.

Chapter 56

"Is he dead, Daddy?"

"I'm afraid so, peanut."

"Why did they kill him?"

"It was a long, long time ago," Corey said, although he knew his explanation would fall flat.

Perched on her father's shoulders, Heather was not quite eye-to-eye with the towering, snow-white polar bear. The poor guy, Corey was thinking—shot, skinned, gutted, probably stuffed with cotton, and transported from the Arctic. Namuq (the bear's name, according to a plaque) had been standing, silent and motionless, by the museum's front door for over a hundred years. One more century, Bill Wiggin was telling a group of VIP guests, and this exquisite species would likely be extinct.

"I think this is my favorite place," Heather told her father as they followed their guide from one intriguing room to the next. "Can we live here like that old lady did?"

"I'm afraid it's too crowded for the Caswells. Too many snakes and bugs and birds and butterflies."

"And polar bears," Heather added.

"Exactly. But we can come here anytime you want," Corey promised.

They were hand-in-hand now, climbing the stairs to the second floor, having lost Claire and Levi among other invited guests at the museum's holiday fundraiser.

"Wait, wait!" Levi was saying with only a slightly detectable slur. "You're telling me it was the real estate guy's idea to forge those Lucy pages? I didn't see that in your article."

A fish out of water, the caretaker was three beers into the annual holiday gala.

"Shush, you lush," Claire said, a finger to her lips. She tugged him gently away from the crowd and into the Natural History room. They huddled together next to a stuffed Alaska gray wolf as a mixed herd of mounted moose, deer, antelope, and elk heads gazed forlornly in their direction. Unlike most of the men at the party, Levi did not own and had refused to rent a tuxedo. He had, however, resuscitated an old corduroy sport coat and was wearing his only tie. Claire, meanwhile, was decked out in a strapless black number that matched the formal occasion perfectly.

"We couldn't talk in the car because the rugrat has big ears," she whispered as soon as they were alone. "But Jenna had a lot more to say off the record."

In a nutshell, Claire explained, the whole thing started when a distant member of the Chandler family retired and leased an apartment at Founder's Point Estates. As soon as the new tenant moved his stuff into the ritzy retirement complex, Wagner Hilton spotted Lucy's dresser. He offered the tenant a couple thousand dollars for the dresser, Jenna told Claire and loaned it to the museum.

"Did Hilton know about the secret drawer?" Levi asked.

"Definitely," Claire said. "He then hired Jenna to create the sample pages. He told her it was just a prank. He's no fan of Bill Wiggin. Jenna didn't like the idea, but she needed the money."

An elegantly dressed couple wandered into the Natural History room and recognized Claire. It was ten minutes before she could politely escape their questions. Levi, who had been pretending to read the exhibition labels, rushed back over.

"Then it was Mr. Hilton who sent out the fake diary copies, not some unidentified associate like you said in the article." Levi quivered with excitement.

"Looks that way," Claire said softly. "Jenna thinks the whole thing was a scam. The more publicity Lucy's diary received, the more valuable her dresser became. Remember, Hilton had the right to reclaim it at any time."

An intricately crafted, antique Spanish dresser with a hidden drawer that belonged to a woman with a romantic connection to Abraham Lincoln's killer—Levi did a fast calculation.

"It could be worth a fortune," he said. "The wilder the story, the greater the value."

Claire shushed him again. "Meanwhile, the controversy cost Bill his job."

"What I still don't get," Levi said, his tone now hushed, "is why you didn't go all Claire Caswell on this real estate developer guy. You had him dead to rights."

"Not without Jenna going on the record," the well-dressed reporter replied. "Think about it."

Levi thought, but came up empty.

"Could be a coincidence, but I hear Jenna's mother is moving into the assisted living wing at Founder's Point Estates," she said. "And at a shockingly low rate."

Levi's eyes widened to match Claire's smile. "But isn't that blackmail or extortion or something?"

"I'm sure I don't know what you are referring to, sir." Claire gave him a comic wink.

"You are some piece of work," Levi said admiringly. "Are you going to tell Billy?"

"Tell Billy what?" Billy Wiggin said as he rounded the corner, arm in arm, with Emily Smyth.

Chapter 57

"Tell Billy what?" Bill Wiggin said. "I found this lovely young lady searching for her date." The curator's face, flushed with joy, bubbled out of a well-worn tuxedo. He danced Emily towards Levi and launched her into the caretaker's arms with a final pirouette.

"Sorry I'm late," Emily said.

"But you do know how to make an entrance," Levi grinned. In her red party dress—hair, heels, and hem high—she reminded him of no teacher he had ever known.

"Tell Billy what?" the curator repeated, breathing heavily.

"Oh, we were just saying how much we enjoy being invited to this party," Claire said unconvincingly.

"Sure you guys weren't talking about Jenna agreeing not to rat out my old pal Mr. Hilton?" Bill was enjoying the moment.

"So you know," Claire said.

Emily gave Levi a questioning look. "I'll tell you later," he whispered.

"You hadn't left her driveway before Jenna called and filled me in," Bill kidded Claire. "She and I go way back, and her mother is in decline. She did what she had to do."

Like a vaudeville magician, the joyful curator whipped

an envelope from his vest pocket and handed it over. Claire opened it, skimmed the contents, and squealed with delight.

"Congratulations! Now the museum owns Lucy's dresser," she summarized as Levi and Emily applauded.

"In perpetuity," Bill added. "Plus $50,000 to install a small, permanent exhibition about Dover's founding Hilton brothers, sponsored by Founder's Point Estates."

"Not to mention," Emily spoke up, "the museum has offered Billy his job back."

The curator raised his hands against another round of applause. He had decided, he said, to stick to his plan to write a book, after taking his wife on a well-earned vacation.

"I'll still do tours, as a volunteer, and pop my head in now and then," Bill explained.

"I'm jealous," the journalist admitted, giving him a congratulatory hug. "But I think it's time to find my family."

"I left them in the Old Damm Garrison after my VIP tour," the curator said. "Corey was teaching your daughter to churn butter in the hands-on display area. She said something about working here when she grows up, and I quote— saving the polar bears, so they don't GO-STINK and die out."

"That's my Heather," Claire said. "Saving the world from polar bear farts." She gave Levi a peck on the cheek, smiled at Emily, and turned to leave.

"Let us know if you need a ride home," she told Levi and disappeared.

"Let us know if you need a ride home," Emily repeated with a snarky nasal edge. Levi cocked his head. "Okay, maybe there was no subliminal message," she said, taking his arm, "but the woman can be pretty intimidating."

"I have to second that," Bill Wiggin agreed and winked

at the teacher. Now it was his turn to be distracted. A cluster of donors, drinks in hand, began pelting the curator with questions about the strange stuffed, dried, and bottled creatures all around them. Levi took the opportunity to update Emily on the "Bessie hoax" and the "Hilton scam." Bill rejoined them as Levi was wrapping up.

"You're part of the inner circle now," the curator told Emily. "I wouldn't want Mr. Hilton to know we know he tried to pull a fast one."

"At least you were right about the dresser," Levi noted. "It was floating around in the Chandler family. Lucy's only son must have passed it on to a relative who never tripped the magic switch to the secret hiding place."

"Orrrrr . . ." Emily cleared her throat for effect. "Maybe . . . someone found the real journal and it's still out there."

"Emily, please, my ticker!" Bill clutched his heart in mock terror. "I don't think I could survive another scandal from Lucy Lambert Hale Chandler."

"Lambert?" Emily perked up. "I've got a Lambert in my class this year."

"Lucy's mother was a Lambert," the curator told her. "It's a local name."

Emily was fiddling with her phone. "Hey guys," she was laughing. "Ever heard of a Pink Lambert?"

She held her cell phone at arm's length, the screen pointed in Bill's direction. It showed a photograph of a bright pink cylinder. It was roughly the size and shape of the cardboard tube inside a roll of toilet paper.

"Can I see that?" The curator's hand was shaking as he accepted Emily's phone. Bill studied the image for a few seconds, then handed the phone to Levi, who lifted the glowing screen within inches of his eyes.

"Oh, my God!" Levi said. He returned Emily's phone, gripped both her hands and kissed her.

"Let's go!" the curator said, waving the couple towards the door and pulling a set of keys from his pocket. The trio hurried through the museum guests and into the bracing December air. They followed an asphalt path strung with holiday lights to the Keefe House next door.

"What did I do?" Emily asked Levi as they wormed their way, hand-in-hand, through another cluster of well-dressed partiers in the downstairs art gallery and up a flight of stairs to the research room.

"I think," Levi said, his breath hot and close, "you just made history."

Chapter 58

The two Pink Lambert wax cylinders in the museum collection could not have been less conspicuous. The shiny pink recording tubes were hidden inside drab cardboard sleeves printed with the word "indestructible." They sat upright on a shelf in the media archive, surrounded by competing brands. Prominent among the collection were the Edison Gold Molded cylinders in their bright yellow tubes featuring a portrait of Thomas A. Edison himself. Other labels advertised companies named Columbia, Busy Bee, Pathé, Sterling, and more. They announced classic song titles like *Twinkle, Twinkle, Little Star*, and *Turkey in the Straw*, plus *Auld Lang Syne*.

"We hardly ever play them," Bill said, opening a low cabinet door. He pulled out a heavy machine made of wood and metal and set it gently on a table, then continued his tutorial.

"Edison, as usual, got all the credit for the original phonographs when they came out in the late 1880s. The first cylinders were actually coated with beeswax, so you can imagine how delicate they were. They ran for only two minutes and fell apart after 20 plays. The Lambert brand came later. They were made from some kind of early plastic and could play up to four minutes. But by the 1910s, they were being edged out by 78 RPM flat vinyl records with up to five minutes on each side. Then came 45s, 33^1/$_3$, cassette tapes, 8-track, mp3 players."

"I miss my old Discman," Emily said.

"We're all tomorrow's dinosaurs," Bill added and began wiping down the antique phonograph with a crisp white cloth.

"Are these cylinders valuable?" Levi wondered.

"Historically, perhaps," the curator said. "Some are rare, but most have been cataloged and digitally re-recorded. Many titles were sold by the thousands and you can pick them up for a few bucks in an online auction or at a flea market. Then people give them to us, which is why we have so many."

"It's the players like this the collectors want," Bill continued. "A good one in working condition can be worth hundreds, maybe thousands, of dollars."

"Fascinating," Emily said. "But why are you guys all fired up about listening to an old scratchy song?"

The curator turned to Levi. "She doesn't know?"

"There was a note," Levi told Emily. "Just a slip of paper. It was stuck at the back of that hidden drawer in Lucy's dresser. I found it, but, you know, with all the forgery going on, I figured it was probably nothing."

Emily asked the obvious question with her eyes—What the hell did it say?

Levi recited the message on the note from memory: I'M SORRY. PLAY LAMBERT. Emily opened her mouth, but nothing came out.

"We had no idea what it might mean until you showed

us that picture on your phone," the curator admitted. "Could be a pig in a poke, but we're about to find out."

Levi handed Bill the first of two Lambert cylinders. The couple watched as he removed a paper cap. He slipped two fingers into the opening and removed the dull cardboard sleeve, revealing a gleaming pink celluloid tube.

"It looks brand new!" Emily gasped.

"I can't do it," Billy said, his tension evident.

"How about a dry run?" Emily's voice was calm and reassuring. She selected another cylinder from the collection, glanced at the label, and snickered. It read, *All She Gets from the Iceman is Ice.*

Bill accepted the alternate gratefully and unwrapped it. He opened a metal loading gate on the machine and, being careful not to touch the grooves on the surface of the recording, slid the cylinder onto a long horizontal rod. He snapped the gate shut, positioned the playing needle onto the disc, and attached a black, metal, speaker horn shaped like a giant tulip. Grasping a metal crank on the side of the machine, he gave it a few gentle turns, then stopped, calmer now.

"The beauty of these affordable home units," he said to the tiny audience, "was their ability to record as well as play. Besides music, we have uncounted early speeches, poetry, dramatic readings, jokes, vaudeville acts, animal noises, babies' first words, Bible verses—sounds never captured before."

"And you think Lucy might have . . . ?" Emily let her question drop.

"It's just a wild theory," Levi jumped in. "Right, Billy?"

"Billy?"

The curator had taken a worn-looking ledger from a shelf. Levi watched as the man in a tuxedo flipped through the pages, oblivious to anyone else in the room.

"Hey, Billy!" Levi said. "How about some tunes?"

"Sorry," the curator said. "Here goes nothing."

Releasing a lever, he let the needle meet the spinning plastic tube. A male voice like a sideshow barker announced the title as sung by Ada Jones on Edison Records. A blasting introduction by a brass band was followed by a lilting soprano.

> One fine day
> The sun was shining hot;
> I was standing
> On the corner lot.
> Saw the iceman
> Slowly going by.
> As he looked
> He winked his eye.
> After that in
> Any kind of weather,
> He and I
> Would always be together.

The scratchy 1908 hit filled the room. Billy, absorbed in research, was back at his ledger. Levi gazed towards Emily in her party dress, a splash of color in a monochrome world. She saw him looking and leaned provocatively against him.

"I guess this is what happens when you go to a party with history nerds," he apologized over the music.

"Why, Mr. Woodbury," she cooed. "I would be charmed to accept this dance."

They waltzed among the books and artifacts, past card

catalogs and rows of gray archival boxes, past vertical files, computer monitors, old maps, and stacks and stacks of cardboard boxes. Bill Wiggin never looked up until, like a man struck by the Holy Spirit, he raised his arms to heaven. The imaginary orchestra went silent and the couple froze in place.

"I knew it, I knew it!" Bill cried out. "It was hers!"

He stabbed his finger into the ledger and, as if seeing them for the first time, addressed the dancers.

"CH-052-1910," he read aloud. "Edison gramophone, 1910 model. Excellent condition. Includes two dozen wax cylinders, various titles and manufacturers. Gift of the Chandler family, Warner, NH."

Emily and Levi separated but found themselves holding hands.

"It's been here all these years," the curator sighed. "I never made the connection."

"Not to be a buzz kill, Billy," Levi spoke after a reverential pause. "But if this is a 1910 machine, wouldn't Lucy have been in her 70s when she bought it? She died in 1915, right?"

Bill nodded. "That's true, Levi. And for all we know it was her husband's hi-tech toy. Maybe he used it for dictation. One thing for sure, the two Pink Lamberts were not commercially recorded. There's no printed title on either. Whatever is on them, was a home recording."

"If there's anything on them," Levi warned.

"It says here," Emily had her phone out again, "that Thomas Lambert got the patent for celluloid cylinders. They could be played thousands of times without deteriorating, and were largely unbreakable. Edison eventually bought out Mr. Lambert's business."

"That said, how would the teacher like to do the honors?" Edgy, but no longer frozen, Billy removed the Edison disc and loaded the Pink Lambert. He ushered Emily to the phonograph and showed her how to position the needle and flip the switch.

"Let's do this thing," she said as the metal speaker began to hiss and crackle again. There was a good five seconds of nothing but static. Emily crossed herself in silent prayer as all three leaned an ear toward the metal horn. Then came a faint voice.

"Hello?" the speaker, discernibly female, was tentative and distant, like someone calling from the bottom of a well.

"Hello," she said again, this time louder and resolute. "My name is Mrs. Lucy Lambert Hale Chandler."

Chapter 59

Half an hour and one text message later, the three Caswells joined the private history party in the Keefe House second-floor research room. Seated at the curator's computer, Claire was tapping notes into her online account. Heather and Emily were seated nearby, happily drawing pictures of polar bears and other ex-stinky creatures.

The first Lucy recording had turned out to be both a revelation and a disappointment. The elderly Mrs. Chandler had apparently used the family phonograph to record a pitch for her favorite charity. In a dry, dull monotone, Lucy summarized the work of the Ladies Benevolent Society and thanked her listeners, in advance, for their generous contributions.

It was, at least, the first time anyone had heard her voice in over a century. It wasn't the young, flirtatious belle of the ball for whom all things were possible. That voice was gone forever. But it was truly Lucy, the flesh and blood, unforged, fiction-free woman who had known and loved the actor who shot the president and altered the course of history with a single bullet.

They listened to the recording three times before Bill removed it from the machine. When it was safely back in its wrapper, Levi handed him the second Lambert cylinder. Heart racing, hands sweaty, the curator loaded the pink plastic tube.

"Any final words before I hit the switch?" Bill nodded towards his fellow historian, also sporting a vintage tuxedo.

"I hate to speculate," Corey said, causing Levi to laugh.

"All right," Corey corrected, "I love to speculate." He cleared his throat as Claire slid her tiny tape recorder in his direction.

"Let's recap. We know Lucy or her husband bought a new phonograph around 1910. We know she knew how to use it. I'm guessing she was attracted to the indestructible Lambert recording brand. We know from a newspaper clipping that a lot of her dead mother's possessions were shipped from Dover to the Chandlers' summer home at Warner in 1910. And we can safely assume her Spanish-made dresser was among those items. What happened next?"

"I bet she opened the secret drawer and found her old journal," Claire announced.

Emily's hand shot up as if in school. "I think option one should be—there never was a secret journal."

"Emily's right," Claire said. "This whole thing may just be tilting at windmills."

"Point taken," her husband said. Corey seemed to have appointed himself master of ceremonies for the world premiere of cylinder two. Bill was up next.

"Let's say she did write the diary, but then forgot all about it. Lucy got married, had a kid, grew old. Almost half a century passed and—BANG!—the dresser lands back on her doorstep in 1910. She can't let her husband see it. She obviously left it in Dover when they got married. He was in denial that Lucy ever knew John Wilkes Booth. What's her next move?"

"She didn't need a move," Claire countered. "She and her dead dad were probably the only ones who knew her diary was hidden in the dresser."

"If there ever was a diary," Emily reminded the jury.

"If there was no diary," Levi couldn't help saying, "then why did she hide an apology note and a clue in a secret compartment? Doesn't that mean she anticipated that someday someone might discover her hiding place?"

"Which means," Corey interrupted, "she either got rid of the diary when it resurfaced in 1910 . . ."

"Or she opened the hidden compartment—and her diary was gone." Levi concluded.

Heather looked up from her latest drawing. "Emily says there was no diary, so she's right!" Having made her point, she went back coloring a butterfly.

"Heather, please be polite to grownups!" Claire scolded. She turned to smile at Emily, who smiled back.

"Sorry, grown-ups," Heather pouted, obviously bored.

"What I don't get," Claire said to the three well-dressed history men, "is why Lucy would give a hoot about a missing journal almost 50 years after the Civil War."

"We need to remember," the curator responded, "that this must have been a stressful time for Lucy. The late 19th and early 20th century saw an explosion of interest in the Civil War. Monuments, both Confederate and Union, popped up in town after town. Abraham Lincoln had become a martyred god. His image was everywhere—on stamps and on framed portraits hanging in schools next to George Washington."

"We're talking about 1910," he continued. "In 1909, Lincoln showed up on the penny, the first president pictured on an American coin. Plans were in the works in Washington to build the Lincoln Memorial—a huge Greek temple with a 50-foot tall statue. Lucy couldn't buy a piece of gum without being reminded of the greatest mistake of her life. This was the woman, after all, whose date to Lincoln's second inauguration was John Wilkes Booth."

"Point taken," Claire said, somewhat irked by the lecture. But the curator wasn't finished. He backed carefully away from the old phonograph and pulled a book off a shelf.

"Pardon my passion," he said, directing his attention to Claire. "But this woman's predicament has been on my mind for decades. Think of it. Caught in the line of fire between the two most famous, most photographed men of her era. And worse, the speculation and the publicity never let up."

Bill placed a battered hardcover on the table. "As if living with the ghost of a beloved dead president wasn't hard enough, Lucy had to contend with this."

At the phrase "dead president," Claire gave a worried glance at Emily.

"You know," Emily announced, "while all this grown-up stuff is interesting, I believe Mr. Polar Bear is about to serve hot cocoa and cookies to all the five-year-olds at the party."

Heather shot out of her seat. "Can I go, Mommy?"

"Well . . ." Claire teased. "No more than two cookies." And just as quickly, the teacher and the student were gone.

"You were saying?" Corey prompted the curator.

"Forgive me, again. This isn't exactly G-rated." Bill held up the book featuring a crude painting of Booth on the cover. "We have a rare hardcover copy of the book that claimed

John Wilkes Booth died by suicide. When it appeared, the Associated Press reported there was no doubt the dead man was Booth. Lucy must have seen those disturbing stories. Had he been alive all this time? When the book came out in 1905, it sold 70,000 copies."

"Is this the same guy whose corpse was on display at state fairs for the next 50 years?" Levi asked.

"The same," Bill said. "Meanwhile, the body of the real Booth was making headlines too. The Booth family had it exhumed and moved in 1901. Believe it or not, that's the same year Lincoln's corpse was exhumed. Robert Todd Lincoln had the coffin opened to confirm the president's identity. Then it was reburied and covered in concrete to discourage any grave robbers."

"That's horrible!" Claire gasped.

"Horrible, but true," Corey stepped in. "Newspapers and magazines were jammed with stories about Booth and Lincoln. They faded from the headlines during two world wars, but the media frenzy and conspiracy theories have only picked up speed since."

The curator put an end to the discussion by giving the crank on the side of the phonograph a few turns. "These old springs sometimes snap," he said. "Winding them makes me as nervous as a cat."

The tension was infectious. The foursome held their collective breath as the curator set the needle on the spinning cylinder. A crackle of static was followed by what sounded like shuffling sheets of paper. Then came the now familiar voice.

"Hello," Lucy said again.

Chapter 60

TRANSCRIPT
LUCY LAMBERT HALE CHANDLER
LAMBERT WAX CYLINDER
RECORDED CIRCA 1910-1915
WOODMAN MUSEUM ARCHIVE

Hello.

This private recording is for my dear husband Willy and son Johnny, should they find it after I'm gone.

[Pause. Sound of paper shuffling. The speaker appears to be reading.]

As you well know, I have lived three lives. I was a gay and silly schoolgirl who became a young woman of privilege. That all ended one horrible night. In my second life, following the tragedy, chastened for my sins, I devoted myself to Father, first in Europe and then in our beautiful Dover home. Those were hard and heavy years. When he passed, I could see no future before me.

[Sound of paper. Speaker clears throat.]

Then, suddenly, I was reborn as a wife and a mother, for which I have been eternally grateful. My third life has been a blessing.

But there are things we never speak of, and speak of them now, I must. The honor of our families requires it. Perhaps, through this mechanical method, you may be able to listen to the words I could not speak in life.

[Pause. Speaking with increased emotion.]

In my youth, like many of the fairer sex, I was in the practice of committing my deepest thoughts privately to paper. Father encouraged it. Towards the end of our great American conflict, while living at the National Hotel, and later in Europe, I continued to find solace in the written word. Those words were hidden from prying eyes in a secret place.

I never took up my pen again. I do not recall or wish to know what my young, agitated mind composed during that tumultuous and traumatic year. No one should ever know.

The purpose of this message is to inform you, my beloved husband and son, that my record of that fateful time is missing. The diary, once secreted in the Spanish dresser father gave me, is gone. The space was violated by parties unknown and the contents taken away.

[Speaker's voice halting or choking after pause.]

Forgive me for my tears. If God is good, then my foolish words will never see the light. If I am cursed, as sometimes I have believed was true, then the villain who robbed my soul may yet attempt to tarnish the name of Hale and the name of Chandler.

[Speaker's voice highly emotional.]

If my diary should reappear, for all our sakes, for the honor of our families, I beg you, my men, to make haste to obtain it by any means possible. Bind the pages shut and send it to the bottom of the ocean, commit it to the flames, or bury it deeper in the ground than my grave.

[Distant voice, sobbing.]

Farewell, my men. There are so many things a mother

and a wife can never say. Please know I love you both. Please hold me in your hearts. And may God in Heaven bless and keep you always.

[End of recording.]

Chapter 61

Pine Hill Cemetery lives up to its name. From a long granite wall not far from the Woodman Museum on the city's main road, acres of Dover's dearly departed rise heavenward amid a cluster of towering pines. Even with Bill Wiggin's hand-drawn map, it was 20 minutes before Claire and Levi spotted the Hale family memorial. The blocky stone slab, topped with a ponderous triangular roof, was intended to echo the shape of a Greek temple. To Levi, it looked more like a Monopoly game hotel, enlarged to an obscene size and painted gray.

Two days before the new year, an eerie warm spell had erased the moderately white Christmas. Patches of green again poked through a carpet of pine cones and dried fir needles. Confused clumps of ground flowers and the occasional dandelion wondered openly what season was in play.

A century and a half earlier, the same spot had been a dark sea of mourners and muslin-draped carriages. Church bells rang and shops closed following the death of Senator John P. Hale. The "ancient agitator", as one obituary described him, had been ill since returning from Spain four years earlier. But Hale had put the city on the map, and its residents turned out in droves to usher him into Eternity.

Claire read the bold embossed letters on the stone aloud:

HE WHO LIES BENEATH SURRENDERED
OFFICE, PLACE AND POWER RATHER
THAN BOW DOWN AND WORSHIP SLAVERY.

"Not too shabby," Levi said, kneeling to read three small markers below the bulky Hale tomb. "I see mom, dad, and daughter Lizzie, but where's Lucy?"

"She's over here," Claire called back and rested her gloved hand on a distinctly modern and unadorned stone. It read: "Lucy Hale Chandler, wife of Sen. William E. Chandler, 1841-1915." Nothing more.

"Bill says he didn't even know Lucy was here in an unmarked grave until he dug through the cemetery records a few years ago," Claire explained, tapping Lucy's stone. "The museum and the Chandler family kicked in for this."

"Her husband never even bought her a headstone," Levi said. "That's cold."

"Do you think he ever listened to her message?" Claire wondered aloud.

"I doubt it," Levi said, "considering he died two years later and is buried in Concord with his first dead wife."

"I forgot that! So sad."

Claire tried making a muddy snowball, but it fell apart in her hands. "What about her son?"

"If he heard it, then why leave the wax cylinder hanging around for someone else to find? It makes no sense. Neither of them discovered the note I found stuck in the dresser."

"So the diary might still be out there, waiting to go off like a forgotten land mine." Claire pondered the thought.

"I guess," Levi said. "But if any of the Chandler

descendants found it, they sure aren't sending up flares."

"Which leads me to one of the reasons I offered to give you a ride to your therapy appointment this morning," Claire said. She was wearing her serious-face, but Levi was too far away to read it.

"Oh no," he wailed. "You're finally joining a convent!"

Claire offered a polite half-laugh.

"I outgrew that dream long before I met you. But I do want to apologize for the way I treated your new Catholic school-teacher-friend."

"She isn't a nun," Levi protested, still not reading the mood. "She's a comedian."

"Please, just tell her, for me, that I think she's great. I really do. Heather says Emily is cooler than a polar bear on an ice cube. That's a direct quote."

"I'll tell her," Levi promised, then hesitantly added— "She thinks you're kinda scary."

He had moved close enough to see her face fall. "Do you think I'm scary?" she asked.

"Not anymore," he said. They were shoulder to shoulder now, the only living beings in the land of the dead in the late morning of late December. "Well, not most of the time."

"I know I can come on a little strong," she said, suddenly sounding not strong at all. "It's probably just a midlife crisis thing."

Levi wasn't sure how to respond, so they stood for a minute, letting the birds, and a light breeze, and the distant sound of traffic fill the vacuum. They had been together long enough to share the comfort of silence.

"You know I always wanted to write a book," she said at last.

"A million-dollar bestseller, if I recall," he said.

"Exactly," Claire smiled. "I love being a reporter, but lately, you know . . ."

"Too many store openings?"

"Exactly. At least with the Lucy story, we had a little excitement. I got to investigate something. It felt good."

"There's no biography of this mysterious lady," Levi said, tapping on Lucy's stone marker.

"I don't think I could do it," Claire said. "That's a history book. We never found the journal. A good crime story needs an ending, hopefully a twist at the end."

"I guess," Levi agreed. He cupped his hands at the sides of his mouth and shouted towards the half-frozen soil. "Sorry, Lucy! No blockbuster for you!"

At this point, Claire almost confessed. It would have been the perfect moment, the two of them alone in a sweeping landscape of tombs, with Levi on his way to a therapy appointment, just in case things went badly.

"I want to write a book about Julianne," she wished she could say, imagining his reaction. Claire wanted to tell him about the true crime publisher, the one she had queried. The advance money being offered wasn't much, barely three week's salary at the newspaper. It was nothing they could live on. She couldn't quit her job, of course. But the added income would help cover their rising property tax bill.

And maybe it would sell. Cold cases were very popular, the publisher had told her. Claire had an outstanding reputation for investigative reporting. She had been at the scene of the crime. She even knew the dead woman's boyfriend. Her book could be a powerful account of a tragic unsolved crime.

And if it did well, there would be more income, perhaps the start of a whole new career.

A book, she thought, might fill that gnawing empty space. Her renewed attention might crack the 20-year-old murder case wide open. Or, as she looked into Levi's warm smile, might crack her best friend in half. She could lose him altogether. And what of Heather and Corey, who loved him too? This was, she told herself, the most dangerous writing assignment she had ever considered. And yet, chapter by chapter, the book was assembling itself in her mind.

"Where did you go?" he said, gazing back. "Are you picking up voices from the dead?"

"Kind of," Claire said. And instead of confessing, the reporter threw her arms around the caretaker and kissed him for real.

"That was . . ." he exhaled, blinking back to reality.

"Yes, it was the contracted annual kiss. One per year, payable on demand, till death do us part."

"Is that a calendar year or a fiscal year?" he asked, trying to break the thrill.

"Calendar," she confirmed. "The next kiss-year begins in two days. Date and location of event to be determined. And for the record," she studied her watch, "your therapy appointment begins in 16 minutes and 32 seconds. We should get moving."

"I can walk from here," he said. "The office is right nearby."

"But, but, I'm going to give you a ride home after," she stammered.

"I'll be fine," he said. And she knew he was right.

Claire had brought a single rose for Lucy and, drawing

it from her bag, placed it atop the gravestone. It looked so forlorn against the gray that she took out her camera and grabbed a few shots for a future story.

"Can I say something?" she asked as they walked down the steep hill and out of the land of the dead.

"That you're proud of me?" Levi guessed.

"Even more," she said, as they reached her car. "I'm sorta proud of us both."

"Me too," he agreed.

Levi held the car door open as she settled in, then closed it gently. She lowered the window.

"Are you sure?" She gave it one more try.

"I'm sure," he said and began walking purposefully, eagerly forward.

"The funny part," he was saying minutes later to Gerome "Gerry" Goldman, sunk safely into the comfortable therapy couch, "is that we still don't know any more about Booth and Lucy than when the whole thing started. Her journal is still out there. The conspiracy theories keep swirling around."

"And that funny part is?" the therapist nudged.

"There's no final act," Levi said. "We didn't solve the big puzzle. We were like a team playing a really good game that ended in a tie or was called on account of rain."

"Lawyers talk a lot about closure," the therapist proposed, gesturing with his imaginary pipe. "But a lot of therapists, myself included, think closure is overrated. Not all wounds heal. Most mysteries never get solved—except, perhaps, in books and movies"

"Are we talking here about Lucy or Julianne?" Levi wondered where this was going.

"Take your pick," the therapist said. "It sounds like you

are pleased with the way you and your friends handled . . . can we call it *The Lucy Case?*"

Levi was nodding as he thought. "Yes. It's true. We all did the best we could with our piece of the puzzle."

"And that made you feel . . . ?"

"Happy?" Levi offered. "Satisfied? Accomplished?"

"But you didn't find the Fountain of Youth or the Holy Grail or the Great White Whale?"

"Well, let's not get carried away here," Levi laughed.

"My point, exactly," the therapist laughed back. "I'd like to take what you just said and paint those words on the walls of my office. If it's not too Yoda of me, can I tell you what I think is happening?"

"By all means," Levi said.

"Thanks," Gerry said. He wiggled his butt in his chair, settled both hands on the armrests, and leaned towards Levi.

"We're all trying desperately to manage the bubble we live in, right? One minute, we're in control. The next minute our lives are blasted into chaos. It happened to you 20 years ago and, based on what you've told me, it also happened to Lucy Hale. Not your fault. The tragic event ends, but the negative emotions—the uncertainty, the guilt, the fear, the sadness continues. We can't undo the tragedy, but our brain won't stop trying. It needs to understand what happened, to explain it, to get justice, to prevent it from happening again. We need to make the bubble we live in livable."

"Isn't that why we need closure?" Levi asked, leaning in.

"Need it, yes. Maintain it, not likely. True closure, if you ask me, means accepting the idea that pain and sadness and disappointment are part of life. Negative emotions always follow. Once you can identify them and where they come from, then you can learn to let them go, one by one. That's what I call closure. It's a process. And you, my friend, are doing a kick-ass job at it."

Levi had no comeback. He bit his lower lip and let the wisdom wash over him.

"Poor Lucy," he said eventually. "She lived just down the street and could have used a few sessions here in your office."

"Bad timing on my part," Gerry said, warmed by the compliment.

"Oh, hey," he added. "How are things going with your new relationship? What was her name?"

"Emily Smyth. I think you know each other."

That one caught Gerry by surprise.

"Things are promising," Levi confirmed. "She says, hello."

"Good to hear," the therapist said as if he wanted to hear more.

"Love to chat," Levi said, sliding out the door. "But I'm afraid our time together has run out. Catch you later, dude."

Chapter 62

HALE HOUSE
DOVER, NH
SEPTEMBER, 1873

John Parker Hale struggled with the cursed buttons on his breeches, but it was no use. His fingers refused to obey. He was not accustomed to dressing himself lately. But today was special. He was on a mission, perhaps his last.

Emptying the house had not been easy. Both Lucys, his wife and his daughter, refused to leave his side. He was fully recovered—Hale and hardy—-he insisted. The dislocated hip from that fall from his rocking chair was fine, but they knew better. It was only when the older daughter grew ill that he could convince his loyal caregivers to attend to Lizzie in New York. He would be fine. Cassie, the family cook, at his command, was en route to Portsmouth by train to pick up his medicine. Peter, a long-time servant, had been dispatched to Durham by carriage with an "urgent" letter. The house was finally empty.

JP Hale stood painfully. He steadied himself, hugging the hand-carved pillar at the foot of his bed. The touch of the wooden post brought back a memory. It was another piece of the beautiful furniture he had imported from across the

Atlantic. It was also the reason his job as U.S. Minister to
Spain had been cut short.

"Damned Gideon Welles," Hale muttered. The ancient
rivalry stirred his blood. Welles, once Lincoln's Secretary of
the Navy, was as corrupt as the day was long, Hale believed.
And he had said so, loudly, on the Senate floor and in the
newspapers during the Civil War. His rival had shot back. JP
Hale, Welles told President Lincoln and everyone who would
listen, was unfit to serve as ambassador to any country. Hale
was nothing but a boorish demagogue and a "used-up man,"
Welles told the world.

Hale got the foreign appointment, thanks to Abraham
Lincoln, but Welles got his revenge. The ambassador was
accused of overusing his duty-free privileges by importing
and reselling Spanish goods, including furniture, cases
of wine, and six carriages. Always a fighter, Hale blamed
the scandal on his secretary, but the "smuggling" charge
lingered and he was replaced in 1869.

Returning to his beloved Dover house was, at first,
joyful. The townsfolk had welcomed him home "like a king,"
the press reported. Hale liked puttering in the garden and
riding around the countryside in his carriage with Lucy.

But the evidence of his decline was indisputable, a
fact made brutally clear when the local newspaper reported
that "his vigor, both in body and mind, is gradually failing."
In truth, he hadn't been himself since that outbreak of
dyspepsia back at the National Hotel. Then came the
chronic skin rashes and mental lapses, not to mention the
stroke.

What mission was he on? Hale's hip throbbed as he
leaned against the sturdy Spanish bedpost. John Parker Hale

was no smuggler. Devil take that Gideon Welles, he thought again. Then he remembered.

The waning days of summer had gone chilly and, before taking the shay to Durham, the family's longtime houseman had kindled a warming fire in the bedroom hearth. Grabbing his trusty cane for balance, the senator managed to settle into his wheeling chair.

The journey to Lucy's bedroom was uneventful. The wooden wheels rolled smoothly down the hall. The bottom drawer of his daughter's dresser slid open. JP pressed the secret spot and felt a surge of satisfaction as the hidden space revealed itself. The journal, he knew from earlier reconnaissance missions, had not been moved in almost eight years.

JP Hale did not feel like a thief, or a smuggler, or a used-up man. He felt, truth be told, like the loving father of a daughter who still needed his help. Back in his bedroom, seated in the wicker wheelchair, he looked down at the journal resting on his knees. JP opened the leatherbound cover and read his own inked message—To my sweet child on her birthday from her proud father, January 1, 1865, Washington, DC.

Hands now shaking, he turned the first page. He read Lucy's account of the hotel party that New Year's afternoon. Her description, though spare, flooded his memory. The long war was winding down. General Grant was on the move. Hope was on the rise. JP Hale remembered, and then he dreamed until a voice, garbled at first, drove him from sleep.

"Are you all right, sir?" Peter said from the doorway. "May I turn up the lights?"

"Yes," the old senator managed to reply, his throat dry and sore. He cast his eyes around the darkened room as the servant adjusted the gas lamps and added more wood to the embers in the fireplace.

"Cassie has returned with your medicine and will bring it up with your dinner. Is half an hour acceptable?"

"Thank you, Peter. That will be fine," JP said, having gotten his bearings. His hands, he noticed, had instinctively covered the book in his lap.

He almost dozed again. What was the mission? He had been reading something.

Suddenly he knew. Hands gripping the oversized wooden wheels, John Parker Hale inched toward the marble hearth of the reinvigorated fire. Bending dangerously forward, he pushed the iron gate aside. It was time. Lucy's father picked up the diary in one hand and, with the sudden strength of an Olympian, he hurled it into the flames.

* * * THE END * * *

What's Real & Where to Go

The Woodman Museum is among New Hampshire's most intriguing and colorful hidden gems. The four-building campus at 182 Central Avenue in Dover, NH is truly a must-see stop for visitors of all ages. The Hale House there was owned by Senator John Parker Hale, but Lucy's dresser, secret diary, and recordings are imaginary, as are the key characters in the novel. Most of the historical research and references, however, are authentic, including the 1878 Mrs. Temple article reprinted in the appendix here. For tours and to support the work of this unique museum established in 1915 visit: WoodmanMuseum.org online.

* * *

To visit the **John Paul Jones House** (1758) and explore the latest activities at the Portsmouth Historical Society across the street, check out their website and museum shop at PortsmouthHistory.org online. Ask about becoming a member or volunteer.

* * *

The **Portsmouth Athenaeum** in Market Square, founded in 1817, is a membership library supported by friends and proprietors. It offers frequent exhibitions, lectures, and research assistance to the public, plus a detailed virtual catalog available at PortsmouthAthenaeum.org online.

Notes from the Author

The original idea for this trilogy was to murder someone at a different historic house in each new book. But I'm a reluctant killer. The teacher in me insisted this was an opportunity for likable, make-believe protagonists to explore real events from the past in and around my hometown. *Point of Graves*, therefore, borrowed true tales from the Portsmouth Black Heritage Trail.

I was working on a plot about John Paul Jones for this sequel when Lucy Hale rose from the grave and demanded to be heard. I first learned about Lucy decades ago while living in Dover, NH. After visiting her home at the Woodman Museum, I fell down the Hale/Booth research rabbit hole. Top of the list is an article by Richard Morcom, reportedly based on letters in his private collection. "They All Loved Lucy" appeared in the hardcover monthly magazine, *American Heritage* (October 1970, volume 21, number 6). I found a copy on eBay. Morcom promoted the legend of Lucy Hale as a rare beauty whose power over men "goes mysteriously beyond anything that can be pictured or described." Really?

Lucy drove my research into Booth and Lincoln. I scoured related biographies and history books for hints of the Hale connection. I made a pilgrimage to Ford's Theatre to view the killer's gun and portraits of the women found in Booth's pocket after he was shot. I corresponded with a distant relative of the Chandler family, plumbed the conspiracy theories, watched every Lincoln assassination documentary, and winced at every made-for-TV dramatization. In Concord, I stood before John Parker Hale's statue at the State House and white-gloved my way through one of Lucy's journals at the New Hampshire Historical Society. A nonfiction book about Lucy Hale was always on the back burner. However, as Claire Caswell discovered, it was a book with too few facts and no ending. Lucy might work as a novel, but I didn't do fiction.

Time marches on. A dozen nonfiction history books later, I was hanging out with a successful novelist friend. "It must be nice," I teased "to simply invent stories unshackled by reality." He countered that my job, merely regurgitating the work of earlier historians, must be a breeze. I accepted his challenge. Years later, *Point of Graves* appeared, the first of a planned series.

Except for a few scenes, *Lucy's Voice* is not historical fiction that, by definition, attempts to recreate a former period. My "history mystery" concept sticks to modern times with rare flashbacks. I'm also leaning toward the "cozy" mystery genre here. A cozy (think Agatha Christie) attempts to unravel a puzzle without explicit and forensic detail. But while CSI-style crime stories have grown increasingly violent and gory, the cozy has become even lighter, often featuring recipes and lovable animal detectives. Neither direction was appealing.

It's never a good idea to get caught between genres, but this original format pleases me. As a historian, I get to burrow deep into fresh territory with each volume. When Frederick Douglass speaks at the dedication of the John Parker Hale statue in *Lucy's Voice*, those are his precise words. The assassination conspiracy books Levi discovered online are the same ones sitting on my bookshelf. As a fiction writer, meanwhile, I'm never certain what Claire, Levi, and the others will say or do next. They surprise me every day.

Other authors have faced the same Lucy dilemma. The earliest effort to depict the romance between JW Booth and Lucy Hale was the Alexander Hunter article, "Booth and Bob Lincoln." It appeared in 1878 and, yes, it is real. Real fiction, that is. I've reproduced the entire article here for readers only starting to climb down this rabbit hole.

In her 1923 novel, *Booth and the Spirit of Lincoln*, Bernie Babcock accepted Hunter's imaginary story of Mrs. Temple and Bessie Hale as gospel. Babcock also embraced the "documented fact" that John Wilkes Booth was not killed in 1865. In her book, Booth gets his comeuppance when the ghost of Abraham Lincoln haunts him into committing suicide. TIME magazine called it a "semi-fictional romance," the modern equivalent of "based on a true story." Unfortunately for readers of historical fiction, neither of Babcock's foundational stories was true.

The more one studies history, the more it turns out to be a mash-up of fact, conjecture, legends, and lies. Samuel Johnson said it best: "Many things which are false are transmitted from book to book and gain credit in the world." I mention all this because, for many years, I also passed on Alexander Hunter's stories about Bessie Hale as fact. Some Booth biographers use the names Lucy Hale and Bessie Hale interchangeably. Even prominent scholars, perhaps unknowingly, have borrowed tidbits from Hunter's article to flesh out the mysterious senator's daughter who, according to Booth family letters, had won the actor's heart. It wasn't until returning to my Lucy Hale files for this book that I searched out the full Hunter essay in newspapers from 1878. In my story, curator Billy Wiggin feels Lucy begging him to get her story straight. She's been after me, too.

Conspiracy theories about the Lincoln assassination
are as prevalent today as ever. I leave that stuff up to each of
you. For readers who can't leave Lucy behind, I recommend
E. Lawrence Abel's book *John Wilkes Booth and the Women
Who Loved Him* (2018). Abel devotes a couple of chapters to
the Hale affair. He begins his analysis this way:

> *If opposites attract, John Wilkes Booth and Lucy
> Lambert Hale were made for each other. John was an
> ardent racist; Lucy was an abolitionist. John was trim;
> Lucy was stout. John was an Adonis; Lucy was a plain
> Jane.*

As to the "Bessie" question, Abel is equally frank. "Lucy
was never called Bessie," he writes. Hunter's story was "total
fantasy." Abel then notes, regretfully, ". . . some historians,
professional and amateur, still refer to Lucy by that name,
a legacy of the Temple article." Was Mr. Abel referring, in
part, to my early work that lingers online like a long-lost
shoe? *Lucy's Voice*, submitted for your approval, is my effort
to set things right and have a little fun in the process.

J. Dennis Robinson, Portsmouth, New Hampshire

"Booth and Bob Lincoln"

CHICAGO DAILY INTER-OCEAN
BY ALEXANDER HUNTER
JUNE 18, 1878

Among all of Bessie Hale's admirers Booth was the most ardent and devoted, distancing all competitors except one, and that was the President's eldest son, Robert Lincoln who was madly in love with Bessie. He courted her again and again, and wouldn't take no for his answer. He had a heavy backing for both the senator and his wife, aware of the splendid advantages of the match, urged their daughter to marry Robert Lincoln, and queen it at the White House, which in those days was like the palace of royalty itself. She would have given in, I am confident, but for Booth, who, with his charm of person, manner, and intellect, carried the day, and won her heart but not her hand; for her parents frowned down and most emphatically vetoed the intimacy between their daughter and the actor. Indeed, both father and mother considered it a great piece of presumption for the 'player' to make love off the scenic stage. John Wilkes Booth they considered divine in the princely role of Hamlet, or wearing the slashed doublet and habiliments of the half-prince, half-Melnotte; but as a son-in-law to the first senator in the land: there the charm ceased, and they commanded the daughter never to think of him.

How much BESSIE HALE cared for Booth none of us know; probably not even himself could tell. No one was aware of the absorbing, true, devoted affection that Bessie had for him—a love great in its purity and singleness, firm in its attachment, as true as death itself, and stronger than life and death combined. Only in the fearful trial, and the awful times of menace and of peril, did this love shine out in all its brightness, lighting the lured darkness with its beams, even as the rays of the lighthouse gleam out across the waste of angry waters.

Bessie Hale was passionately fond of seeing Booth assume the character of Hamlet the Dane and often would make him repeat the famous soliloquy.

Booth's was the most jealous temperament I ever knew; he was insane, sometimes, it seemed to me, and when Bessie accepted any attribution from any other man, Booth would act like a patient just out of Bedlam. One night—I can never forget it—there was a large hop at our hotel, and the salons were crowded with the wealth, the beauty, the bravery, and the talent of the land. The bench, the bar trade, and the soldier were all represented, and the scene in the ballroom was one calculated to excite the imagination and dazzle the eye. I well remember the night; it was in the late winter of '65. A series of heavy skirmishes had taken place before Richmond with heavy loss to our side, and there had been a hard battle before Atlanta, and the telegraph told us of the blood that had been poured out like water. Though throughout the whole length and breadth of the land a wall of sorrow could be heard, yet society never was more gay nor given away more utterly to the abandonment of mirth. The moans of the bereaved, the groans of the funeral cortege, the plaintive strains of the dead march, and the beat of the muffled drum, were stifled and lost in the mad shout of revelry and the light laughter of careless hearts. Wars are terribly demoralizing, and we in Washington lived as if there was no future, and that the present was all there was to exist for. I really believe that not even in the French revolution, when men worshiped the goddess of Reason, was there a more mad rush after wild excitement, and all plunged into the vortex and joined the whirling throng.

MR. LINCOLN CAME VERY EARLY TO THE RECEPTION

that night. He never liked to attend these gay gatherings, especially during the season of doubt and despair, when the very air came laden with the sulfurous smoke of the battle-field. He never came except as a duty, and to carry himself high before his people. The president came into my private parlor, and sat for an hour or so talking; he was unusually sad and seemed buried in deep thought. He turned and commenced to speak of the war. Mr. Lincoln was a man of broad, generous nature, and his heart was tender and soft as that of a woman's. He spoke of the rivers of blood that were always flowing from thousands of veins, and, turning to me, said with a pathos and feeling I can never forget, and with the tears rolling down his rugged, honest, kindly face: "Mrs. Temple, it almost breaks my heart to witness the death and desolation that this once happy country is going through: and God knows, if by sacrificing my own life I could restore peace to this distracted land, I would cheerfully do it; but my hand is on the plow and I cannot turn back. My people have put me forward, and I cannot turn back until the object of all our spilled blood has been accomplished, and the Union restored. For nearly an hour Mr. Lincoln remained with his face buried in his hands, lost in deep, painful thought, and then, with a heavy sigh, shook off his troubles and went into the ballroom. I went with him, and he was soon the center of a laughing, joyous crowd, and seemed to be the most careless and happy in all that joyous throng. "What kind of a man was Mr. Lincoln?" I asked. "The most soft-hearted, strong-headed man I ever knew," answered Mrs Temple. "A man's noblest impulses, which he had to rein in all the time. A pitiful story always touched him—so much so that it was found necessary to keep the relatives of men convicted by court-martial away from him; for, in spite of the necessity of discipline, Mr. Lincoln often pardoned soldiers who were condemned to death for grave offenses. He hadn't a particle of vindictive feeling about him, and cherished no animosity against the Southern people, so he has told me hundreds of times. There were many royally beautiful women there that night, and a fairer scene the lights never shown upon. The band had just commenced to play one of strauss's waltzes, and while I was standing by the door, "a looker on in Vienna,"

I TURNED AND SAW JOHN WILKES BOOTH.

He had but a few moments before returned from Ford's Theatre, where he had been acting. He came over to me. I noticed that he looked very angry and very much excited, and I asked him the cause. He pointed to a couple circling in the rhythmic measure of a waltz. They seemed to be oblivious of everything in the world. Their movements were perfect—the maiden's head almost rested on the youth's shoulder, and with her eyes half closed, she listened to the earnest, tender words that her companion was pouring into her ear. It was Bessie Hale and Robert Lincoln. As he witnessed this scene, Booth's white teeth clenched over the mustache and his face grew very white, while his eyes blazed like fire. He caught me by the arm with a grasp that made me wince, and caused me to utter an involuntary cry, and hissed into my ear: "Mrs. Temple, see that damned villain? Oh I could kill him—AND HIS FATHER TOO; and, by the Lord of Hosts, the sands of his life are fast running out."

"What do you mean?" I asked him, thoroughly startled by his manner and words.

"Oh, nothing," he said, recovering himself. "Only the man had better never been born than come between me and my love. Bessie loves me, I'll swear; but what between her people and his, they will dispose of her as a lamb led to the slaughter."

"I am sorry for you, Mr. Booth," said my husband, who standing beside me, had listened to his words.

"Booth turned fiercely and disdainfully around to him—for he never liked my husband—and said: 'Sir, I would rather be Acteon, chased and devoured by his own beagles, than to be like Lazarus, and have his wounds licked by dogs out of pity."

He left us abruptly and went out of the room, and we saw him no more that night.

I told Bessie Hale of this scene, and she was at first distressed about it, and then got mad, as a woman always does when she doesn't know what to do, and flirted openly with Robert Lincoln, much to that young man's delight.

"The next morning we all awaited Booth's coming anxiously, and Bessie sat in my parlor until dinner expecting him, but not then, nor that whole day, did he make his appearance.

Another day passed, and still another came and went, but no signs of Booth. Instead,

ROBERT LINCOLN CAME

regularly, and by breakfast-time a most exquisite bouquet of flowers from the White House conservatory would always be sent to Bessie; and Robert Lincoln pressed his suit boldly and ardently. I think she was piqued at Booth's silence, for she gave Robert much encouragement, and his visits became longer and more frequent.

One day, about a week after the ball, as the two were sitting alone together in my parlor, John Wilkes walked abruptly in, and sitting down with only a slight nod of recognition to both, took a book and commenced to read. An hour passed on, and his rival, seeing that Booth was determined to sit him out, got up, made his adieu, and left the field open. Bessie told me afterward that she was much incensed at his behavior, and gave him a piece of her mind. He retorted; she grew more angry, he more curt and contemptuous. She recriminated sharply, and then he, losing his temper, flung himself with a muttered curse out of the room.

She cried often and openly over this misunderstanding, and would have sent for him but that her pride withheld her.

Matters were at this state for some time. The long winter passed away, the long days came and went, each bringing some dreadful story. The very air brought tidings every hour, and the whole continent seemed to resound with the clash of arms; troops everyday passed toward the front, and, passing our hotel with their bands playing and colors flying, each day brought the news of some new triumph, and victory, so long frowning on the Union arms, came now, perched on its banners; and nearly every night there was a joyous gathering at our hotel, and mutual congratulations were the order of the day. Mr. Lincoln was happier than I ever saw him, and wherever he moved was a circle of cordial friends.

At last the great event happened that we had all wished for, hoped and prayed for, during all the four weary years—

LEE SURRENDERED

at Appomattox Courthouse!—and it seemed as if the people were delirious with joy. At our hotel there was one round of congratulations and rejoicings. Every night the parlors would be thronged with an anxious, eager, excited party who would discuss, drink, and dance the night through. Amid all these scenes Booth moved—calm, stern, silent, cold. His manner was utterly changed; and, instead of a ranting, romantic boy, he seemed a composed, practical man. We all knew that the triumph of the Federal army was a blasting of his most cherished hopes, and none of us said anything to him on the subject. And so the fated days sped swiftly by; and while a nation was drunk with joy—while the ringing of the bells, the crackling of the bonfires, and the blaze of martial music all united into a *Te Deum* in honor of Victory and peace—this would, if told make the world stare with horror.

In all this din one head only kept cool and plotted dark deeds, while the face bore a calm, inscrutable look that no search could read, no eye could pierce. None of the misgivings of Cassius, nor the torturing misdoubts and fears of the noble Brutus, disturbed him. Instead, he arranged all the minute details of the horrible conspiracy that was to convulse the country in throes of terror with a coolness that was wonderful. No dark mutterings and cantations of the shrinking Macbeth, no remorse of the French Georges, seemed to disturb his serenity of mind. Instead, he went his resolved way—cool, determined, and deadly.

So time passed until the sun rose on that fateful Friday morning, April 14, 1865. John Wilkes Booth came into the Parlor at noon, and stayed there only for a few moments. He seemed restless and excited, but not enough so to attract any attention from us. He left in an hour, and went down, as he said, to witness the rehearsal of the new play, 'Our American Cousin.' Mrs. Hale and myself thought of going

THAT NIGHT

but he strongly advised us not saying, I remember, that it was Good Friday, and that few people would be present, and the play would drag on that account. After this we decided to postpone our intention, and go the night after.

Dinner passed off pleasantly, and we had retired to our rooms for our post-prandial nap, and did not reassemble together until the evening, when about a half an hour before supper we all met in the parlor. There were Senator Hale and his wife, I and Bessie, and an English lady who was staying at the hotel. A few moments after we were seated John Wilkes came in and greeted us all with the utmost cordiality and the same old graceful bow that he, and only he, could make. He seemed to be in good spirits, and laughed at the machinery of the play. After a little desultory conversation, he and Bessie drew off together, and carried on an earnest conversation in low tones. I recollect thinking what a pretty picture the two made. The room was brilliantly lighted in front, but leaving the lower portion of it in the shadow. The two seemed to be utterly unconscious that anyone in the world existed save themselves. Bessie Hale reclines on a huge velvet armchair, her black silk contrasting and well set off by the red velvet back-ground. Her eyes were luminous, and shone like the stars, as she listened with her soul in her face to Booth, who sat beside her. He seemed to be inspired, and the musical murmur of his voice could be heard, but not his words. He was evidently impassioned to the highest degree, and Bessie sat like the charmed Princess in the Arabian Nights—spellbound. I do not think that any woman on Earth could listen to Booth unmoved when he chose to exert himself. His beautiful language, tender ways, personal beauty, rich voice, and magnetic presence, all combined, made him a romantic maiden's ideal actually personified. God knows he was passing in his heart as he sat there with the only woman he ever loved, and only He who knoweth all things could read the stormy working of the heart that was torn with the battle of contending passions. No wonder the dark eyes gleamed with an unnatural luster and softened with an unutterable longing as he gazed his last on the fair woman beside him. And she looked up at him as only a wholly loving woman looks upon her heart's king.

At last the whole party rose to go to supper, and the two were brought back to themselves again. They followed us slowly, and just as I left the parlor I heard Booth say, 'Ah! Bessie! Bessie! Can I trust you utterly?' and her reply came clear, but with a world of melancholy in the tones:

"Even as Ruth said, so say I—Even unto death."

We took our seats at the table—a small round one. Booth and Bessie sat together, then the English lady, I next to her, and the Senator and his wife completed the group.

The supper passed off pleasantly enough; I noticed nothing whatever excited in Booth's manner; he was unusually entertaining, and his laugh rang out as loud and clear as any man whose mind and conscience were at perfect ease. It was the last meal he was to take on earth, and yet he was careless and at rest.

At last Booth arose from the table, and drawing out his watch said: "It is after 8 o'clock; I must go"—and then dropping into a quotation, as was his wont, he added: "But when shall we three meet again?"

Bessie who had cultivated a strong love of Shakespeare under Booths tuition, took the part of one of the weird sisters, and answered promptly—

> "When the hurly-bury's done,
> When the battle's lost and won."

And then Booth threw himself into a melodramatic attitude and replied—

> "Hark! I'm called, my little spirit see!
> Sits in a foggy cloud, and stays for me."

He then made us all one of his grand bows, and walked to the door, and just as he passed out, some recollection of memory seemed to strike him, and he returned abruptly to the table, and said to Bessie, using a familiar quotation of Hamlet:

> "Nymph, in thy orisons
> Be all my sins remembered."

He took her hand, and gazed with one long, lingering look in her face. I noticed his eyes grow soft with a beautiful mystic radiance, and his sensitive mouth quivered and showed the pearly teeth beneath the mustache, and then he shook his head with a determined movement, dropped her hand, turned and disappeared through the open doorway, and as we gazed, none of us thought our eyes were looking the last in this world upon the Wayward genius who had won so upon all that we loved him.

I cannot tell you how we passed that fearful evening— much, no doubt as the rest; we laughed, talked, and just did, as was our wont, and no shadow of the impending awful event fell upon us. The hours sped swiftly by, until 10 o'clock struck, and then our little circle broke up. As I kissed Bessie good night, I couldn't help saying to her, 'My dear you look exquisitely lovely tonight sweeter and prettier than I ever saw you.' She only smiled and left the parlor.

I went to my own room, and being tired, undressed and went to bed. It seemed as if I had been asleep but a minute when I was aroused by an indefinable noise that served to wake, but was not loud enough to startle one. Doors were slamming all over the house, and a murmur of voices was heard. I thought at first that someone was sick, and that a doctor was being hurriedly sent for; but the noise still continuing, I imagined that there must be a fire in the vicinity. This idea caused me to jump up at once and open the window—and I heard the sound of many horses' feet striking the pavement in a full run, but no fire bells or alarms; but still the inexplicable sounds continued.

The rebels have stormed the city! was the next impression, and with that I hastily threw on my wrapper and hurried to my parlor. There was no one there, and I kept on until I got to the grand salon, and there I found a crowd of people—mostly like myself, guests of the hotel and in Dish dishabille.

To our scared looks and frenzied interrogations of 'What has happened?' The reply came in hushed, awful accents, that President Lincoln had been murdered by Booth while he sat in his box in the theater.

"By Booth!" I incredulously asked; "by John Wilkes Booth!!"

"Oh no! That is impossible." As the crowd surged to and fro in uncontrollable excitement, Bessie Hale came in, and as she heard the dreadful news she screamed, and then, before anyone could reach her, fell prone upon the floor. She was carried up to her room.

That night of horror seems like a frightful dream to me now. None of us retired, but sat in the parlor in a kind of dumb terror. Our gentlemen friends were out all night, and the ladies sat close clustered together. Not until the gray dawn came stealing in did we retire, sick at heart and with heavy, wet eyelids; for we then knew the worst—the President dying, the Secretary fatally wounded, and our favorite flying from justice with the burden of a mighty sin upon his guilty soul.

During the whole time of the pursuit of Booth we awaited, in a dreadful state of suspense, the end. A thousand rumors were flying about, and all people seemed nearly crazed with all the startling events that followed so rapidly each other in succession.

In all these hours Bessie Hale kept in her room, and none but her mother and physician was admitted to see her.

A day or two after the assassination—a never-to-be-forgotten day—the report came, substantiated, that John

Wilkes Booth had been captured and was being brought back to Washington. It was told Bessie and she came into my room in a fearful state of excitement, and the proud, haughty, cold woman seemed to have lost all control over herself.

I did the best I could to calm her, and finally succeeded. She wrote a letter to Booth telling him she loved him, and concluded by saying she would marry him even at the foot of the scaffold. At last the news came of his capture and death, and finally all Washington turned out to view the remains, though but few men were allowed to look upon the corpse. On the 27th of April a small boat received the remains of the actor, and they carried the body off into the darkness, and from that darkness it will never return.

Robert Lincoln never met Bessie Hale afterward, but, ere long, married a daughter of Senator Harlan, of Iowa. Bessie never recovered from the shock. The shadows of the past, full of mingled sweetness and pain, and of ecstatic dreams and abhorred reminiscences, left its imprint on mind and brain, and like one touched by Ithurial's spear, she shivered, cowered, and changed in an hour from happy, radiant maiden into a sad, silent pale woman, who lived in a live world while she herself was dead. The Senator carried her to Europe, hoping the change of scene would make her forget the past. Vain faith! I saw her years ago, and the fair, sweet, though pain-drawn face, the hollow eyes, the sad, patient smile haunts me like a dream.

"But, Mrs. Temple," I said. "That was years ago. What has become of her now? I saw a marriage of Miss Hale announced in the papers a few days ago. Was it Booth's Bessie Hale?"

"Yes," she said. "It was. But if I were to write her future life, do you know what I would denominate it?"

"I cannot tell."

"I would call it: A DEAD WOMAN'S LIFE."

*** THE END ***

Hale Family Portraits

Lucy Lambert Hale Chandler
(Courtesy Thom Hindle Collection)

John Wilkes Booth
(Courtesy US Library of Congress)

John Parker Hale (Lucy's father)
(Courtesy Thom Hindle Collection)

Lucy H. Lambert Hale (Lucy's mother)
(Courtesy Thom Hindle Collection)

Elizabeth "Lizzie or Eliza" Hale Jaques (Lucy's sister)
(Courtesy Thom Hindle Collection)

William Eaton Chandler
(By Mathew Brady, Courtesy US Library of Congress)

About the Author

J. Dennis Robinson has written 20 history books, so far, and well over 2,000 published articles, mostly about regional history and culture. He lives in Portsmouth, NH just across the swirling Piscataqua River from Maine. His author website is jdennisrobinson.com online.

Made in the USA
Columbia, SC
02 November 2024

45405917R00163